She thought she was the luckiest woman in London . . .

Surviving on a seamstress' income and a steady stream of fantasies, Prudence Bosworth has always longed for love and romance. Then she inherits a fortune from the father she's never seen, with the stipulation that she wed in one year. Prudence is determined to marry for true love, and after seeing first hand the splendid chivalry of a certain duke, only one man will do. . .

Rhys de Winter, the Duke of St. Cyres, hides his cynicism behind a quick wit and an even quicker smile. He must marry an heiress, and as luck would have it, the pretty little seamstress-turned-heiress is exactly what he needs. But he never expected to fall for Prudence, and when his shocking deception is revealed, he will stop at nothing to win her back . . . even if it means renouncing every last one of his wicked ways.

By Laura Lee Guhrke

THE WICKED WAYS OF A DUKE
AND THEN HE KISSED HER
SHE'S NO PRINCESS
THE MARRIAGE BED
HIS EVERY KISS
GUILTY PLEASURES

If You've Enjoyed This Book,
Be Sure to Read These Other
AVON ROMANTIC TREASURES

BEWITCHING THE HIGHLANDER *by Lois Greiman*
IN MY WILDEST FANTASIES *by Julianne MacLean*
JUST WICKED ENOUGH *by Lorraine Heath*
THE SCOTTISH COMPANION *by Karen Ranney*
UNTOUCHED *by Anna Campbell*

Coming Soon

THE PERILS OF PLEASURE *by Julie Anne Long*

Laura Lee Guhrke

The Wicked Ways Of A Duke

AVON
An *Imprint of* HarperCollins*Publishers*

This is a work of fiction. Names, characters, places, and incidents are products of the author's imagination or are used fictitiously and are not to be construed as real. Any resemblance to actual events, locales, organizations, or persons, living or dead, is entirely coincidental.

AVON BOOKS
An Imprint of HarperCollins*Publishers*
10 East 53rd Street
New York, New York 10022-5299

ISBN: 978-0-06-114361-8
www.avonromance.com

First Avon Books paperback printing: January 2008

Printed in the U.S.A.

10 9 8 7 6 5 4

This book is for all my readers. Your support and encouragement mean more to me than I can ever express. Thank you.

The Wicked Ways Of A Duke

Chapter 1

Duke of St. Cyres sinks to new depths of depravity! Peeking beneath young ladies' skirts at charity balls? We are appalled.

—Talk of the Town, *1894*

Miss Prudence Bosworth's opinion of the incident in question would prove somewhat different from that of the society papers, but during the evening itself, she was unaware of what the scandal sheet scribblers would have to say and too busy to care. The goings-on of dukes, depraved or not, was of no concern to her.

For weeks now, she and the seamstresses under her at Madame Marceau's had been frantically making up gowns for the fashionable young ladies coming to London for the season, and at the moment, one of those gowns had a hem in need of repair. If Lady Alberta Denville would only stand still.

"Hurry up, Bosworth!" Lady Alberta jerked impatiently at her skirt, ripping the blond silk away from the seed pearl trim in Prudence's fingers, tearing the fabric in the process. "Must you be so slow?"

Prudence sat back on her heels, staring in dismay at this new damage to the gown. And she'd been nearly finished. She pushed damp hair back from her forehead and reached into her sewing basket for her spool of gold thread and her scissors. "I shall try to sew faster, my lady," she murmured, striving to maintain the air of humble, apologetic deference so necessary to her position.

"You had best do more than try! The Duke of St. Cyres has engaged me for the next dance, and it could be the most important event of my life. He's just returned from Italy, and he's looking to marry, you know."

Prudence didn't know and didn't much care. This ball was the first significant social event of the season, and the preparations of the past few days had been grueling, with little time for either food or rest. Missing meals she didn't mind so much. As the lead seamstress for a fashionable London dressmaker, she was acutely conscious of her plump figure, and was always making attempts to reduce its proportions. Sleep, however, was a different matter. She longed to go home to her cozy flat in Little Russell Street and crawl into bed, but knew rest was a good twelve hours away at least. "Yes, my lady. Of course."

These subservient murmurs did not seem to placate Lady Alberta. The young lady heaved an aggravated sigh, folded her arms, and tapped one satin-slippered foot on the floor, fuming. "I cannot believe this is happening to me. First, Sir George Laverton treads on my lovely dress and tears it, the clumsy oaf. And then I find myself saddled with the slowest seamstress in Madame Marceau's employ."

The seamstress in question decided she was saddled with the most odious debutante. Such a pity she couldn't say so. Prudence set her jaw, reminded herself that self-restraint helped to build one's character, and sewed as fast as she could.

"If your ineptness causes me to miss this waltz and lose my chance with Rhys," the girl went on, "Madame Marceau shall hear of it."

A pang of alarm shot through Prudence at those words. It had taken her eleven years of hard work to be elevated to the position of lead seamstress, and with one unfavorable word from Lady Alberta, she could lose her post in an instant. Lord Denville was one of the few peers in Britain able to pay tradesmen's bills promptly, and his daughters were some of Madame Marceau's most valued clients. Without pausing in her work, Prudence took as deep and steadying a breath as she could manage in her tight stays. "Yes, my lady."

Another silk skirt moved into Prudence's line of vision. "Planning your wedding to St. Cyres, are you, Alberta?" a laughing feminine voice inquired, a voice that to Prudence's ears was tinged with malice. "A bit precipitate, don't you think, to leap from acquaintanceship to matrimony because of one waltz?"

"I've a better chance of securing him than most, Helen Munro, and you know it. Our families possess some adjoining lands and we've known each other all our lives."

"All your life, you mean. Don't you think you're a bit young for St. Cyres? He's thirty-three, my dear, and you're barely twenty. To him, you are still a child."

"I'm not! It's true I was only eight when he went away, but he certainly doesn't see me as a child any longer. Why, the moment he set eyes on me again, he engaged me for a waltz. It must mean something."

"I daresay it does!" another woman said, joining the conversation with a laugh. "Home less than a week, and he's already ascertained the amount of your dowry and income!"

"He'll need every penny of it, too," Helen Munro assured her companions. "St. Cyres likes to live well, and he's head over ears in debt, they say. The fact that he's inherited the title from his uncle won't save him from the creditors. The old duke's debts were ten times greater than his, and the estates are a shambles. Munro and I are in Derbyshire every summer to stay with Lord and Lady Tavistock, and I've seen for myself the sorry state of St. Cyres Castle. It's a deserted ruin. God only knows what condition the other ducal estates must be in."

"Winter Park looks well enough," Lady Alberta answered. "We'd live there, of course, since those St. Cyres lands adjoin ours. As for his debts, most peers have those. Not my own papa, of course. He has heaps of money."

"Yes, and London has heaps of pretty American heiresses who'd love to snare a duke and whose fathers have far more money than yours!"

"Americans? They've no breeding at all. Rhys would never choose an American to be his duchess."

"Those American girls have a great deal of charm."

Lady Alberta seemed undaunted. "I am much more charming than any dreadful American." She gave Prudence's knee a none-too-gentle kick with her foot. "For heaven's sake, Bosworth, aren't you finished yet?"

"Nearly done, my lady," she answered, keeping a firm grip on the skirt lest the girl yank it away again.

"Mind you, I expect the gown to be as flawless

as it was when I first put it on. If anyone notices the repair, I'll have your head for embarrassing me—"

"Still abusing servant girls, Alberta?" an amused male voice behind Prudence said, interrupting the tirade. "How refreshing to know that some things never change."

Shocked murmurs from the other ladies rippled through the room at the unexpected arrival of a man in their midst, for this alcove and the retiring room that adjoined it were reserved exclusively for women. But Lady Alberta didn't seem to notice.

"Rhys!" she greeted him with a cry of delight. "What are you doing back here?"

"I came in search of you, of course," he answered, and though Prudence did not look up from her work, she could discern him moving closer as he spoke. "We are to have a waltz, are we not? Or was that only in my dreams?"

"You weren't dreaming." Lady Alberta laughed, seeming in a better humor with the duke's arrival. "But you really must leave. You're causing a scandal."

"Am I?" He came to stand beside where Prudence knelt on the floor, and as his shadow fell across her hands, she paused in her sewing to take a quick peek up at him, for she'd never seen a duke in the entire twenty-eight years of her life, and such a daring one would arouse any woman's curiosity. But her one cursory glance told her little. The gaslights were behind him in the small alcove, making his tall frame no more than a silhouette of black broadcloth, snowy linen, and blond hair.

Returning her attention to her work, she was dismayed to find that his wide shoulders were blocking what little light she had to work by. Asking him to move, however, would be a gross impertinence, and she didn't want to risk raising Lady Alberta's ire even higher by irritating the girl's potential future husband. Prudence bent her head close to her sewing and tried to carry on with what little light she had left, but it was slow going.

"Rhys, you have to leave," Lady Alberta repeated, still laughing. "You shouldn't be back here at all, you know."

"Why ever not?"

"It's not done."

"But that's what makes it worth doing. Besides, I couldn't find you in the ballroom, and was emboldened to venture within this feminine enclave in search of you. Though I fear I am too late, for I detect the strains of Strauss."

"Strains of what?"

"Strauss, darling," he said patiently. "They have begun the waltz without us."

The girl let out a shrill cry of dismay.

"No need to shatter the window glass, Alberta," he said at once, and Prudence smiled to herself, fancying that perhaps the gentleman wasn't as enamored of Alberta as she was of him.

"It is only a waltz," he went on. "We'll have another sometime."

"We ought to be having one now, but Bosworth here cannot seem to manage a simple repair to my gown."

Prudence's smile vanished and she felt an overwhelming desire to prick Lady Alberta in the leg with her needle. Just a harmless little jab, she reasoned to herself. She could always offer profuse apologies afterward for her clumsiness.

Even as she savored the idea, Prudence knew she couldn't carry it through. This girl was the daughter of a wealthy earl, and she was a seamstress of no consequence. She could not afford to risk her post for a little momentary satisfaction. Sometimes life was very trying.

Desperate to speed things along and send this horrid girl on her way, Prudence nudged the gentleman's leg with her elbow to gain his attention. "If you please, sir," she said without taking her eyes from her work, "could you move a bit to the side? You are blocking the light."

Lady Alberta made a sound of outrage. "What impudence!"

"Pert, isn't she?" The gentleman sounded amused rather than irritated, but if Prudence hoped she would escape unscathed, she was mistaken.

"This is the Duke of St. Cyres," Lady Alberta said, as if Prudence were too dense to know that already, and kicked the sewing basket near her feet, spilling the contents across the Aubusson carpet. "How dare you presume to give him orders?"

Prudence stared at her scattered sewing supplies and feared that despite all her nauseating attempts at subservience, she was destined to lose her post before the night was over. If she couldn't find another, she'd have to return to Sussex and live with Uncle Stephen and Aunt Edith again. Horrible thought.

"It's no more than I deserve for coming between a woman and her modiste," the duke said in a good-humored voice that made her breathe a sigh of relief. "I'd best do as she wishes, I think."

To her astonishment, he complied with her request not by moving away, but instead by kneeling down beside her. She watched his hands as he righted her basket and reached for her pin box. "Oh, no, sir," she whispered, realizing his intent with dismay. "Don't trouble yourself."

"No trouble, I assure you."

As she pulled her needle through the silk, Prudence darted a glance at him, and found that he was staring at her. Their eyes met, her heart twisted in her breast, and she stopped sewing.

He was beautiful. Beautiful the same way an autumn morning in Yorkshire was beautiful, when the beech woods had turned a thousand shades of gold, and the meadows, still green, were swathed in silver frost. She caught the scent of him, an earthy scent like the peat sheaves, smoky wood fires, and spicy cider of her childhood.

Her lips parted and she swayed toward him, inhaling deeply. He smiled at her, a slight curve of his lips that made her wonder if perhaps he could read her thoughts and was laughing at the country girl. But she didn't care. He smelled heavenly.

His silver-green eyes studied her face with unnerving openness, yet she couldn't seem to look away. Still smiling a little, he leaned closer. His wrist brushed her knee, and she jumped, unnerved by the contact, but he merely took up her scissors from the floor and dropped them into her basket. Then his thick brown lashes lowered to her hands and his smile widened, showing teeth that were remarkably even and as white as his linen. "Resume your sewing, I beg you," he murmured just loud enough for her to hear. "I couldn't bear it if Alberta started wailing again."

Smothering a laugh, Prudence forced her attention back to her work as he gathered up wayward spools of thread. But such splendid masculinity had never come this close to her before, and she continued to study him covertly as she worked.

His evening clothes, she noted, were impeccable and exquisitely cut in the most current mode. Other things about him, however, hinted at a disregard for fashion. His hair, burnished and tawny beneath the gaslights, was thick, with a hint of curl that scorned the use of any disciplining hair oil. He was clean-shaven, an unfashionable choice, but a wise one, to Prudence's mind. A beard would have hidden the lean planes of his face and the strong edge of his jaw, and a mustache would have detracted from the beauty of his mouth and the aquiline line of his nose. Never in her life had she seen a more handsome man.

"Rhys, what are you doing down there?" Lady Alberta's laughing voice interrupted Prudence's observations. "I cannot believe you are on your knees playing the gallant to a seamstress."

There was an unmistakable tone of petulance beneath the girl's laughter, and Prudence tensed. She looked at the gentleman and gave a tiny shake of her head, imploring him with her eyes.

He made a sound of impatience. Whether that impatience was with her or Lady Alberta, Prudence couldn't tell, but he tilted his head back and gave the girl standing before him his full attention. "Me play the gallant?" he said, a hint of disdain entering his well-bred drawl. "What a notion!"

"Then what in heaven's name are you doing?"

He dropped another spool of thread into Prudence's basket with one hand as he grasped a handful of blond silk in the other. "Having a peek under your petticoats, of course," he answered, and lifted the girl's hem a few inches from the floor, earning himself startled gasps from the ladies around them. "What else would I be doing down here?"

Lady Alberta gave a squeal of shocked delight, and Prudence felt the tension slide away from her.

"What pretty ankles you've got!" he added, giving the girl's feet a judicious study and ignoring the murmurs and stares of the other ladies. "Why, I believe little Alberta's all grown up."

The girl was now giggling in the silliest way, but Prudence found that sound a welcome relief after all the whining that had come before. Her task completed at last, she reached for her scissors, and as the move brought her closer to the duke, she inhaled the wonderful, earthy scent of him one last time. "Thank you, sir," she whispered as she cut the thread.

"Not at all," he murmured in her ear. "It has been my pleasure." He straightened Lady Alberta's skirt and rose to his feet.

Prudence sat back. "I've finished, my lady."

"Finally!" The girl curled her arm through the man's offered one, and they left the alcove together. Prudence turned her head and watched them depart, her relief at being rid of Lady Alberta tinged with disappointment as the duke vanished from view. Never again was she likely to encounter such a man.

Ah, well. She gave a philosophical shrug and stuck her needle in the pincushion the duke had placed back in her basket, then stood up. Pressing a hand to her spine, she arched her back to stretch her aching muscles, and as she did so, spied Maria beckoning to her from the nearby corridor.

Her dearest friend, Maria Martingale shared a flat with her and worked in a bakery shop during the day. At night, Maria supplemented her income by assisting at public balls such as this one.

After a quick glance around, Prudence picked up her basket and walked over to her friend, who was standing by the corridor that led to the kitchens, a heavy silver tray in her hands.

"Who was that man?" Maria asked.

"A duke."

"Stuff!" Maria said in disbelief. "Really?"

Prudence nodded. "Lady Alberta, the girl whose dress I was mending, called him the Duke of St. Cyres."

"Well, his chivalry seemed *sincere* enough," Maria answered, laughing at the adjective that matched the pronunciation of his title. "If I'd been in your place, I wouldn't have been able to sew a stitch!"

"It was difficult," Prudence admitted, grinning, "but I managed. A treat to look at, wasn't he?"

"Rather! You should have seen all the other ladies watching him while he helped you. And then he took a look under the girl's skirts and scandalized 'em all, the saucy fellow!"

Prudence felt a delicious little thrill. He'd done

that for her, she knew, and it amazed her that a man of such exalted rank would bother.

"The girl didn't like it, not by half," Maria told her. "She was staring daggers down at you the whole time. He didn't seem to care, though." She shifted her weight from one foot to the other and grimaced. "My feet hurt."

"I should imagine so. You've been trotting back and forth from the kitchens to the dining room all night with those trays of supper."

Maria's grimace of pain changed at once to a grin that lit her pixy face. "It does have some compensations. I've sampled my share of the goods." She held up the nearly empty tray. "These crab cakes are too delicious for words."

Prudence groaned, a pang of hunger twisting her insides. Her mouth began to water. "Don't! I've eaten almost nothing these past few days."

"Listen to you. Always trying to slim, and those tight corsets you wear! Hurts me just lacing them for you. I don't know why you torture yourself." Maria glanced around to be sure no one was watching, then pulled the last three bite-size crab cakes off the tray and shoved them into Prudence's hand. "Here."

Tempted beyond bearing, Prudence popped one of the stolen canapés into her mouth and groaned again, looking at the other woman with heartfelt gratitude. "I don't think anything has ever tasted this delicious," she said around the bite of crab cake. "How are things in the kitchens?"

The girl lifted her gaze heavenward. "Andre is the most temperamental fellow. Throws a tantrum if things on the trays aren't just so. These French chefs are all the same. Fuss, fuss, fuss. And the other maids—" She broke off with a sound of contempt. "Lightning strike me dead if Sally McDermott isn't the flightiest bit of goods! She's too occupied with chatting up the footmen to give the work any attention."

"She is a terrible flirt," Prudence agreed. "Still, if I were as pretty as she, I'd flirt, too."

"Sally McDermott does far more than flirt."

"We don't know that."

Her friend gave an exasperated groan. "You're too nice, Pru, that's your trouble. Believing the best about everyone, mild as milk, and hiding your own lights under a bushel. Make me quite cross sometimes, you do."

Prudence felt compelled to protest. "I'm not nice! Whenever I look at Sally McDermott, I want to pull every pretty blond curl out of her empty head. Her, and that awful Lady Alberta, too. I wanted to stab her in the leg with my needle. There, you see," she added as they both laughed, "I'm not nice at all."

"Aren't you? If I had your situation, I'd starve. I can manage Andre, for he doesn't mind if I give as good as I get. Rather likes it, in fact. But those women you make dresses for? I wouldn't last a day. I saw how that girl kicked your basket and abused you up and down, while you just kept sewing and saying, 'Yes, my lady.' You should've stabbed her, I say."

"Be glad I didn't. I'd have lost my post, and then you'd be paying all the rent on our flat." Prudence glanced at the window, noting it was still pitch-black outside. "Isn't this ball almost at an end?"

"We've two more hours, at least. It's barely three o'clock."

Prudence's shoulders slumped a little at that discouraging news. The thrill from her encounter with the handsome duke had faded, and she was once again feeling the effects of exhaustion.

Maria studied her with concern. "You look all in, Pru."

"I'm all right. It's just so warm in here, and the fumes from these gaslights give me a headache."

"When this ball's over, we'll take a hansom home, shall we?"

She shook her head. "I'm not going home. Madame told me I have to be in the showroom at seven o'clock. We're to make things ready for a group of Austrian ladies who want gowns for the Embassy Ball. They come at nine, so there's no point in returning to Holborn."

"Madame Marceau's a slaver." Maria set the empty tray on the floor, leaning it against the wall, and reached out to grasp the handle of Prudence's sewing basket. "Go get some air and clear your head. I'll take your place for a bit."

"You can't!"

"Well, I like that!" Her friend sniffed, pretending to take offense. "I can sew on a button or fix a torn hem, I daresay. Not as well as you, but—"

"I didn't mean it that way. Someone will notice you've taken my place."

"No one ever notices a servant or a seamstress," Maria responded blithely. "We're part of the furniture, don't you know?"

"I meant Madame. She'll notice."

Both of them glanced at Prudence's employer. The dressmaker was on the other side of the alcove, her back to them as she supervised the efforts of the seamstress who was making repairs to the torn frock of Lady Wallingford. In her phony French accent, the dressmaker from Lambeth was exclaiming over the marchioness's beautiful figure and the elegant arrangement of her hair.

"She's too busy bootlicking to notice anything," Maria said.

"We can't risk it. We'd both lose our posts, and then there'd be no one to pay the rent." Prudence shook her head. "Besides, if I take a rest now, I'll just drop."

Her friend let go of the basket with a reluctant nod. "All right, but come find me after the ball. We'll share the cab as far as New Oxford Street. The driver can leave you in front of the showroom then take me on to Little Russell Street."

"All right. I'll come to the kitchens and find

you after. And Maria—" She hesitated, wavering, then added in a rush, "If there's any more of those canapés left—"

"Girl?" A commanding voice rose nearby, and both Prudence and Maria turned their heads to see a very stout woman encased in an ice-blue gown so tight it made her look like a sausage.

"Yes, ma'am?" both younger women answered in unison, bobbing deferential curtsies.

The stout lady perched a lorgnette on her nose and peered at Prudence as if she were some sort of insect. "You are one of Madame Marceau's seamstresses, are you not?" Without waiting for a reply, she beckoned Prudence with an impatient wave of her white-gloved hand. "Come with me," she ordered. "I've a split seam to be mended. And you'd best be quick about it, girl. I don't have all night, you know."

The friends exchanged wry glances.

"Yes, ma'am," Prudence murmured, and turned to Maria with a grin as the woman flounced away. "I've changed my mind. Take my place."

"Too late," Maria told her with a wink. "You lost your chance, luvvy. But I'll save you all the crab cakes I can." She departed for the kitchens, leaving Prudence to stitch the sausage lady back into her dress.

It was indeed two and a half hours later before the ball finally ended, just as Maria had predicted.

Dawn was breaking by the time the guests began to depart and Prudence went in search of her friend. When she entered the kitchens, however, she found Maria still occupied with her duties.

"I'll wait for you in the alley," Prudence said, pulling her cloak from the row of hooks near the entrance to the kitchens. "I need some air."

"Right-ho," Maria called back. "I'll be along in just a few minutes."

Prudence donned her cloak and fastened the buttons as she walked down the corridor toward the servants' entrance. She opened the door and stepped out into the alley, inhaling the cool air of early spring with gratitude, savoring it after the stifling heat and horrid gas fumes indoors. She started down the alley, intending to stroll up and down its length while she waited for Maria, but came to a halt almost at once.

A couple stood in the back corner where the alley ended, and though the man had his back to her, blocking her view, it was clear the pair were engaged in an amorous encounter. Hotly embarrassed, Prudence started to turn around and go back inside, but the woman's voice stopped her.

"No, sir! No!"

In the woman's voice was the violent protest and raw fear any other woman immediately understood. Realizing her initial assumption had been a mistake, Prudence turned back around, further alarmed as she saw the man grasp the woman's wrists and pin them against the wall over her head.

"No, sir, please let me go," the woman sobbed as she twisted in a violent effort to free herself. "Let me go."

"Don't carry on so, my girl. There'll be a bob in it for you afterward." Holding her wrists with one hand, he began pulling up her skirts with the other.

Heart in her throat, Prudence started forward, but before she'd taken three steps, she was shoved aside. She looked up to see the handsome duke who had collected her sewing supplies earlier in the evening. "Stay back," he muttered to her as he passed. "Keep well out of the way."

She let out her breath in a sigh of relief as she watched the duke stride down the alley toward the struggling couple in the corner. Without preliminaries, he grabbed the man by the arms and hauled him away, his action revealing the sobbing woman in the corner.

It was Sally McDermott.

Prudence gave a gasp of surprise, but had barely registered the other girl's identity before Sally dodged sideways, scrambling to get clear as the duke spun the other man around.

"St. Cyres?" the man cried in amazement. "Are you mad? What in blazes are you doing?"

"Rescuing a damsel in distress, it seems."

"What?" The other man twisted his shoulders as if to free himself from St. Cyres's grip. "She's a scullery maid, for God's sake!"

"A scullery maid who said no, Northcote."

"What does that matter?"

Whether it was that question or the laughter accompanying it that ignited the duke's temper, Prudence couldn't tell. He slammed the man called Northcote against the wall of the alley. "It matters to me," he said, drew back his fist, and landed a blow to the other man's jaw.

Northcote's head snapped sideways, but St. Cyres did not seem content. He dealt the other man several more punishing blows, giving him no opportunity to strike back. When he finally stopped, Northcote fell to the ground, where he lay unmoving on the cobblestones.

St. Cyres watched him for a moment, as if to be certain he was thoroughly incapacitated, then turned away just as Sally hurled herself into his arms.

"Oh, sir, thank you, sir!" she cried, clinging to his neck. "Thank you!"

Behind Prudence the door to the alley opened and banged against the brick wall of the building. "I'm finished, Pru," Maria cheerfully called as she stepped into the alley. "Let's be on our way before all the hansoms are—crikey!"

That last startled exclamation came as her friend paused beside her and took in the sight of the unconscious man on the ground and the terrified Sally McDermott sobbing into the shirtfront of the gallant duke.

"What's happened here?" Maria asked.

Prudence didn't answer. Instead, she walked down the alley and put her hand on Sally's arm. "Are you all right? What can we do to help?"

"Nothing," Sally said from the depths of the duke's shirtfront. "I'll be all right." She shook off Prudence's hand, then lifted her head, gazing up at her savior. "If I could just sit down for a bit?"

"Of course." St. Cyres glanced around, then gently disengaged himself from her embrace and reached for a large wooden crate from a nearby rubbish heap. He removed his jacket and draped it over the crate. "Will this do? Alleys don't come furnished these days, more's the pity."

Sally gave a shaky laugh and sank down onto the crate, grasping his hand in hers. "Thank you, sir," she said again, holding onto his hand as if it were a lifeline.

The duke looked at Prudence. "It might be best if you and your friend went home," he advised. "After all Alberta's abuse," he added with a smile, "you must be exhausted. And it's bloody freezing out here. If you linger, you'll catch a chill."

Was it cold? Prudence wondered. She couldn't tell, for this man's smile warmed her all through. "You're very kind, but—"

"I will arrange for the girl to be taken safely

home," he assured her, seeming to know just what concern she'd been about to express. "You needn't worry."

"Thank you." She could feel Maria tugging on her cloak, and turned away, following her friend toward the street, knowing there was nothing more they could do. But when she reached the corner, she was unable to resist one last look at the duke. Glancing back down the alley, she saw him hovering over Sally with the solicitous regard of a true gentleman.

He's splendid, she thought. Brave, considerate, and utterly splendid.

Quite a low pass he'd come to, he supposed, shagging servant girls.

Rhys De Winter slid his palm over one of Sally McDermott's bare buttocks, and it occurred to him that seducing a serving maid only minutes after rescuing her would inspire a bout of conscience in most men, at least once lust had been sated. Rhys, however, suffered no such inconvenient pangs. When a plum dropped into his lap—or, to be accurate, hurled itself into his arms—he'd be a fool not to take advantage of the moment. Rhys was not a fool, and Sally had turned out to be quite a tasty plum.

Rather a surprise that, since she hadn't been his first choice. He'd originally had his eye on that delicious little seamstress with the dark hair. She had just the sort of generous curves he favored in a woman, and when he saw Alberta kick over the sewing basket, it provided him the perfect chance for a closer, much more thorough perusal. He'd been quite pleased to discover she had a pretty complexion, fine brown eyes, and hair with the fresh scent of lavender, a fragrance he'd always liked. But after only a few moments, he'd been forced to banish any amorous inclinations about her. Those big, soft eyes had gazed at him as if he were king of the earth just for retrieving a few spools of thread, but she jumped and shied at the mere brush of his hand, making it clear his little seamstress was innocent as a baby. Innocence had never held much charm for him.

It was just as well, he'd told himself at the time. His reason for attending the ball hadn't been skirt chasing anyway, but heiress hunting. He had returned to the ballroom with Alberta, one of the richest heiresses in Britain, and for the rest of the evening was a very good boy, doing his best to seem virtuous, marriage-minded, and responsible, particularly in front of her father.

Rhys rolled onto his back and stared at the painted cherubs and gilded ceiling moldings overhead. God, Milbray has gaudy taste, he thought. Still, a hideously decorated town house borrowed for the season from an old school friend was better than nothing. At least it was a fashionable address. He might be stone broke, but he was also a duke, and if he was going to find himself an heiress to marry, he had to maintain a residence worthy of his position.

Alberta had a dowry that could rescue him from the mire of his debts, but a few hours in her company had rid him of any notion to marry her. He had no intention of going to hell until he was actually dead.

Though Lady Alberta Denville had proved an untenable solution, he couldn't complain about how the evening turned out. The ball had ended with the usual crush of people waiting out front for their carriages to be brought around, and Rhys, tired of standing amid the suffocating mass, had ducked out the back, thinking to fetch his carriage from the mews himself. In so doing, he had ended a rather unsatisfactory evening on a very satisfactory note.

Turning his head, he glanced at the naked woman who lay on her stomach beside him with her head pillowed on her folded arms.

Yes, he'd come to a very low pass, indeed, when a maid or seamstress in need of a few bob was all he could afford. But he had no taste for streetwalkers, and keeping a mistress was out of the question. He hadn't been able to afford that particular luxury for quite some time, an unfortunate circumstance unlikely to change in the near future. Though he'd only returned to Britain five days ago, any courtesan worthy of her trade was already well aware that the newest Duke of St. Cyres couldn't scrape together the blunt for his own household, much less provide one for her.

Sally stirred and lifted her head to find him watching her. She smiled at him sleepily amid the tumble of her wheat-colored curls, and his desire began to stir. He returned her smile with a wicked one of his own, rolled onto his side and pressed a kiss to her shoulder as he eased his hand between her thighs.

"Wantin' another toss already, are you?" Her smile widened. "Greedy bloke."

"Very greedy," he concurred, and nipped her shoulder. She giggled, and he pushed his hand deeper. Finding the result of that exploration satisfactory, he slid his free arm beneath her stomach.

"All right, all right, I'll give you second helpings," she murmured, her body stirring in response to these amorous advances. "But only because you rescued me."

He lifted her hips and positioned himself behind her, thinking it a damn fortunate thing he was such a chivalrous fellow.

Chapter 2

Indebted Dukes Now Available at a Discount. Heiresses, What Shall You Bid?

—The Social Gazette, *1894*

The scrape of the coal scuttle woke him far too soon. Rhys rolled onto his stomach and covered his head with a pillow, cursing the efficiency of English household routine. In Italy, a servant wouldn't dream of intruding upon a gentleman's rest until the sun had moved to the western side of the horizon. No such luck in England.

He took a peek from beneath the bedclothes and saw beside the fireplace the unmistakable striped gray dress, white apron, and cap of a chambermaid. Only the most obtuse servant could have failed to notice that there were two people in the bed, and with a pretty wench beside him, he hardly needed the warmth of a fire, but Rhys didn't point that out. Speaking seemed too much of an effort at the ungodly hour of eight o'clock in the morning, especially since he'd fallen asleep less than an hour ago. He closed his eyes again.

The second time he was awakened, it was by his valet, a servant who damned well ought to have known better.

"Fane," he muttered, shrugging off the hand on his shoulder, "if you don't remove yourself from my room this instant, I will sack you."

An empty threat, since he owed the fellow at least six months' wages and couldn't afford to find someone new, at least not someone loyal enough to stick with him as Fane had. The valet was clearly aware of this, too, for he didn't leave. Instead, he gave Rhys another gentle shake.

"Sir, I'm terribly sorry," he murmured, "but it seems there is a domestic crisis that requires your immediate attention."

"Domestic crisis? Have Hollister take care of it. He's Milbray's butler, isn't he?" Rolling away from the persistent shaking of the valet, he wrapped one leg and one arm around the slumbering woman beside him and began drifting back to sleep. "I have no intention of leaving this bed until at least two o'clock this afternoon unless it is the end of the world."

"Your mother is in the drawing room, and footmen are bringing in her trunks. She appears to be moving in."

"Good God." Rhys rolled onto his back and sat up, staring at Fane in horror. "It *is* the end of the world. Don't just stand there, man. Fetch my dressing gown at once."

Five minutes later Sally was on her way home in a cab and Rhys was dressed—more or less. In trousers, shirt, and dressing gown, he headed down a flight of stairs to the drawing room, pausing along the way to peer over the rail at the foyer below, confirming that there was indeed a pile of trunks, valises, and hat boxes stacked there. His mouth set in a grim line as he watched a pair of footmen maneuver another trunk through the front door.

He strode to the drawing room, wondering how Letitia could think for one moment he would allow her to stay under the same roof as himself. He'd spent the past twelve years on the Continent for the sole purpose of keeping as far from her and her lecherous brother-in-law as possible. Thankfully, Uncle Evelyn was dead, but Rhys was still as intent on avoiding his mother as ever. He hadn't been able to stomach more than five minutes in her company since he was twelve. She was equally fond of him.

When he entered the drawing room, she was sitting in one of the chairs closest to the fire, and as she rose and turned to face him, he was startled by how much the years had aged her. As far back as he could remember, Letitia had been a stunning woman, a dazzling ice-blond beauty who, when he was a small boy, reminded him of the magical and remote Snow Queen. Now, only the vestiges of her beauty remained. Her papery skin had a sallow hue, and her cheeks were sunken beneath those high, perfect cheekbones. She was rail thin and haggard, making her seem far older than her fifty-six years. But her eyes, the same gray-green color as his, had not changed. They studied him with all the warmth of an arctic glacier as he crossed the room and paused before her. She gave him no smile of greeting.

"St. Cyres," she said with the barest of curtsies.

He didn't even bother to offer an answering bow. "Mother. How delightful to see you."

His voice dripped mockery, but Letitia was far too callous to be bothered by it. They stood silent, studying each other a bit like duelists *en garde,* and he noticed that she had not yet taken off her cape and hat. Her umbrella was in her gloved hand. It was almost as if she had come merely to pay a call.

Too late, he realized the truth. "You have no intention at all of moving in, do you?"

She didn't even hesitate before replying. "Live with you? God, no."

He made a wry face at the distaste in her voice. "As always, your maternal affection warms my heart."

She sank back down in the chair, and it did not escape his notice that she leaned heavily on her umbrella as she did so. "You have ignored my letters. I have called upon you three times since you arrived in town, and each time, you have refused to receive me. Threatening to move in with you was the only way I could think of to garner your attention."

"Trunks in the foyer is carrying things a bit far, don't you think? Besides, you have never seemed particularly eager for my attention. Why, I think we've spoken less than a dozen times in my entire life. Why the sudden pressing need for my company?"

"I'm here to make you aware of the family situation."

Rhys did not reply. Instead, he rested his forearms on the top of the wing-back chair opposite hers and studied her resolute expression as he weighed the two alternatives open to him. He could toss her out on her ear right now, or he could endure the unpleasant, but inevitable, discussion of their financial status and have it over and done. He decided on the latter route. Though not as satisfying, it would prove less aggravating in the long run. Circling to the front of the chair, he sat down.

"The family has a situation?" he asked in a murmur as he leaned back. Elbows on the arms of his chair, he steepled his fingers together, his head tilted to one side, his pose deceptively relaxed. "How ominous that sounds."

"Let's not waste time beating about the bush. I know you've already been to see Mr. Hodges and that he made you aware of where things stand."

"Astonishing how you ferret things out, Mama. Since you already know I've seen the family solicitor and you're aware of what he told me, your purpose in coming here was obviously not to apprise me of the family situation." He gave her his most provoking smile. "Come for a touch, have you?"

"Must you be vulgar?"

"Your efforts are in vain," he was delighted to inform her. "You carted all those trunks over here to no purpose. My dear, I haven't a bean."

She made a sound of contempt. "You are such a liar."

"Yes, so you've told me before." Rhys pressed his fingers tighter together, so tight his hands began to ache. His smile, however, did not falter. "But in this case, I'm not making any attempt to deceive you. I'm absolutely flat."

She gave him a hard stare, as if to determine the verity of that statement. "The money from your father is gone, then? You've squandered it all?"

"Every shilling," he confessed with cheer. "Had jolly good fun doing it, too, shameless libertine that I am."

She paled, seeming to grow older right before his eyes. "The debts incurred by the estates are enormous, and our credit is already extended as far as it can be. You have to do something."

"What would you suggest? I thought about earning a living, but I decided I simply couldn't subject you to that. It would shame you beyond belief if I took on a profession. Besides, I should have to work." He shuddered. "A very bad habit. I try never to engage in it."

"Don't be absurd!" she snapped. "You're the Duke of St. Cyres. Of course a profession is out of the question."

"You and I in agreement about something? The warm climes of Italy have made me far too easy-going and amenable, I see. But to return to the matter at hand, we have very few options. I could appeal to the Salvation Army to come to our aid, I suppose, though I doubt they'd help a family of bankrupt aristocrats. Awfully uncharitable of a charity to be so stingy, but—"

"Everything is mortgaged to the hilt," his mother interrupted, reiterating the material point as if he were too dim-witted to appreciate its significance. "Interest payments take what little income we have from the land rents, and the creditors have been circling like vultures for several years. They'll be hovering over you as well before the week is out."

He didn't tell her they already were.

"Unless you act, and quickly, they will call our loans and take what little we have left. We will be destitute."

Rhys did not respond. Perhaps it was his innate

laziness, but he'd never seen the point of beating dead horses.

In the wake of his silence, his mother stirred with impatience. "Well?" she prompted. "What are you going to do?"

"What I always do when faced with a crisis," he answered, then rose to his feet and walked to the liquor cabinet. "I'm going to have a drink."

"A drink?" she repeated with contempt. "You think a drink is an appropriate response to our difficulties?"

"No," he answered as he poured himself a stiff measure of whiskey. "It's an appropriate response to *my* difficulties." Turning, he met her gaze and smiled. "About your difficulties, dear Mama, I couldn't care shit."

They stared at each other for a long time. He kept his stance relaxed. His mouth kept smiling. Letitia was the one who looked away. "Rhys, your uncle hasn't paid my jointure for four years."

He flicked a glance over her, noting her luxurious fur-trimmed cape and the jeweled pin that held it closed at her collar. "Yes, you appear awfully down-at-heel."

She looked at him again, and when she saw the direction of his gaze, she lifted her hand to her throat. "It's paste. All my jewels are paste. I've been selling the real ones, one by one. Now, there are none left to sell. I haven't enough money to last the spring."

Hodges hadn't told him that. Rhys set his jaw and lifted his gaze to her face. "Once again you are assuming I give a damn."

She stiffened in her chair, and her momentary attempt to play on his sympathy went to the wall. "Still thinking only of yourself, I see," she said with the disdain he knew so well. "You were always selfish, even as a boy."

Her voice was as sharp and cutting as a razor, but Rhys had developed his thick skin years ago. "Terribly selfish," he agreed, and raised his glass. "And a liar. Let's not forget that."

One elegant blond brow lifted, a sure sign that she was about to fire off the heavy guns. "If Thomas were still alive, he would never have allowed this to happen to me," she said. "Thomas was a good boy, always. Unlike you, he respected his mother. He would not have abandoned me and run away to Italy."

The reference to his younger brother shattered Rhys's carefully cultivated nonchalance in an instant. His smile vanished. He slammed down the glass, straightened away from the liquor cabinet, and took an involuntary step toward her. Satisfaction curved the corners of her lips, and he stopped. Some things never change, he thought, as angry with himself as he was with her. No one, no one, could flick him on the raw like Letitia.

He pasted his smile back on. "Ah, but Thomas did run away, didn't he, Mama?" he countered softly, watching her satisfaction fade. "He ran as far as he could go. Heaven's a pretty fair distance north of here, I'd say."

She didn't answer. Rhys leaned back, flattening his palms on the polished marble top of the cabinet, striving to regain an easy, relaxed demeanor. "I just love these family reunions," he drawled. "So heartwarming. Since you are in a mood to reminisce, shall we talk about the day Thomas hanged himself?"

She flushed a dull, deep red.

"Shall I tell you how he looked when I found him?" As he spoke, he worked to keep just the right note of careless indifference in his voice. "I can describe the scene for you, if you like. His body was hanging over the stairwell—neck broken, of course. Really, he looked like a marionette on a string, and his skin was the oddest shade of blue—"

"Stop it."

"Don't want the physical description? Then perhaps we should talk about the reason *why* he did it. Do you ever wonder about that, Mama?"

The tip of her umbrella hit the floor and she jerked to her feet. "I said stop it!"

"You brought up the topic."

Letitia's eyes narrowed. When he was a small boy, that glittering gaze had held the power to shred him to ribbons. Rhys was heartily glad he'd grown up.

"God," she choked, "how did I spawn such a son as you?"

"With the devil. How else?" He stretched out his arm to yank the bell pull on the wall nearby. "It certainly wasn't from something as distasteful as bedding your own husband."

She opened her mouth to reply, but before she could do so, Hollister appeared in the doorway. "Your Grace?" he inquired.

Rhys spoke to the servant without removing his gaze from Letitia's. "My mother has changed her mind. She will be staying elsewhere for the season. Please show her out, and arrange to have her trunks sent wherever she intends to stay."

With a sound of contempt, Letitia turned and started for the door.

As she walked away, he called after her, "Does this mean I won't have the pleasure of seeing you again for another twelve years, Mama?"

The drawing room door slammed behind her, which he hoped was an affirmative answer. He reached for his glass, downed the remainder of his whiskey in one swallow, then leaned back against the cabinet and closed his eyes, pressing the cool glass against his forehead.

He drew deep breaths, striving to banish the image of his brother's lifeless body from his mind, forcing all the rage and pain back down deep where they belonged, working bit by bit until he was numb again. He stood there a long, long time.

* * *

It was a well-known fact in London that omnibuses were like cats, for whenever it was pouring rain, both made themselves scarce. Prudence rose up on her toes and leaned out over the curb, keeping her umbrella carefully over her sewing basket to protect the piecework it contained from the deluge as she studied the various vehicles lumbering up New Oxford Street.

After a moment she fell back onto her heels with a discouraged sigh. Not an omnibus in sight. Either she would have to stand here and wait, or she would have to take a hansom. Cabs cost so much, and she and Maria had already splurged on the luxury of one twelve hours earlier, but Prudence was so tired, she couldn't bear the thought of walking even part of the way to Holborn. Nor did she want to stand here on a cold, rainy afternoon waiting for an omnibus to pass by. After the ball last night and a full day at the showroom, she was utterly done in.

She once again leaned out over the curb and scanned the traffic to her left, this time looking for a hansom cab. If only she could afford to take hansoms every day, she thought with longing, then immediately shook off such wasteful wishes. Wanting what one couldn't have was such a pointless game, and yet, on days like this, it was such a tempting one to play. If only she could afford to leave Madame and find a better post. If only she could afford not to work so hard. If only she were rich . . .

Just then a clatter of wheels to her right warned her a vehicle was coming around the corner. She jumped back, dropping her umbrella and cannoning into the person behind her as a luxurious brougham rolled past. With no way to escape the inevitable, Prudence lifted her basket high overhead to protect her piecework, turning her face to the side as she was doused with a spray of cold, muddy water from the gutter.

"Oh!" She looked down at her dress, impossible dreams forgotten as she stared in outraged dismay at the brown stains across the pretty beige and white stripes of her skirt. Gutter mud was awful. She would have to launder the garment the moment she got home or the stains would set and her best showroom dress would be ruined. Then she'd have to buy a new one from Madame and have the cost taken out of her wages. That meant she'd have to work even harder next week to make up the difference. Suddenly, everything in the world seemed too overwhelming to bear, and Prudence felt the stupid desire to weep.

Instead, she gave vent to her feelings by shouting one of Maria's best curses after the inconsiderate driver of the brougham, then picked up her umbrella, hailed a hansom, fought mightily with the two horrid men who tried to jump into it ahead of her, and went home.

She fell asleep and was jolted awake three times before the cab reached the lodging house in Little Russell Street where she lived. She paid the driver and went inside, wanting only to wash out her dress and fall into bed, but when she stepped into the foyer, she found that sleep was destined to elude her a little while longer.

Just inside the door, she was greeted by her landlady, Mrs. Morris, who must have been watching for her arrival from the window. "You have a visitor," the older woman informed her, closing the front door as Prudence set her dripping umbrella on one side of the coatrack and her sewing basket on the other. "A gentleman caller," she added in an animated whisper, her face alight with understandable curiosity. This was a respectable ladies' lodging house. Gentlemen callers were infrequent, and always generated a great fluttering of excitement and speculation.

Even so, Prudence was too tired to find this news exciting, especially since she knew it had to be some sort of mistake. She was a twenty-eight-year-old spinster of average looks who worked twelve-hour days in a post where she was surrounded by women. She never had gentlemen callers because she didn't know any gentlemen. "Who is he?"

"He says his name is Mr. Whitfield, and he has been waiting for you for nearly an hour." She glanced downward. "Oh, heavens, look at your dress. Perhaps you should change."

Prudence had no intention of going to that sort of trouble for a stranger. Pulling at the ribbons of her hat, she removed the damp concoction of straw and feathers and set it on a hook of the coatrack, then leaned sideways and peeked around the doorjamb into the parlor.

Seated on the horsehair settee was an older gentleman with a precisely groomed goatee. His hat, a fine felt bowler, was beside him, and his hands were folded over an ebony and gold walking stick. A black leather dispatch case sat at his feet. He met her gaze with a genial smile, and Prudence ducked back out of sight.

"I've never seen him before in my life," she whispered as she began to unbutton her cloak. "What does he want with me?"

"He says he's come all the way from America to meet you, but he refused to say why." Mrs. Morris's face, round as a currant bun, scrunched into lines of concern. "Dearest Prudence, you didn't perhaps answer one of those advertisements, did you?"

Attempting to engage her wits enough to figure out what Mrs. Morris was talking about proved beyond her. "Advertisements?"

"For wives, you know," the older woman whispered back. "American men are always putting advertisements in our newspapers. They do seem to have quite a shortage of women over there." A hint of disapproval mingled with the concern on her face. "Of course you wish to be married. Every young woman does, and husbands are so difficult to find nowadays, but America is such a long way off. And, really, dear, to answer an advertisement rather implies a sense of desper—"

"I didn't answer any advertisement." Prudence cut her off, knowing that sometimes interrupting her landlady was the only way to get a word in. She hung her cloak beside her hat. "I cannot imagine why he wishes to see me."

"Should we offer him tea?"

Prudence's empty stomach twisted, reminding her of how hungry she was, but she told herself to be strong. "I hardly think tea is necessary."

"But Prudence, it is coming on five o'clock. And he seems a most respectable and courteous gentleman. For the sake of civility, tea, sandwiches, and cake seems the least we can do."

Her mouth began to water. "Mrs. Morris, you know I'm banting," she said, valiantly resisting temptation.

"You girls, always banting, so conscious of your figures that you refuse to put decent nourishment in your mouths. Why, I don't know why I bother serving meals at all in this house. But striving for a twenty-inch waist simply isn't *healthy*, dear."

To obtain the coveted and fashionable twenty-inch waist, Prudence would have pledged to go on banting for the rest of her life. But her body seemed to care little about what was fashionable, for despite her continual efforts to whittle down the size of her waist, it seemed stubbornly fixed at a number equal to the years of her age. She ran her hands along her ribs, disheartened that her stays felt as tight as ever. Two days of nothing but a handful of crab canapés and a few cross buns at the showroom, she thought, aggrieved, and she didn't seem the least bit slimmer. "Tea, then," she agreed, capitulating at last, and tried to console herself with the irrefutable fact that she had to eat sometime.

"Dorcas and I shall bring it directly." The landlady bustled away in search of the maid, and Prudence shoved down any glimmers of guilt over her lack of gastronomic fortitude as she entered the parlor.

The gentleman, silver-haired and quite handsome, rose as she came in. "Miss Bosworth?"

"I am Prudence Bosworth, yes." She took in his finely tailored clothes with an experienced eye. A prosperous gentleman, she knew at once. A bit of a dandy as well, she judged, going by the gardenia in his buttonhole and his ornate walking stick.

"My name is Elliot Whitfield," he told her, offering his card with a bow.

She accepted the card and read it as she moved to the overstuffed chintz chair closest to the fireplace. "Why would an attorney come all the way from America to pay a call upon me?" she asked as she sat down, feeling a hint of alarm at the impressive sound of a firm called Whitfield, Joslyn, and Morehouse, Attorneys-at-Law, with offices in New York, London, and Paris. Lawyers, she suspected, were rather like the police. Getting entangled with them could not possibly be agreeable.

The gentleman once again took his seat and set aside his walking stick. "I have come on behalf of your father, Mr. Henry Abernathy."

She blinked at this unexpected announcement and set the card aside. "Sir, I believe there's been some sort of muddle. I do not know of anyone named Abernathy. My father was Henry Bosworth, of Little Furze, Yorkshire."

To her surprise, the dapper man across from her nodded. "Yes, exactly so. When Henry Bosworth went to America, he changed his name to Abernathy."

Prudence sniffed. "To prevent my mother from finding him, I've no doubt."

Mr. Whitfield gave a discreet little cough. "Be that as it may . . . " He paused, then went on, "I have come to offer you news both good and bad, Miss Bosworth. First, I must inform you that your father recently died."

That, she concluded from the somber expression of the man before her, was the bad news. But since her father had been a deceiving scoundrel who refused to do the honorable thing and instead abandoned her mother before her birth, she did not feel inclined to weep over his death. "And the good news, sir?"

"He has left you a legacy. That is the reason I am here."

This information didn't stir her emotions much more than the news of his death. From what little she'd been told of her father, he'd seemed a worthless fellow. A legacy from him was most unlikely. "He had something to leave?"

"I wouldn't have come all the way from New York otherwise, Miss Bosworth." Mr. Whitfield reached for his dispatch case. "I have here a duplicate copy of his will. You are the only beneficiary."

Astonished, she watched as the little man opposite her took up his case of black leather, placed it on his lap, and opened it. He lifted from its interior a thick sheaf of papers, and at the sight of such a substantial-looking document, she felt a throb of hope. Perhaps there really was a legacy, enough that she could resign her post at Madame Marceau's and find a better situation, one that did not involve working such long hours or bowing and scraping to people like Lady Alberta Denville. Oh, if only . . .

"Per the terms of his will," the attorney went on, "all income generating from his estate comes to you. In addition, you are to inherit his personal assets, which are considerable."

Words like "assets" and "income" made things sound so promising, and Prudence's hopes broadened. Perhaps she wouldn't be forced to seek a new post at all. Perhaps, there would be enough to give her a cozy nest egg that would protect her from the ravages of old age and give her a home of her own. She began to envision a quaint little terrace house in Hackney with bobbin lace curtains.

"The income from the estate," the attorney went on, "is to be placed in a trust fund for you."

She felt compelled to quash the longing sweeping over her before it took hold. This had to be a dream. Legacies out of nowhere didn't happen in real life. Any moment now she would wake up and find herself still in that hansom cab on the way home from the showroom. Still . . . a trust fund did sound wonderful. She would love to have a trust fund. She swallowed hard, wanting to believe. "Is it very much money?"

"Much money?" The attorney began to laugh. "Miss Bosworth, as I said before, your father was Henry Abernathy." At her blank stare, he went on, "Surely, even here in England, you've heard of Abernathy's Department Stores?"

Of course she'd heard of them. Abernathy's were the most famous department stores in all of America. Their emporium on Fifth Avenue was said to be grander even than Harrods here in London, though Prudence's staunchly British heart was doubtful on that point. "My father owns the Abernathy stores? He is—was—one of those American millionaires?"

"Yes, indeed." Mr. Whitfield smiled at her snort

of disbelief. "As I said, there are conditions attached to the inheritance, but if you meet those conditions you will be a very rich woman, one of the richest women in the world."

She simply could not credit it. This had to be some sort of trick or confidence swindle. Prudence jumped to her feet, ready to send this fellow off with a flea in his ear, but she was hit at once with a wave of dizziness. Pressing a hand to her forehead, she choked, "I do not . . . believe . . . you."

"Nonetheless, it's the absolute truth, I assure you."

"It can't—" Whatever she'd been about to say vanished from her mind. The room was starting to spin in the strangest way, and she closed her eyes, trying to think. She was inheriting money, the man said. An entire fortune. She'd be one of the richest women in the world. "How . . . how much—"

Though she could not manage to finish her question, Mr. Whitfield comprehended at once. "The income fluctuates with economic conditions, of course," he said, his voice barely discernible past the roaring in her ears, "but at the current rate of exchange, it amounts to approximately one million pounds per annum."

With those words, the past few days of grueling work with little food and almost no sleep finally took their toll. For the first time in her life, Prudence Bosworth fainted.

Chapter 3

American millionaire Henry Abernathy leaves entire fortune to illegitimate daughter!

—The Social Gazette, *1894*

The horrid odor of ammonia penetrated her consciousness, and Prudence shook her head in protest, pushing away the hand that held a vial of foul-smelling stuff beneath her nose.

As if from a great distance away, she heard Mrs. Morris speaking. "She's coming around now."

"That is good news, indeed," a man answered, and it was the sound of his voice that recalled Prudence to the incredible situation at hand. She jerked upright.

"Don't move too quickly," Mrs. Morris cautioned, putting a hand on her shoulder. "No sense having you faint again."

"I fainted?" Prudence blinked and tried to get her bearings. She was sitting in her chair, Mrs. Morris was hovering at her elbow with a bottle of smelling salts, and standing on her other side was the attorney who had just told her she was to inherit a fortune. "Is it true?" she whispered.

"Quite true, Miss Bosworth." Turning, he crossed the room and resumed his seat. "A bit overwhelming, I suppose."

"To say the least! One million pounds a year?" Saying the amount did not make inheriting it more believable. "Heavens."

"One million pounds a year?" Mrs. Morris glanced at the attorney, then at her. "What's this?"

"Your Miss Bosworth has come into a legacy from her father. She is set to become a very rich woman. One of the richest women in the world, as a matter of fact."

"You don't say so!" Her mouth open in amazement, Mrs. Morris groped for the arm of the chintz chair beside Prudence's own and sat down. "But . . . " She swallowed hard and tried again. "But Prudence, dearest, I thought . . . that is, I believed your father had died years ago when you were a little girl. At least, that's what you told me when you came to live here."

Prudence gave the older woman an apologetic look. "I deceived you about that, I'm afraid. You see, my father deserted my mother before I was born. He—" She broke off, her cheeks heating with shame. "He never married her, and he went off to America."

"Eleven years you've lived in my lodging house and you could never tell me the truth?"

"I didn't want you to know that I was . . . " Her voice wobbled. " . . . that I was illegitimate. This is such a respectable lodging house. When I applied to you for rooms here, I was afraid you would turn me away if you knew the truth."

"It's your father who should be ashamed!" Mrs. Morris answered, and her obvious outrage filled Prudence with relief. "To abandon your mother so callously. Dishonorable cur!"

Mr. Whitfield cleared his throat. "Yes, well, he's redeemed himself now, I hope? He has left Miss Bosworth his entire fortune."

"Well, I don't know what to say to that," Mrs. Morris answered. "One million pounds a year. My goodness." She gave a breathy laugh. "No wonder you fainted, dear."

Prudence laughed with her, her mood swinging back to dazed exhilaration. "I can't seem to take it in," she said, and put a hand to her forehead, still a bit light-headed. "I can't think."

"Perfectly understandable, given the circumstances," Mr. Whitfield assured her. "I'd be rather topsy-turvy myself. But we must discuss the specific terms of your father's will. There are conditions to the inheritance of which I must make you aware—"

"Begging your pardon, sir," Mrs. Morris interrupted, "this news is most exciting—we're all overwhelmed by it, I am sure, but we must allow Miss Bosworth a few moments to recover herself."

"I'm all right now," Prudence said, sitting up straighter in her chair. "I want to hear about the will."

"No, no, your landlady is quite right. Forgive me for being much too precipitate." He gestured to the table between them. "Perhaps we should have tea now?"

"I hope it's not gone cold," Mrs. Morris said as she returned to her seat and reached for the silver teapot. "I was just bringing in the tray when I saw you faint, Prudence. Then I had to run for the smelling salts, and it took me forever to find them."

"I've never fainted before. I hope I did it gracefully."

"Yes, dear. You sank right down into your chair, one hand to your forehead in the proper manner, just as we were always taught. Sugar, Mr. Whitfield?"

"Yes, thank you," he answered, but shook his head as she held up the milk jug. "Taught?" he echoed as he accepted a cup of tea. "Girls are taught how to faint?"

"Oh, yes," Mrs. Morris assured him as she poured another cup for Prudence. "We were always practicing when I was a girl." She handed the sandwiches and tea cakes around as she began to explain the necessary precepts of a gentlewoman's education to Mr. Whitfield. Prudence paid little attention to the conversation. She ate her food and drank her tea and tried to comprehend this amazing thing that had happened to her, but a strange sense of unreality pervaded her mind.

One million pounds.

She couldn't conceive of such a sum. It was too much. It was enormous. And to have that much money every year? Why, even Lady Alberta Denville didn't have a fortune that could compare. With that thought, a burst of joyous glee shot up within her like a rocket. She set aside her empty plate and teacup with a clatter and jumped out of her chair, a squeal of delight escaping her as if she were a five-year-old on Christmas morning. Before she knew what was happening, she was whirling Mrs. Morris around the drawing room, her dance steps more exuberant than graceful.

"I'm richer than Lady Alberta," she singsonged as they galloped across the carpet. "I'm richer than Lady Munro. I'm rich, I'm rich, I'm the richest girl I know! Oh!"

Her landlady laughed with her, stifling the merriment only long enough to issue a warning about their proximity to the potted fern.

"If we tumble it over, I'll buy you a new one," Prudence promised, and began singing again as they took another turn across the carpet. "I'm richer than Lady Alberta . . . "

"Miss Bosworth?" Mr. Whitfield called to her over her faulty soprano. "We must discuss the conditions of the will."

She glanced at him as she twirled Mrs. Morris in a circle. "Conditions?"

"There are certain things you must do in order to receive the full inheritance. For one thing, you are required to marry."

She stopped, letting go of Mrs. Morris so abruptly that the poor lady went spinning away and nearly demolished the potted fern. "Marry?"

"Yes. In your life, is there . . . " He paused delicately. " . . . is there perhaps some suitable young man?"

"No," she answered, trying to catch her breath and consider the ramifications of this newest development. "There's no one at all. That is to say," she amended at once, a bit embarrassed that she had not a single suitor to her name at present, "I have been very occupied with . . . with other things. Work, you see."

"I see." Mr. Whitfield took up the sheaf of documents from the settee. "Your father has stipulated that you be given one year to find a suitable husband. During that time, a generous allowance will be portioned to you each month from the income of the trust—for clothes, living expenses, and such—but at the end of the allotted time, you must be married, or the inheritance goes to various relatives of his wife."

"Wife? My father married?"

"Yes. A New York heiress named Elizabeth Tyson. She died a few years ago. She and Mr. Abernathy had no children of their own."

"So my father left all his money to me?" She shook her head. "But he never even knew me. Never wanted to know me," she added with a hint of bitterness.

"Blood ties are often stronger than we think. Which brings me back to the point. Your father badly wanted heirs of his own blood. Once you marry, the income of the estate is yours, and your husband's, of course, for your lifetime, then it passes to your direct heirs. The man you choose to wed must be approved by the trustees. I am remaining in London until that situation is resolved and you are married, and then I shall return to New York. Your income after that will be managed by our London offices. I hope you will find our firm satisfactory in—"

"Wait." Prudence held up her hand to stop him, trying to take it all in. "You must approve my marriage?"

"Yes, but I am sure that with the guidance of your aunt and uncle, you will make a suitable matrimonial choice, one we can wholeheartedly endorse."

"My aunt and uncle?" Prudence's ebullient joy faded a little. "They know of this?"

"Of course. My first task upon arriving in England was to locate you, and I journeyed first to the home of your uncle in Sussex, assuming you lived with him and his wife. But when I called upon them, they informed me that you were living out. Naturally, they would not tell a perfect stranger your exact whereabouts without knowing the reason for my inquiry. They are delighted by your good fortune and will be arriving in London shortly to assist you."

"Assist me?" Prudence did not like the direction this conversation was heading. A knot began to form in her tummy, a typical reaction to thoughts of Aunt Edith, and one that threatened to overshadow the joy of the present moment. "Assist me with what?"

"Your introduction into society, of course. Your aunt will act as your chaperone."

Prudence suppressed a groan. The last person in the world she would choose as a chaperone would be Aunt Edith. After her mother's death, when she was fourteen, she had lived with her mother's brother, his wife, and their two daughters. For three years she had been the illegitimate poor relation, the burden, the obligation, and being reminded of that by the women of her uncle's household had made life so intolerable that she had moved to London to make her own way in the world.

"Can't Mrs. Morris act as my chaperone?" Even

as she said it, she knew how impossible a notion that was.

"My dear Miss Bosworth, with all due respect to your friend . . . " He paused to give a nod to the other woman. " . . . you must marry well, and to do that, you need introductions into a higher echelon of society than that to which you've been accustomed. Your uncle is a squire, and your aunt the cousin of a baronet. These connections provide you with the necessary entrée."

Prudence knew that was probably true, but she still resisted, hoping for an alternative. "I should like to make a different choice."

"Have you other suitable connections?"

She thought of her friend Emma, who had also lived in Mrs. Morris's lodging house until her marriage one month earlier. Emma had wed her former employer, a viscount. "I am acquainted with Viscountess Marlowe. She is, in fact, a friend of mine."

"You know Emma and Marlowe are in Italy for their honeymoon, dear," Mrs. Morris reminded her. "They won't be home until June."

Prudence looked hopefully at Mr. Whitfield. "I don't suppose I could wait until then to make my come-out?"

The attorney shook his head. "I should strongly advise against that course. The London season will be coming to an end, and you do have only one year in which to make a suitable match. Also, there is the matter of the newspapers. Journalists will learn of your situation very quickly. You cannot hope to keep it a secret. Within days you will be much talked of, your attentions sought by all manner of people, many of them not the right sort. Being a young lady, you are blissfully unaware of the more unsavory aspects of human nature. You need your relations to protect you."

"I have been living out since I was seventeen. At twenty-eight, I hardly think I need protecting now."

"Miss Bosworth, there is an enormous amount of money at stake, and money is a strange thing. It brings out the worst in people. In choosing your future spouse, you need people whose judgment you can trust, people upon whose advice and guidance you can rely."

She had no intention of relying on Aunt Edith's guidance about anything, especially about someone to marry. Still, to go into society, she did need a chaperone. And Uncle Stephen had always been kind to her. "I suppose you are right," she said, resigning herself to the inevitable. "They are family, after all. Living with them is probably the best course. At least until Emma returns in June."

"If you're not married by then," Mrs. Morris put in. "With your dowry, you won't lack for suitors!"

Prudence's spirits brightened at once. "That's true. Why, the gentlemen will be queuing up outside my door now!"

"That is more true than you realize," Mr. Whitfield said, and leaned forward on the settee. "Though I can appreciate your joy, I feel impelled to caution you, Miss Bosworth. Wealth can be an enormous burden."

"Burden?" That notion was so absurd, Prudence couldn't help laughing, despite the man's grave countenance. "How can wealth be anything but a blessing? With money, one can do anything. Why, all my life I've wished I were rich!"

The solicitor studied her with a thoughtful expression. "The only thing more difficult to bear than an unfulfilled wish, my dear, is a wish come true."

Prudence got her first inkling of Mr. Whitfield's meaning the following day after church. Aunt Edith arrived.

She and Maria were in their flat, removing their gloves, cloaks, and hats in preparation to join the other ladies of the lodging house for Sunday-afternoon tea downstairs, when the news of Edith's arrival was brought to them by Dorcas, the parlor maid. .

"That didn't take long," Maria murmured after Dorcas had departed. "They must have taken an express train."

Prudence made a face as she began pulling off her gloves. "My aunt has never been in that much of a hurry to see me."

"Until now."

There was an emphasis in Maria's voice that caused Prudence to pause. She gave a sigh of acknowledgment. "Because of the money, I suppose."

"Of course it's the money!" Maria skewered her hat with her hat pin and tossed it onto her bed. "It isn't out of concern for you."

"No," she agreed mildly as she resumed her task. "I know that."

Maria bit her lip, looking contrite. "I'm sorry. I'm happy for you, of course I am. You'll never have to work or scrape by or any of that again."

"Only if I marry, and that's by no means certain."

"Oh, you'll find someone. You'll be leaving us behind, moving in high circles, meeting all sorts of gentlemen, and one of them's bound to catch your fancy. Your life is going to be so different from now on, and everything is going to change—" Her voice broke and she turned away. "They'll be waiting tea. Let's go down."

Maria took a step toward the door, but Prudence stopped her, putting a hand on her arm and turning her around. This was the first opportunity she'd had to discuss her new situation with her friend. Maria had served at another ball the previous night and was very late arriving home, too late for Prudence, who had tumbled into bed, still excited but also exhausted, at ten o'clock.

She'd barely had time to tell her friend the news this morning on the way to church.

"Maria, everything's going to change for the better. I'm not the only one who won't have to work. If I do marry and inherit this money, I'm giving some of it to you. Yes, I am," she added when her friend started to protest. "I want you to have a share."

"I don't want your money."

"But I want you to have it. You can use it as a dowry for yourself or as a nest egg or—"

"I said I don't want your money!" Maria spoke with such vehemence, Prudence was startled.

"But why not? There will be plenty to go around."

"That's not the point. Wealth is a curse. It . . . it does things to people."

This statement was an almost exact echo of what Mr. Whitfield had said, but Prudence didn't understand it any better now than she had yesterday. "How can you say that? Why, you and I are always buying sweeps tickets and dreaming of what we'd do if we had pots of money. And now we do."

"No, we don't. You do."

"What's mine is yours," she said firmly. "You're having some of it, and I won't take no. And I want our other friends to have some, too. Lucy and Daisy and Miranda and Mrs. Morris—I want everyone here at Little Russell Street to have some of it. And I'll give some to charities, too."

"Oh, Pru." Maria pulled free of her hand and sat down on the edge of her bed with a sigh. "You can't just go around giving your money away to everyone who needs it. It's not that simple. Don't you see that?"

"Of course, I'll only give it away to those who are deserving," she began, and sat down opposite her friend on the edge of her own bed. "I've been thinking about it all morning, and I have some ideas. I want to give some for orphans, and illegitimate children, and—"

The sound of the front door opening interrupted this outline of her plans, and a high, arch voice floated through the open doorway from the parlor of the flat. "Prudence?"

She groaned under her breath, but when her aunt came bustling into the bedroom, she forced herself to smile as she stood up and turned to greet her.

"Prudence, there you are!" The older woman entered the small bedroom, her hands outstretched in greeting. "My dear."

"Aunt Edith," Prudence said as she accepted a kiss on the cheek. "This is quite a surprise."

"I don't know why. Mr. Whitfield was to have informed you to expect us in town."

"He didn't tell her you were taking the overnight express," Maria said, her voice cheery.

Prudence started to laugh, but managed to transform it into a tactful little cough as she gestured to the woman standing nearby. "Aunt, you do remember Miss Martingale?"

Edith's smile froze in place. "Of course," she said. "I believe we met on my last visit."

"What a wonderful memory you've got, Mrs. Feathergill," Maria answered at once, "to remember something that happened so long ago."

The rebuke was plain, and Aunt Edith began bristling. "Now see here, young woman, there are reasons I haven't been to London for some years now, and I resent your implication—"

"Will you take tea with us, Aunt?" Prudence interrupted, compelled to jump into the breach before a quarrel could begin.

Edith recovered herself with an effort. "Tea? Oh, no, dear, not today. You and I are having tea with Sir Robert and his mother. You do remember Steven's cousin, Sir Robert Ogilvie, and his mother Millicent? They stayed with us one summer when you were living with us."

"Yes, of course," she answered politely. She was lying, of course, for she barely remembered Robert and his mother, and she doubted they remembered her, for they hadn't ever bothered to answer any of her letters when she first arrived in London eleven years earlier. "They've invited us to tea?"

"Yes. Sir Robert is a baronet now, you know. You didn't seem much impressed with him when you were fifteen, but you might change your mind when you see him now. He's turned into quite a handsome gentleman, and he is most eager to renew his acquaintance with you."

"Of course he is," Maria muttered, but at Prudence's imploring look, she turned away. "They'll be waiting tea, I expect, so I'd best go down. I'll tell them you won't be joining us today, Pru. If you'll pardon me?" She bobbed a departing curtsy to Edith and practically ran out of the room. Prudence watched her escape with a hint of envy.

"Impertinent girl," Edith pronounced the moment the door of the flat closed behind Maria. "Is it necessary for her to be so forthcoming with her opinions?"

Already Prudence was remembering all the reasons she'd left Sussex. "Maria is my friend. She has my best interests at heart."

"As we all do, dearest. Though you didn't particularly appreciate my guidance and advice when you were a girl. You were so rebellious then. So stubborn."

Prudence remembered the three years she'd lived with her uncle's family somewhat differently, but she knew there was no point in discussing the topic at this late date.

"Heavens, look at the time," Edith exclaimed with a glance at her brooch watch. "We'd best get on with things. There is so much to do."

"Is there?" she asked, happy to change the subject.

Ignoring the question, Edith gestured to the armoire against one wall. "Your gowns are in here, I suppose?" Without waiting for an answer, she crossed the room and opened the doors of the armoire to examine Prudence's wardrobe. As she perused the garments within, she gave a heavy sigh. "Just as I thought. Not a thing here fit to wear."

Prudence, who had made all the clothes in question, set her jaw, folded her arms and did not reply.

"My dear child," Edith said as she continued rooting through Prudence's clothes, "how have you been spending the two pound and six allowance your uncle sends you each quarter?"

Lodgings. Food. Minor things like that. She bit her lip.

Edith glanced over her. "The green wool you have on will do well enough for today, I suppose, but we simply must have you fitted with suitable gowns as soon as possible. It's fortunate that even the most exclusive dressmakers keep a few ready-made dresses to hand. We ought to be able to find you something decent to wear for Tuesday evening."

"Tuesday evening?"

"Yes, dear. We are attending the opera. Sir Robert has a box, and he has invited us to join him. We must find you a gown suitable to the occasion." She pulled out a gray serge walking suit and looked it over, then put it back. "At least we won't have to pack any of these. They can be bundled up and taken to charity."

Prudence was a placid sort of person, not generally prone to fits of temper, but such high-handedness was too much to bear. "I have no intention of giving these to charity!"

The moment the words were out of her mouth, she felt silly and unreasonable, for she had already decided to give her old clothes away.

At her sharp reply, Edith turned, looking wounded. "Well, of course, dear, if you prefer to give your castoffs to your friends, by all means do so."

Prudence intended all her friends to have their own new dresses as well, but she decided not to mention that. She hated rows, and she didn't want to have one with Edith after only five minutes. Taking a deep breath, she reached for the gloves she'd cast aside a few minutes earlier. "You're right, of course," she said, striving to be gracious. "Donating them will be fine."

Edith smiled in a conciliatory fashion as she tucked her arm through Prudence's and began leading her out of the bedroom. "Your uncle is meeting with Mr. Whitfield to make the arrangements regarding your allowance from the trust. Oh, and he is seeking to purchase a brougham for us. In the interim, I have hired a carriage. We can make several calls on our way to tea."

"Calls?"

"Yes, but there is no need to be alarmed." She patted Prudence's arm as they crossed the parlor toward the front door of the flat. "We are only calling on my daughters today."

"That's a relief," Prudence murmured without enthusiasm as she lifted her reticule from a hook of the hat rack. Beryl and Pearl were as enjoyable as a Presbyterian funeral. "I was worried we'd be calling on horrid people."

It was probably a good thing that sarcasm was wasted on Aunt Edith. "Moving in good society is always a bit nerve-wracking, but try to put your mind at ease. Your uncle and I shall take very good care of you, you know. The most fashionable address, the best entertainments, the finest company. I will ensure you are presented to the right sort of people, dearest. I intend to devote myself entirely to your needs from now on."

"Lovely." Suppressing a sigh, Prudence closed the front door of the flat behind them. June, she reflected as she shoved her latchkey into the lock, seemed a long way off.

"Your uncle will find a suitable house for us here in town," Edith went on as they started down the stairs. "But until then, we are staying at the Savoy. I've arranged for your room to be right beside mine. Won't that be nice?"

Prudence began to feel rather like a cornered animal. "I don't wish to be any trouble," she said in desperation. "I would much rather stay here for the time being."

"Here?" Aunt Edith paused on the landing and looked askance around the dim stairwell. "Don't be silly," she remonstrated with a tinkling little laugh. "This is a lodging house."

"A respectable one."

"A most respectable one, I am sure, but Prudence, you are an heiress now of substantial means. You cannot stay here on your own. Why, without your uncle and I to watch over you, every fortune-hunting scoundrel in London would be on your heels!"

Rhys spent Monday reckoning up what little he had in ducal income, and Tuesday wading through the complicated mire of the De Winter family debts. After studying reports from various land agents, bankers, and attorneys, his spirits were nearly as low as his bank balance, and he had no choice but to dine Tuesday night at the Clarendon. He consoled himself with a superb beef fillet and a fine bottle of French Bordeaux, and by some clever timing he was able to duck out without paying the bill, a practice at which he'd become quite adept in the past few years.

"No peer should ever pay at the Clarendon," he explained to Lord Standish later that night at the opera. "Thank heaven for middle-class sensibilities."

Standish, an old acquaintance from days at Oxford and his host for the evening, laughed. "What do middle-class sensibilities have to do with you caging meals at the Clarendon?"

"Everything," he answered at once, turning to accept a glass of champagne from a footman. "The middle class won't dine at any establishment unless peers frequent it. A fortunate thing for us they are able and willing to pay. Without them, restaurants would be forced to close, and we should never dine out again."

Lord Weston, whose friendship with Rhys also went back to boyhood, flashed him a wry grin. "Only certain peers are able to get by with that in London nowadays, St. Cyres. Having a duke dine at your establishment still carries a certain cachet. I, however, am merely a baron, and can never get by with such things. I know this because whenever I try to evade the bill, they forward it to my residence."

"All the more reason not to have a residence!" Rhys countered, making everyone laugh.

"But how does one live without a residence?" asked Standish, looking puzzled. But then, Standish had always been one of those upright, scrupulous sorts who wouldn't dream of spending beyond his means and evading his bills.

"Travel, of course," Rhys answered him. "It's very simple. One goes abroad to escape one's debts at home. One comes home to escape one's debts abroad. In this way, a man can explore the entire globe for less than five hundred pounds."

Everyone laughed, including Standish. "But where does a gentleman live while here in town?" the earl asked.

"Off his friends, of course!" Rhys clapped Weston on the back. "Have you a spare room, Wes, by the way? I can't abide Milbray's town house much longer. His butler's far too courteous. Let my mother in a few days ago. It was ghastly."

"Have you in my house?" Smiling, Weston shook his head. "Not a chance of it. I have my sister to think of."

He grinned back at the other man. "Don't you trust me?"

"With my sister? Not for a moment."

A gong sounded, informing everyone in the Royal Opera House that the performance was about to begin, and Standish's guests began moving toward the seats that overlooked the stage to the left and the floor below.

Rhys started to do the same, but Weston stopped him. "Have you been north since coming home?"

"Visit my own estates? God, no. Inflicting such depressing sights on oneself is unhealthy. If you ever tell me you are paying your estates a visit, Wes, I shall be quite concerned for you."

Weston didn't laugh. "I've seen St. Cyres Castle. Went hunting near there with Munro last autumn. It was . . . not in the best condition."

"Exactly my point. Visiting one's country houses is too depressing for words."

"Rhys—" He broke off, then sighed. "You know the rumors floating through town, I suppose?"

Rhys's smile flattened, but he kept it in place. After all, a gentleman was required to put up a good show. "I say, did you know I have the singular honor of possessing two ducal titles?"

Weston blinked at this seeming change of subject. "Two?"

"Yes. The day after I arrived home, *Talk of the Town* proclaimed me not only the Duke of St. Cyres but also the Duke of Debt. And, according to the *Social Gazette,* I can be had at a discount." He took a sip of champagne and grinned. "So clever, these London journalists."

"How can you laugh it off?"

He shrugged. "No sense losing one's sense of humor."

"All joking aside, my friend, are things as bad as they say?"

"If things were that good, I'd be celebrating. Unfortunately, they're not. Evelyn, being an idiot as well as a prize bastard, kept everything in land. As if land is any use to anybody nowadays."

"He had no funds? No other investments?" Weston was understandably astonished. "Even my father, as old-fashioned as he was, put a bit of money into Newcastle coal mines and American railroads. Those are the only things saving us now."

"How fortunate for you. I, on the other hand, am the proud owner of over ten thousand acres of mortgaged farmland and pasture. But I am choosing to look on the bright side. I'll wager my estates are the prettiest in Britain. Not a coal mine or railroad in sight to spoil the views."

Weston laid a hand on his arm. "I'm sorry, Rhys. Truly. I'm mortgaged pretty heavily myself, but I might be able to raise another loan if you need—"

Rhys, who loathed pity, never gave it to anyone, and never accepted it when it was offered, turned away. "We're missing the opera."

"God forbid we should miss Wagner," Weston murmured behind him, but being a tactful chap, he let the matter drop.

Rhys took his seat but paid little heed to the performance. For the first time, a feeling of genuine gloom began settling over him. He might make light of obtaining free meals at the Clarendon and sponging off friends, but beneath his laughter at his own expense was the inescapable taint of desperation.

He'd always been cynical, believing the worst because the worst was so often true, and in regard to the family holdings, he'd been particularly pessimistic. But after seven days home, he was realizing he'd been somewhat out in his assumptions. Things were far worse than he had thought possible.

If the reports he'd read that afternoon were accurate, then Winter Park was the only property he possessed in decent condition, no doubt because that residence was the one where Uncle Evelyn had spent most of his time. It was also a house Rhys loathed, the house where he and Thomas had spent that god-awful holiday the summer he was twelve. He had no intention of living there at the end of the season. He'd rather live on the streets. Winter Park would have to be leased.

The other estates, he'd been told, could not be let to anyone in their present condition, with the ducal seat of St. Cyres Castle being in the sorriest state of all. The fortified manor house, its original keep held by his family since the time of Edward I, was apparently a deserted ruin, though he'd been assured it could be made fit to live in. It would cost about a hundred thousand pounds to replace the sold furnishings, fix the roof and the rotted timbering, repair the drains, stock the larder, rebuild the tenant cottages, till and plant the crops, and clear all debts to the village tradesmen.

A hundred thousand pounds? What a good joke. He couldn't even afford beefsteak at the Clarendon. Rhys rested his head against the back of his chair and closed his eyes. Over the lurid music of Wagner, he heard Letitia's voice, a voice that beneath her polished veneer of well-bred disdain echoed the sick fear that was forming in his own guts.

What are you going to do?

He thought of the enormous outlays of cash that would soon have to be made. Death duties for old Evelyn had to be paid to Her Majesty's government. First quarter interest payments on the mortgaged De Winter lands were due in June. There were jointures to be paid, annuities, servants' wages, tradesmen's bills—the list was endless. Where was the money going to come from? He would apply to bankers for more credit, but there wasn't a prayer they'd grant it.

A wave of frustration rose within him. He didn't want this, not the titles, not the estates, and certainly not the responsibilities. Hell, if he'd wanted to be the next Duke of St. Cyres, he'd have murdered Evelyn and given the bugger his just deserts long ago. Instead, he hadn't even waited for the ink to dry on his examinations at Oxford before taking the money left him by his father, money Evelyn hadn't been able to touch, and running off to Italy, where he'd spent it all in grand style. He'd never been home, never given a damn, never looked back. Until now.

Now, destitution hovered at his elbow like the grim reaper. But really, hadn't it always been there? Wasn't that why he had lived so high for so long without thinking of the consequences, without contemplating what was down the road? During his days in Florence, plenty of other peers, Weston among them, had stayed with him. They'd been the ones to joke about dodging the bills at restaurants and living off one's friends, coming abroad to escape their own inevitable future just as he had—a future of position with no income to maintain it, possessed of an absolute belief in their superior breeding, yet without the cash to pay for their own meals. He'd known it would come to that for him as well, a brutal truth that impelled him to spend his money twice as fast after each friend who'd come abroad to live off of him was forced to depart for home.

Despite his present circumstances, though, he didn't regret a thing. If he'd been prudent and careful these past twelve years, it wouldn't have made a dent in the mountain of debt already accumulated by his predecessors. Like himself, the past half-dozen Dukes of St. Cyres had lived on their capital, spending their money on extravagance after extravagance and having a hell of a good time in the process.

But now the ball was over. He just happened to be the duke who got handed the bill.

What are you going to do?

Rhys opened his eyes, making a sound of derision under his breath. Pointless of Letitia to ask a question that had only one answer.

He was going to marry an heiress, of course. He'd known that to be his only choice for a long time now. The reports he'd read today only served to underscore the inevitability of his course.

Might as well get on with things. He straightened in his seat and pulled his pair of opera glasses from the breast pocket of his evening jacket to officially begin the hunt for the next Duchess of St. Cyres.

He tried to banish his gloom by reckoning up what he had on his side of the ledger. He was a duke, and as Weston had pointed out, that still counted for something. He was also well aware of his appeal to women, and a most fortunate talent it was, too, when one had to marry for money. As an added bonus, he was sitting beside Cora Standish tonight, a woman who knew everyone in London society and could give him their financial status as well as their social position. If he came across a pretty face, Cora would know the name and dowry that came with it.

He began to scan the boxes opposite, and almost at once found his attention caught, not by an heiress, but by a far more intriguing sight. In a deliciously low-cut gown of pink silk, a simple strand of pearls at her neck and another woven into her dark hair, was the delectable wench he'd seen a fortnight ago mending gowns.

Since when did a seamstress wear pearls and silk and attend the opera? Rhys straightened in his chair and leaned forward, certain he had to be mistaken.

But after studying her for several moments, he knew there was no mistake. It was her. Desire began thrumming through his body, just as it had the moment he'd first seen her down on her knees in that deceptively submissive pose. He imagined her now as he had then, with his hand in her hair.

He shifted in his seat with a grimace. Such erotic imaginings, as delicious as they were, could not lead anywhere, not with this woman, and certainly not at this moment. Despite that, he found himself unable to look away.

He wondered why she was here. Her silk dress had been borrowed, no doubt, and the pearls had probably come from some Manchester manufacturer rather than from oysters, but that did not explain her presence in an opera box at Covent Garden. Perhaps his little seamstress had decided to embark on a more lucrative career. His gaze slid across a tempting expanse of smooth white skin and came to rest where the low neckline of her gown met the high, round curves of her breasts. Not for the first time, Rhys cursed his present lack of funds.

"What on earth are you staring at?" Cora asked, tapping his thigh with her fan. "I must know what has so captivated your interest that you choose to ignore not only your hostess and your fellow guests, but also the performance."

He took a deep breath, striving to force down his arousal, but he didn't take his eyes from the fetching sight across the theater. "I am ignoring the performance because I loathe Wagner. Valkyries always give me a headache. I am ignoring you because you are already married, my sweet, and one of those rare creatures in love with your own husband, a man who is hovering on your other side with tiresome possessiveness. And since Standish practices such strict economies nowadays, you can't even grant me a loan."

"So you have turned your attention in a more profitable direction? Some rich heiress, I suppose?"

"Alas, no." He lifted his gaze, somewhat reluctantly, from Miss Bosworth's splendid breasts to her face. It was not a beautiful face by any means, but pretty enough, with its dumpling cheeks, turned-up nose, and quite kissable mouth. But it was her eyes—those big, soft, dark eyes—that would make a name for her, if she were truly intent to become a woman on the town. "Much to my regret, the woman in question is no heiress."

"You intrigue me. Point her out."

"Straight across," he obliged, "then two boxes to the right. Dark hair, pink silk dress and pearls."

Lady Standish peered through her own opera glasses, scanned the boxes across the way, and gave a cry of triumph. "How you do tease, St. Cyres, to say you were not staring at an heiress when you've set your sights on the richest one in the room!"

That gained his full attention. "I beg your pardon?"

"The woman you've been gaping at is Miss Prudence Abernathy, the daughter of that American millionaire."

Rhys began to laugh. "You've gotten muddled somehow, Cora. Her name's not Abernathy. It's Bosworth, and she's no millionaire's daughter. She's a seamstress."

"She *was* a seamstress, darling. But she's also Henry Abernathy's illegitimate daughter. You've heard of Abernathy's Department Stores, I trust?"

Rhys decided to humor her. "How do you know this?"

"I saw the girl myself at Madame Marceau's this afternoon."

"Exactly. The Marceau woman is who she works for."

"How you know which seamstresses work for which dressmakers baffles me, St. Cyres."

He grinned. "I have devoted a lifetime to the study of feminine apparel."

"Learning how best to remove it, no doubt," she countered dryly, but didn't give him the chance to reply before she went on. "At any rate, the girl wasn't at the dressmaker's to work, believe me. She was with her aunt, being fitted for gowns, and Marceau was in such a flutter as I've never seen, tripping over herself to make the girl happy. A friend of mine, Lady Marley, was with them—she's slightly acquainted with the aunt and knows their cousin—Sir Robert Something. He's a baronet, I think. Anyway, she introduced me, and later, after the girl had gone, told me the whole story."

Cora leaned toward him, eager to share London's latest gossip. "Henry Abernathy, the girl's father, wasn't always so rich. He was originally a Yorkshire farmer named Bosworth who had a fling with the daughter of the local squire."

"How naughty of him."

"Very naughty." Cora edged closer and whispered, "Bun in the oven."

"Ah. Our heiress, I presume?" When Cora nodded, he went on, "I take it the squire had no dowry for his pregnant daughter?"

"Just so. The income from Squire Feathergill's land wasn't more than a few hundred a year. So instead of doing the honorable thing and marrying her anyway, Bosworth ran off to America, changed his name to Abernathy, and married some heiress from New York."

"Clever bastard," Rhys said with appreciation.

"The girl's mother died some years ago, and the girl lived with her uncle's family for a time. The uncle, being the squire's son, inherited the estate, but the family was still quite badly off, and the girl came to London, got a flat, and began to earn her own living as a seamstress."

"Sounds like something written by a lady novelist."

"Doesn't it? But so many girls are doing that

nowadays. 'Girl-bachelors' they're called. Scandalous notion. Anyway, the father made a fortune in those department stores of his. He recently died, and in his will, he left every penny to the girl."

Rhys crossed his fingers. "How many pennies, Cora?"

"The income is over a million pounds a year, so they say."

Staggered, he swallowed hard. "Good God. Even I might find it hard to spend that much money."

"But there's a catch. This is the part you'll be interested in, darling. She has to marry in order to claim the inheritance."

An image of those big brown eyes gazing up at him in obvious adoration flashed through his mind, and the gloom that had been haunting him began to dispel. He lifted the opera glasses for another look at Miss Bosworth-cum-Abernathy, and found that she was growing more luscious by the moment. "Over a million pounds a year, you say?" he murmured. "Fancy that."

Chapter 4

A certain duke and a certain heiress have been spied tête-à-tête at the opera. What can it mean? Is love in bloom in Covent Garden?

—Talk of the Town, *1894*

Prudence wasn't sure she liked opera. She was just as fond as anyone of a rollicking penny revue or a Gilbert and Sullivan production, but the performance this evening was like neither of those. It was dark, heavy, and somewhat overwrought. The intermission came as a relief.

The moment the curtains closed across the stage and the lights came up, she leaned forward in her chair to survey the scene spread out before her. Between opulent crystal chandeliers that sparkled with electric lights, elegantly dressed ladies and gentlemen sat in luxuriously appointed boxes.

So this is how the rich people live, she thought, amazed. It was still hard to believe she was now one of them. For two days she had slept in a luxurious gold and white bedroom at the Savoy, with its own marble bath and fresh sheets every day. She had worn silks, dined at the finest restaurants, shopped for jewels, and gadded about London in a brougham with red leather seats, making calls on people her aunt said were "the right sort." Yet, despite all that, her situation still did not seem quite real to her.

Down below, people were strolling toward the foyer, and Prudence decided to do the same. "I'm going to take a turn downstairs," she said and rose to her feet.

In unison, all her relations stood up as well. "Capital idea, cousin," Robert said, offering his arm. "We could all do with a stretch of the legs."

As she and Robert descended the stairs with his mother, Aunt Edith, and Uncle Stephen behind them, Prudence wondered in some exasperation if her relations were going to hover over her this way through the entire season. Only two days of their assiduous attention, and she was already beginning to feel smothered.

"Would you care for some refreshment?" Robert asked as they paused in the crowded foyer. "I'd be happy to bring you a glass of lemonade."

"Thank you, but I don't care for lemonade. I'd like champagne, please."

"Champagne?" Aunt Edith's surprised voice intervened. "Oh, no, Prudence, dear. You aren't accustomed to spirits, and I should so hate for you to wake up tomorrow with a headache. Lemonade will do nicely, Robert, thank you."

Prudence's exasperation deepened. She wasn't a green girl of sixteen, in heaven's name. She opened her mouth to insist on champagne, but then caught sight of one man amid the crowd, and the words she'd been about to say went straight out of her head.

It was him.

There was no mistaking the broad-shouldered frame and windblown, golden beauty of the Duke of St. Cyres. He stood facing her about two dozen feet away, amid a group of acquaintances.

Beside her, Aunt Edith murmured something about a visit to the ladies' retiring room, and though Millicent concurred with this suggestion, Prudence intended to remain right where she was. "Go, by all means," she urged the other two women. "I shall stay here."

Her aunt and Millicent departed, and Uncle Stephen said something about hoping they wouldn't be long, for he wanted to have a pipe before the opera resumed.

"You don't need to wait for them to come back," Prudence told him without taking her eyes from the duke. "Go smoke your pipe. I don't mind."

"No, no," he protested, but without much conviction. "I couldn't leave you standing here all alone."

"Oh, you needn't worry about that," she said at once. "Robert will be returning shortly. In the meantime, I shall remain right by this pillar. I shan't move an inch, I promise. Go on."

Uncle Stephen needed no further urging, and he departed for the smoking room, leaving Prudence alone at last. She continued to watch the duke as he conversed with several companions, and when one of them said something to make him smile, the strangest sensation happened inside of her. Her tummy dipped with a weightlessness that made her feel as if she were in one of those elevator contraptions.

Suddenly, he glanced past his companions and saw her. His gaze caught at her face, lingered there, and everything in Prudence seemed to freeze. She couldn't move, couldn't breathe, couldn't turn away. Would he remember her? Surely not. A duke would never remember a mere seamstress. Yet, he did not look away, and a slight frown creased his brow, as if she seemed familiar and he was trying to place her.

When he murmured something to his friends, disengaged himself from their circle, and started through the crowd in her direction, joy surged up within her, followed at once by sheer panic. By the time he reached her, her heart was thudding in her chest with such force that it hurt.

She hadn't realized until now just how tall he was. Prudence measured her own height at five feet and three full inches. Despite that somewhat optimistic estimate and the fact that she was wearing heels, the top of her head still barely reached his chin, and his powerful physical presence did little to calm her nerves.

"By all that's wonderful, it's Miss Bosworth!" he greeted her. Before she could gather her wits enough for any sort of reply, he took up her hand and bowed over it, lifting her fingers to his mouth in the proper manner, his lips not quite touching the fabric of her glove. "This is a lovely surprise," he added as he straightened and let go of her hand. "I thought I would never see you again."

He'd thought about her? Pleasurable warmth radiated through her body, adding to the quixotic mix of her emotions. "Hullo," she said, wishing she could think of something charming and clever to say, but that short, inelegant greeting was all she could manage. Any further words seemed caught in her throat, suspended there by the sweetness of simply looking at him and trying to believe he was truly glad to see her.

"I hope you haven't had to endure Alberta's tantrums tonight," he said, leaning closer, a teasing gleam in his green eyes. "If you tell me she has been abusing you again, I shall be forced to come to your rescue."

His greeting and his words made her realize

he didn't yet know of her inheritance. The blissful warmth in her deepened and spread. "What a gallant offer," she said, striving to sound nonchalant, as if she conversed with dukes every day of her life, "but it isn't necessary. I've come for the opera." She gestured toward the stairs to her left. "My cousins have a box."

"A box? But surely a seamstress—" He broke off, and looked away as if embarrassed.

"Surely, a seamstress, if she could afford to attend the opera at all, would be in the cheap seats?" she finished for him.

He tugged at his cravat like an abashed schoolboy. "Sorry," he muttered and returned his gaze to hers. "My mistake. Was that terribly snobbish of me?"

"No, it's perfectly understandable, given how we met. But you see, I have had a change in my situation—" She broke off, reluctant to explain. Once he knew of her inheritance, he was sure to discover she was also illegitimate, and when that happened, his manner toward her would change. He was a duke, after all. Legitimacy of birth was everything to people of his class. Though it was probable that he would eventually learn the truth, she decided to postpone the inevitable moment as long as possible. "I have been rather at odds with my mother's family," she said, skirting the vital points. "We are attempting to reconcile."

To her relief, he did not pry.

"Rum thing, families, but I wish you every success, Miss Bosworth. Although for my part," he added, looking doubtful, "I don't think listening to Wagner would put me in a forgiving and amenable state of mind. What is your opinion?"

She made a face, and he threw back his head and laughed. "Wagner not your cup of tea either, I see."

She liked his laugh. It was deep and rich and made her laugh, too. "I suppose it's because I can't understand what they're saying," she told him. "I don't speak German."

"Do you speak Italian?"

"Alas, no. I do speak French, though. My mother taught me French when I was a little girl."

"I only ask because I believe you would like Italian opera far better than the German." He moved a bit closer to her. "This is the closing night of Wagner. Verdi's *Aida,* which is sung in Italian, begins two days hence. If you plan to attend, I should be happy to act as your translator."

Her heart gave a leap of joy. "Thank you. I would—"

"Prudence!"

She almost groaned aloud at the sound of her aunt's voice. Of all the bad timing.

St. Cyres, however, merely smiled and stepped back to a more proper distance as Aunt Edith and Cousin Millicent bore down upon them.

"What is this?" her aunt demanded. "Is it the fashion for gentlemen in London nowadays to accost women who are unaccompanied, sir? Why, I have never seen—"

"Aunt Edith," Prudence cut in, "may I present the Duke of St. Cyres? Your Grace, this is my aunt, Mrs. Feathergill, and my first cousin once removed, Lady Ogilvie."

"Oh . . . I didn't . . . that is . . . " her aunt stammered, then gave a tinkling, rather awkward little laugh. "I didn't realize you were acquainted with a duke, Prudence, dear. What high circles you've been moving in."

There was a bit of fluttering as she and Millicent dipped deep curtsies. The duke bowed in response, and as he straightened, he gave Prudence a roguish wink. "I first met your niece at a ball, Mrs. Feathergill."

"Indeed? How lovely. Prudence, where is your uncle? Off smoking that foul pipe of his, I suppose. I cannot believe he left you here alone."

Prudence wished her other relations would follow that example. "Your Grace," she said, desperate to return the conversation to their previous topic, "I believe we were discussing Italian opera?"

"Here we are, here we are," Robert's voice entered the conversation before the duke could reply. "Refreshments for the ladies."

Prudence spared an impatient glance at the four brimming glasses of lemonade clasped in his hands and took the one nearest her with a perfunctory smile. "Thank you, Robert."

"My pleasure, Prudence. Anything for you." He glanced at the other man and his expression changed, as if he'd just encountered a bad smell. "St. Cyres," he greeted stiffly with a little bow. "I didn't know you were acquainted with my cousin."

"Sir Robert." He nodded to the glasses still in the other man's hands. "Watch out, old chap. You're spilling lemonade on your gloves. Best to hand it 'round before you spill any more."

"Oh. Right." Robert turned away, and the duke moved to claim the place at her side, successfully separating her from the others.

"Now," he murmured, "where were we?"

"Italian opera."

"Ah, yes. Opera. Fascinating subject." He leaned down closer to her and the camellia in his buttonhole brushed her bare arm, tickling her skin and sending shivers of excitement through her entire body. Nervous, she took a gulp from the glass in her hand and immediately grimaced.

"Fond of lemonade, are you?" he asked, laughing under his breath.

"I hate it," she admitted. "Especially when it's lukewarm like this. I wanted champagne, but my aunt said no. I think she's afraid I'll become tipsy and embarrass her."

"I'd like to see that."

"You'd like to see my aunt embarrassed?"

"No." His lashes, thick and golden brown, lowered a fraction, then lifted. "I'd like to see you tipsy."

The way he said those words was soft and low, strangely illicit. For no reason at all, Prudence blushed.

A gong sounded, signaling that intermission was nearly over. The echo hadn't even died away before Aunt Edith was stepping around them to her other side. "We had best return to our seats," she said, and put her arm through Prudence's as if to lead her away.

Prudence, however, did not move. "We have a bit of time still," she said, hoping for a few more precious minutes in St. Cyres's company.

"I don't think so, dear. Forgive us, Your Grace?"

"Of course." He gestured to the stairs on the other side of the foyer. "I must find my seat as well, before my friends wonder what's become of me."

Prudence felt a stab of disappointment, and she ducked her head to conceal it. "Of course," she murmured, and lifted her chin, forcing her voice and her expression to a neutrality she was far from feeling. "It was a pleasure to see you again."

"The pleasure has been mine, Miss Bosworth." He bowed. "Lady Ogilvie, Mrs. Feathergill, Sir Robert. Good evening."

He turned and departed, and after watching him a moment longer, she did the same, reluctantly allowing Aunt Edith to lead her away.

"You see, Prudence? It's just as I said the other day," Edith told her as they mounted the stairs. "We only left you alone for a moment, and fortune-hunting scoundrels began swooping down on you."

"Hardly that!" she countered with spirit. "I know the duke to be a perfect gentleman."

"Of course you would think so, dear. You are such an innocent. But I am a woman of the world, and I know his type. Out for what he can get."

"Your aunt is correct," Robert said behind her. "The man is a rake of the first water. Mama and I met him in Italy a few years ago. Do you remember, Mama?"

"I do," Millicent replied, panting a little from the effort of getting her stout frame up three flights of stairs. "You wouldn't believe the stories we heard about him. Drunken parties at his villa, swimming naked in fountains with Russian countesses, all manner of shameless goings-on."

Prudence supposed that if she were truly good, she would disapprove of such wild behavior, but in truth, she'd swim naked in a fountain, too, if she could get away with it. It sounded delightful.

"And he's deeply in debt," Robert went on. "Thousands and thousands of pounds, I hear."

"A fact which makes him no different from any other peer of the realm," Prudence countered. "I daresay you have a few debts yourself, Robert."

Her cousin grimaced and fell silent.

Aunt Edith, however, was not as easily deterred from the subject. "Robert's situation is hardly the same thing," she said as they entered their box. "He is family. Ah, Stephen, so this is where you've got to," she added, turning to her husband as he rose from his seat. "What were you about, leaving Prudence alone downstairs?" Before he could answer, she returned her attention to her niece. "Setting aside the financial considerations, there is position to consider. St. Cyres is a duke, and far too high for you. It would be an unsuitable match in every way."

"What's this about a duke?" Stephen asked, looking at his wife in bewilderment.

"Ask your niece. She knows him already. Met him at a ball, of all the extraordinary things!"

"I happened to meet the Duke of St. Cyres a few days ago," Prudence explained as she circled the table to her own chair by the rail and sat down. "He paid his addresses to me downstairs just now."

Stephen gave a low whistle. "That didn't take long."

"Exactly," Edith said as she took her own seat beside Prudence. "It's obvious he's after her money."

"Of course, his interest in me could not possibly be genuine attraction!" Prudence shot back, stung. "You attribute the lowest possible motives to him, but I choose not to be so quick to judge!"

"Steady on, Prudence," Uncle Stephen said. "We are your family, and we are only thinking of you. St. Cyres is a thoroughly bad lot, not fit company for a young lady. And as for marrying the fellow, Edith is right. It's out of the question."

"I believe it is I who must decide whom to marry!"

"No need to raise your voice, dearest," Edith said, looking a bit like an abused spaniel. "Our only wish is for your happiness."

Prudencc pressed her fingers to her forehead and reminded herself that June was only twelve weeks away. "Oh, let's not quarrel. Besides, it's far too soon to be talking about my marrying anyone."

Thankfully, everyone let the matter drop, but thoughts of the duke continued to occupy Prudence's mind. She knew her family was right to take a dim view of any romantic connection between St. Cyres and herself. A duke would hardly choose as his duchess a woman whose parents had never married, a woman who until a few short days ago had been a seamstress in a dressmaker's showroom. Yet, he had remembered her, he had gone out of his way to speak to her. He didn't even know about her inheritance. The fact that he had called her Miss Bosworth proved that much. In addition, he had already demonstrated by his actions that he was a thoughtful and gallant man. Her family was prepared to think the worst of him, but she was able to see him in a more balanced light than that.

And of course, there was the fact that he was so terribly attractive. She bit her lip and stared down into her glass of lukewarm lemonade, remembering his words of a few moments ago.

I'd like to see you tipsy.

She couldn't imagine why he would want such a thing. During the fine nights when she'd walked home from the showroom, she had seen drunken people stumbling along the sidewalk or through the open doorways of taverns as they sang boisterous songs at the top of their lungs. Drunkenness didn't seem a desirable state at all.

Still, as she remembered his words, she wished one of Berliner's gramophones could have recorded the moment, so she could relive it whenever she liked, hear again the strange, soft note in his voice that had made her blush all the way down to her toes.

"If you please, sir?" someone said from the doorway, breaking into Prudence's thoughts.

She turned in her chair to see a liveried footman standing by the entrance to their box, a tray in his hands on which reposed several tall crystal flutes and a silver ice bucket containing a bottle of champagne. "I've something for the Ogilvie party."

"There must be a mistake," Uncle Stephen exclaimed as the footman brought the tray to the table. "We did not order this."

"Compliments of his grace, the Duke of St. Cyres," the footman explained as he popped the cork on the champagne. He poured the sparkling wine into the glasses and brought the first one to Prudence, presenting it to her along with a small white envelope. "For Miss Bosworth, from His Grace."

She snatched the envelope before her aunt could do so. Setting aside her glass, she broke the seal and unfolded the note.

Miss Bosworth, the only thing duller than German opera is lemonade. Your servant, St. Cyres.

She read it three times, running the tips of her fingers just beneath the strong, stark lines of his handwriting, then reluctantly tucked the note away into her evening bag.

"How considerate he is," she said, responding to her aunt's sour expression with a sweet smile as she picked up her glass. She took a sip of her champagne and found it every bit as delightful as its reputation warranted, but it was only a temporary diversion from the even more delightful topic occupying her mind.

Turning her attention to the other side of the theater, she took her opera glasses from her pocket and lifted them to scan the boxes opposite.

She found him almost at once, as if she had sensed where he was by some mysterious spiritual connection between them, and it jolted her to discover he was looking at her, too. He was leaning back in his chair, his opera glasses folded in one hand, his flute of champagne held in the other, staring straight at her across the expanse between them, his head tilted to one side, a hint of a smile curving his lips. The sight of him watching her brought a rush of pleasure so acute it hurt.

She lowered her opera glasses and lifted her flute of champagne in acknowledgment of his gift. He lifted his in reply. They each drank at the same time, and the moment made her feel giddy, as if she'd drunk the entire bottle of champagne instead of just two sips.

The lights lowered and the opera resumed, putting an end to the magical moment. She leaned back in her chair and turned her gaze to the stage below, but in her mind she saw only him. Heavy German music reverberated through the theater, but all she heard was the whisper of her own wishful hope.

If only . . .

Prudence pressed her fingers to her lips. Impossible that a devastatingly handsome duke would ever fall in love with a plump, rather ordinary spinster who had calluses from needlework on her fingers and the blood of ordinary Yorkshire country folk in her veins. Impossible, and yet, she sat in the dark and imagined it anyway.

Chapter 5

London's newest heiress demonstrates a profound interest in art. What a happy coincidence some of London's most eligible bachelors share her enthusiasm.

—The Social Gazette, *1894*

Rhys pulled a newspaper from the pile beside his plate of eggs and bacon and grimaced at once. *Talk of the Town.* A journalistic endeavor that made him wish he owned a parrot, so suitable was it as a depository for bird droppings.

Much to his relief, however, London's most sensational newspaper was far too preoccupied today with news of Miss Prudence Abernathy to make snide comments about the financial status and wicked ways of a certain duke. Their account of the seamstress-turned-heiress substantiated what Cora had told him the night before, though it glossed over her illegitimacy and spoke of a halcyon Yorkshire childhood Rhys viewed with skepticism. Bastard children never had an easy time of it, and childhoods were never halcyon. They were the torture one spent the rest of one's life recovering from, though perhaps his own hellish upbringing had given him a rather jaded view on the subject.

The newspaper also waxed volubly on the happy days she had spent in Sussex with her aunt and uncle after her mother's death. Her mother's family, the paper said, had cared for her with overwhelming kindness and generosity, and that statement gave Rhys all the more reason to view this account of her life with a jaundiced eye. He remembered her words from the night before about reconciling with her mother's family, and if her life with the Feathergills had been so blissful, there would have been no reconciliations necessary. Besides, he'd met the aunt. Kindness and generosity were not what came to mind.

Not all the morning papers displayed the sort of treacly sentiments about Miss Abernathy and her family expressed by *Talk of the Town*, but he knew reading about her wasn't going to help his cause, and when his valet entered the breakfast room a few minutes later, Rhys was happy to set aside the morning papers in the hope of more useful information. "Well, Fane, have you determined Miss Abernathy's plans for today?"

The valet paused beside his master's chair. "She intends to visit the National Gallery this afternoon. There is an exhibit of French painters on at present, and Miss Abernathy, I'm told, is fond of art."

"The National Gallery?" He stared at Fane, a bit doubtful that a former seamstress would choose to spend her time looking at paintings. "Are you certain?"

Fane looked affronted by the question. "Sir," he said with feeling.

"Forgive me," Rhys apologized at once. "But it never ceases to amaze me how you find out these things."

His valet gave a discreet cough. "I happened to encounter Miss Abernathy's new maid—Miss Nancy Woddell, her name is—in one of the laundry rooms of the Savoy. She and I are of the same mind, sir, that the laundering of our employers' clothing requires our personal attention."

"I'm delighted to hear it, though it would be a happy day indeed if I could actually afford to stay at the Savoy. But do go on."

"Upon finishing our tasks, Miss Woddell and I were able to take the service lift together. We discovered, to our mutual surprise and delight, that our separate destinations were on the very same floor."

"A most amazing coincidence," Rhys commented, vastly entertained.

"Yes, sir. Miss Woddell and I conversed in the corridor outside Miss Abernathy's suite for quite some time."

"You devil." He began to laugh. "Fane, I had no idea you were such an accomplished ladies' man."

"Five years in your service has been very useful to my education, sir, in many respects. Miss Woddell, by the way, was quite impressed by my position as valet to Comte Roselli. He married that Austrian princess, sir, if you recall. Ladies' maids always enjoy hearing about princesses."

"I shall take your word for it, and I applaud your ability to charm members of the fair sex in the laundry rooms and corridors of hotels, although I feel compelled to point out you are no longer valet to Roselli, but to me."

"Yes, sir. But I thought it best not to volunteer that information. Maids often tell things to their ladies, and Miss Abernathy might receive the impression you sent your valet to spy upon her. We don't want the young lady believing you would do something so desperate as that."

"We? Awfully presumptuous of you, Fane, to take such a personal interest in my pursuit of Miss Abernathy."

Fane's reply was succinct and to the point. "If you marry Miss Abernathy, sir, I get paid."

Rhys couldn't argue with logic like that.

* * *

He arrived at the National Gallery well ahead of Miss Abernathy, Fane in tow to perform the necessary reconnaissance. His valet's forewarning of her approach was perfectly timed, and at the moment she entered the gallery where the works of some contemporary artists were on view, Fane had vanished altogether and Rhys was demonstrating vast interest in a Renoir.

"Your Grace?"

He turned, looking—he hoped—surprised to see her. To his relief, she also seemed surprised to see him. She came toward him, the silk of her pale blue walking suit rustling with each step. Perched on her dark hair was one of those enormous hats shaped like an oversized dinner plate and piled high with a froth of dark blue ribbons and cream-colored ostrich plumes.

"We meet again, Miss Bosworth," he said, and doffed his own hat with a bow.

When Rhys straightened, he found that she was smiling, her upturned face alight with such genuine pleasure at the sight of him that he was caught off guard. Silly of her, he thought, and painfully naive as well, to display her inner feelings so openly. Hadn't anyone ever taught her to play the game?

Even as those thoughts went through his mind, something else stirred within him at the shining pleasure in her face, something he couldn't quite define, something a bit like the feeling one got when an unexpected shaft of sunlight peeked out from between dark clouds on a gloomy day.

Irritated with himself for such fanciful rubbish, he tore his gaze from hers and gestured to the canvases around them. "Are you fond of art?"

"Yes. I used to draw and paint when I was a girl, and I love looking at paintings, though I don't often have the opportunity." She glanced past him. "That's a Renoir, isn't it?"

When he nodded, she moved to stand beside him. *"Dance in the Country,"* she read from the printed sign beside the painting.

He studied her as she studied the Renoir, and he wondered if a direct approach might be best. He could just put it to her in a simple, straightforward fashion: he liked her, she liked him, he needed money and a wife, she had money and needed a husband; it was a match made in heaven, so what about just getting on with it?

"I like this painting," she said, bringing him out of his strategic speculations. "What a vivid expression the artist gives her face. It's clear she's in love."

"Not with the man she's dancing with, poor chap." Rhys gestured to the woman in the painting with his hat. "Her name is Aline. She was Renoir's mistress when he painted this."

"His mistress? Oh, please tell me he wasn't married to someone else at the time! I should hate that. Mistresses are such a detriment to a couple's happiness. And what if there are children?"

Rhys became uneasy. Most women of his own circle would have accepted the inevitability of their husband keeping a mistress without any fuss. Miss Abernathy, he feared, would not be so sanguine. "He wasn't married to someone else. In fact, he married Aline in the end."

"Oh, I'm so glad! I adore stories with happy endings."

He began to fear the worst. "So you are a romantic. I suppose . . . " He paused, striving to put just the right offhand note in his voice. "I suppose you believe in our modern ideal of marrying for love?"

She seemed surprised. "Of course. Don't you?"

He froze. There was nothing for it. He'd been fool enough to ask the question. Forcing a smile to his lips, he lied. "Of course."

To him, it sounded terribly unconvincing, but she seemed satisfied by his answer and turned her attention to another painting.

Damn. He realized he should have known it all along. A woman who'd had a respectable, middle-class upbringing was bound to possess all the staunch moral convictions that came with it. Her sort would never find a marriage of purely material considerations acceptable. She didn't approve of a married man keeping a mistress, so she probably abhorred other sensible, time-honored customs, too, like marriage partners sleeping in separate beds and gentlemen spending their evenings at the club. Hell, she probably collected those commemorative plates of Victoria and Albert in scenes of domestic bliss. It was clear a direct, expeditious approach was out of the question. Rhys resigned himself to courtship.

"This is a beautiful landscape," she commented, causing him to glance at the painting she was studying. The moment he realized what it was, he couldn't help a surprised chuckle.

"By Jove, that's Rosalind's Pond."

"You know this place?"

"I do. I know the artist as well." He gestured to the signature in the bottom right corner with his hat. "This was painted by Earl Camden, an old school friend of mine. Whole family's mad about art, and Cam was always mucking about with paints."

"He's very good."

"Yes, he is. He visited me in Florence one year. Came to study the masters, paint the Arno, that sort of thing."

"Is this pond in Italy?" she asked in some surprise. "It seems a very English setting to me."

"It is English. Rosalind's Pond is on the grounds at Greenbriar, a villa owned by his family. It's quite near here, actually, just past Richmond, no more than an hour by train. I stayed there the summer I was seventeen. Cam and I always liked Rosalind's Pond. Good fishing."

She laughed. "And here I was thinking it a perfect spot for picnics."

"Do you like picnicking, Miss Bosworth?"

"I do, though since coming to London, I've not had much opportunity for it. Having grown up in the country, I miss picnicking and blackberrying."

"Ah, a country girl. Yorkshire, I'd guess, from your accent?"

"North Yorkshire, yes."

"Pretty country up there. No wonder you miss it. Still, picnics and picking blackberries are all very well, but it's the fishing that matters, Miss Bosworth. Excellent trout fishing in that part of the world."

She bit her lip in apology. "I don't know how to fish, I'm afraid."

A cough interrupted them, and they turned to find they were blocking the view of the painting by a group of schoolboys and their tutor. They moved on to the next canvas, a rendering of the Moulin Rouge in which a woman with green skin and orange hair played a prominent role. Miss Abernathy lingered a long time over it, tilting her head this way and that, a puzzled frown on her face.

"You seem quite fascinated by this one," he commented at last.

"I'm just wondering why her face is green."

He didn't tell her it was the artist's oblique reference to absinthe. "Indigestion?" he said instead, making her laugh.

"That doesn't seem very artistic, does it?" She shook her head. "No, Your Grace, I think it must be face paint."

"Couldn't be. This is a depiction of the Moulin Rouge, and none of Zidler's girls paint their faces green. At least not that I ever saw."

"You've been to the Moulin Rouge?"

Rhys turned his head at the surprise in her voice and found that she was staring at him. Her eyes were round as saucers, and he wondered if he'd made a blunder in mentioning he'd seen the Moulin Rouge's infamous cancan dancers. Most women had a weakness for rakes—a fact for which he daily thanked heaven—but perhaps Miss Abernathy was different. Perhaps she preferred an upright, moral sort of fellow. After all, she had displayed the absurd tendency to regard him as if he were some sort of white knight ever since their first meeting.

He briefly toyed with the idea of playing up to that ideal, of prolonging her image of him as a heroic, noble figure long enough to get her to the altar, but he abandoned that notion almost at once. The newspapers brought up his notorious past with such tiresome regularity he couldn't hope to keep it a secret. Besides, acting a role so contrary to his true nature would be deuced hard work, and he was a lazy fellow.

"I have been to the Moulin Rouge, I confess it," he answered her. "I lived in Paris for several years before I went to Italy, and my quarters were quite near Montmartre." His reasons for living a block from the most notorious bohemian district in Paris were quite ignoble, but he spared her the details.

"What is it like?" she asked. "Is there really an opium den there?"

"Several, I'm told, although I've never been in that part of the club. I'm not an opium-eater myself." Absinthe was another matter; he'd been quite fond of the stuff back in his Paris days, but he didn't tell her about that either. An appearance of frankness was one thing, unnecessary honesty was something else.

"Of course you're not an opium-eater!" She shook her head and touched a hand to her temple. "Heavens, what was I thinking to ask such a question? Forgive me. I never meant to imply you had personal experience with opium dens. You're much too good and principled a gentleman for that sort of behavior."

She was gazing at him with such obvious admiration, he couldn't stand it any longer. "I fear you have a mistaken impression of me, Miss Bosworth," he said, letting the chips fall where they may. "I am not good at all. The reason I never entered the opium dens was that my fascination lay with the cancan dancers."

"Oh." She looked away and considered this information, and she was silent for so long that by the time she spoke again, Rhys was sure he'd ruined his chances for good and all. "Do the . . ." She paused and cast a quick glance around. "Do the girls really have little red hearts tattooed on their derrieres?" she asked in a whisper.

He burst out laughing at the unexpected question, earning himself several disapproving stares from the other people in the gallery. They left the room in a huff, but despite their departure, Rhys leaned down toward Miss Abernathy in a confidential manner to offer his reply, ducking his head beneath the wide brim of her hat. "The hearts are embroidered on the backsides of their drawers," he murmured close to her ear. "Rather a treat for us chaps, especially me, since red's my favorite color. As to the rest, they might have tattoos. I couldn't say. We aren't given a view of their bare behinds, more's the pity."

From his view, her face was in profile, but as he watched a wash of rosy color spread over the side of her face and neck, he appreciated again what an innocent she was. The skin of her earlobe, he noticed, looked velvety soft. He was almost close enough to kiss her there, and he wondered if she would like that. He inhaled the lovely lavender scent of her, and as he exhaled, he blew warm breath against her ear with deliberate intent. She moved in response, a slight shift and shiver that gave him his answer.

Footsteps tapped on the marble floor, interrupting this delicious experiment, and he straightened away from her, stepping back as she turned her head toward the door. When a pair of elderly ladies entered the gallery, she returned her attention to him with evident relief. "Thank goodness."

He gave her an inquiring look.

"I'm hiding," she confessed. "My aunt insists upon accompanying me everywhere, and when she cannot, she sends Robert in her stead."

"And which of them are you hiding from at present?"

"Robert. He's somewhere about, and sure to find me any moment now." She sighed, looking quite unhappy at the prospect.

"Your reconciliation with your family is going quite well, I see."

"Do not tease me about this, Your Grace, I beg you. I never have a moment to myself."

"And you don't like that?"

"I'm not used to it. I have lived out since I moved to London when I was seventeen. Being chaperoned everywhere makes me feel quite smothered."

Far be it from him to pass up a golden opportunity. Putting his hand on her elbow, he led her toward one of the doors leading out of the gallery. "Come with me."

"Where are we going?"

"If you wish to hide from someone," he said, pausing to glance left and right before propelling her through the doorway, "you'd best do it properly."

They crossed into another gallery, then another, as Rhys searched for a place that would give him a few minutes to be alone with her. They had almost reached the end of the building before he spied what might serve the purpose—a long, dim corridor, its entrance blocked by a velvet rope hung between two short metal poles. "Now this looks like the perfect hiding place."

"But can we go back there?" She pointed to a sign on a stand beside the entrance. "This wing is closed in preparation for an exhibit from Rome. It is inaccessible to the public."

He reached for the hook that held the rope across the opening and unfastened it. "Nothing is ever inaccessible to a duke," he said, and ushered her into the corridor. "Besides, your cousin will never think to look for you back here."

"That's true," she said as he refastened the rope. "Robert never does anything against the rules."

"Poor fellow. No wonder he's so deadly dull."

"Your Grace!" she remonstrated him, but was laughing as they walked side by side down the length of the empty corridor. At the end, it opened into an enormous room filled with Italian statues, reliefs, and glass display cases containing smaller sculptures. A massive statue of Neptune and his Tritons, half assembled, stood in the center of the room, ringed by metal scaffolding.

He made a show of looking around. "There, you see? Not a chaperone in sight."

"Thank you," she said, looking at him with gratitude and relief, two emotions he knew she would never have felt were she to know his true motives. If he still had a conscience, that might have bothered him. But his conscience, like his innocence, had disappeared long ago.

"It looks a bit eerie in here, doesn't it, with all these white marble statues?" she commented, glancing about the room, bringing Rhys out of his speculations. "An exhibit from Florence, the sign said." She returned her gaze to him. "You lived in Florence, you said?"

"I did, but I hope you're not expecting a lecture tour about Italian statues."

"If I'd wanted a lecture tour, I'd have stayed with Robert. He loves to show off his Oxford education." She gestured to the massive statue before them. "No doubt I'd have received at least an hour-long dissertation on this piece."

"Your cousin spent his days at university far more productively than I. But I can tell you this much: this is a statue of Neptune and his Tritons. Now, before you begin to be impressed with my Oxford education, I must confess I only know it's Neptune because this is a replica of the Trevi Fountain in Rome."

She turned toward him, her face alight with curiosity. "Did you really swim naked in a fountain?"

Rhys groaned. "Lord, is that old story still being circulated?"

"Did you?"

"Yes, although 'bathed' might be a more accurate term. It was too shallow for swimming."

"People say you were with a Russian countess at the time."

She was Prussian, actually. Rhys schooled his features into an expression of earnest dignity. "As a gentleman, I am not at liberty to discuss the details."

"Your discretion does you credit, and I do admire you for it, though I think it must be such a bore to be a gentleman."

He raised an eyebrow. "A bore?"

"Ladies *always* discuss the details," she told him, smiling. "You would not believe the fascinating secrets revealed in a dressmaker's showroom."

"Indeed?" He could only imagine what ladies said about him over the choosing of silks and muslins. "But now that you've patched things up with your family, you no longer have to work as a seamstress, I hope?"

"No, and it seems a bit unreal to me to be choosing gowns for myself instead of making them for others." She turned, curling her gloved fingers around the cross brace of the scaffold, staring at Neptune. "In fact," she added with a little laugh, "my entire life seems unreal nowadays."

Having an income of millions of pounds a year

would seem unreal to him, too, though he suspected he could get used to it. Because he wasn't yet supposed to know about her inheritance, he pretended not to understand what she meant. "Unreal in what respect?"

"In many respects." She turned toward him. "The day before yesterday, I went to my former employer to tender my resignation, and when I was in the showroom, I decided to have a few gowns made up, thinking it a lark more than anything else. Madame was so horrible to me when I worked there, and I wanted to lord it over her a little, show off, you know. I thought it would be amusing."

"And was it?"

"It was at first." She paused and a tiny frown knit her brows. "But the fuss they all made! Heavens, women I've worked with for years tripping over themselves to wait on me! And Madame, with all her gushing compliments that a child could see through. All because I had money to spend. It made me a bit uncomfortable. And the other seamstresses, seeming to be happy for me, and yet, I had the feeling that underneath all the gush, they were not happy for me at all. I didn't . . . " She paused and took a deep breath, her troubled expression deepening. "I didn't like it."

"You'll get used to it," he said, and as he spoke those words, he looked into her soft, dark eyes and thought of what she would become, of what money would inevitably do to her, and something hard and tight squeezed his chest.

"Will I get used to it?" she asked, looking doubtful. "I have been earning my own wages and doing for myself a long time now. I don't know that I will ever become accustomed to being waited on or fussed over."

"Or being chaperoned every moment of the day?"

"Exactly! Though in that, at least, I do appreciate the responsibility that my aunt and uncle feel to watch over me."

You and your millions of pounds.

Rhys drew a deep breath and suppressed that cynical rejoinder. "Their protectiveness seems a rather . . . recent phenomenon," he said instead, choosing his words with care. "Part of your reconciliation with them, I take it?"

"You might put it that way."

"What caused the breach? Did they toss you out? Force you to work as a seamstress?"

"Oh, no, please don't think they were cruel to me," she hastened to say, as if fearing he would receive the wrong impression of her relations. "Living out and working in London was my choice. My mother died when I was fourteen, you see, and her annuity died with her. Her brother and his wife took me into their home, but they had daughters of their own, and there was so little money. I was rather a burden to them. Having to pinch pennies made my aunt quite cross sometimes. It's hard to scrimp and save, and measure out the coal each week and never have beef. And there were quarrels, with their daughters especially, and I hated that. I finally decided I had to go off and make my own way. I don't mean to seem ungrateful."

"Gratitude is one of those things that can't be rammed down our throats with any degree of success. It's a bit like cod liver oil that way."

She laughed. "How comforting it is to talk to you. You're so straightforward."

He didn't even blink. "Quite."

"Still, my uncle has always been kind to me. Whenever he's been in town, he has paid a call at my lodgings to inquire after my situation and be sure I am well."

How generous of him. Rhys did not say that aloud. "Does your uncle come to town often?"

"The first of every month, he journeys up from Sussex on matters of business."

That sparked Rhys's curiosity. What matters of business in London could there be for a poor squire from Sussex who couldn't afford beef for his table?

"Anyway," she went on, returning his attention to the topic at hand, "I am grateful to my uncle. The agricultural depression hit him very hard, and he took me in when one more mouth to feed had truly become a burden. And he sends me an allowance every quarter most faithfully. Besides, they are my only family. So you see, I do feel a sense of obligation to them now that I'm—"

Now that I'm rich.

Her unfinished sentence hung in the air, and he found her reluctance to tell him of her inheritance a curious thing. Any other woman attracted to a man of his position would have made certain he knew of her immense dowry as quickly as possible. And he was not mistaken in her regard for him. It was plain as day. He couldn't understand why she was keeping mum. Didn't she see the advantage money gave her in securing a peer of his rank? God, she truly was a romantic, idealistic sort.

"Oh, let's talk of something pleasant," she said, interrupting his speculations. "Tell me about your family."

He grimaced. "I can't. Not if you wish to talk about something pleasant."

"You do not get on with your family?"

"We used to got on very well," he answered with forced lightness, "when I lived in Italy."

"I understand. My aunt and I rub along much better when we're miles apart, too." She sounded rather wistful.

"If we were in competition over which of us has the more odious relations, Miss Bosworth, I would win hands down. Your aunt is nothing to my mother."

"You are a duke," she said, giving him a look of mock reproof. "Bragging is so beneath you."

"I'm telling you the simple, unvarnished truth. My dear mama is the queen of the cutting remark. She would slice your aunt into pieces, devour her in two or three bites, then feed her bones to the dogs."

"I see." Miss Abernathy tilted her head, considering that information. "Could we arrange for them to meet?"

He gave a shout of laughter. "That's a terribly wicked thing to say, and most unexpected from a sweet girl like you."

She did not seem pleased by his words. "Why does everyone think I'm sweet?" she demanded in consternation. "I am not sweet!"

She was a cream puff. "Oh, very well," he said, making no effort to keep a straight face. "You're hard as nails."

She didn't laugh. "I'm not so pliable as people think, you know," she said earnestly. "It's true I don't like rows, and I do like to think the best of people. But that doesn't mean that I'm weak or don't know my own mind."

"I never meant to imply either of those things. I simply meant what I said. You are sweet." He paused, thinking again of all that money and how it would change her. "True sweetness is a rare and special quality, Miss Bosworth," he found himself saying. "Don't ever lose it."

She frowned a little at those words and the intensity of his voice. "What do you mean?"

Rhys shook his head. "Nothing," he answered, and changed the subject. "Last night when we talked about opera, I mentioned that Verdi's *Aida* was coming on soon. It begins tomorrow night. Will you be attending?"

"Oh, I wish I could! It sounds lovely. But I have to have dinner with my cousins."

"Sir Robert again?"

"No, no, my other cousins. Beryl is my uncle's eldest daughter. We are dining with her and her husband."

"You sound as if you were going to a dentist."

"Oh, I am sure it will all be very pleasant," she said, making a face. "Everything in the garden is lovely with Beryl nowadays. She's being so nice to me, and it's nauseating, because when we were girls she was horrible. She made fun of me all the time." Miss Abernathy looked down at her hands and there was a long pause. "She used to call me a porpoise."

Rhys studied her bent head, a pose that emphasized her chubby chin, and he felt a sudden, fierce flash of anger. He cast aside his hat and grasped her arm, turning her toward him. With his free hand he lifted her face, then leaned closer, ducking his head beneath the huge brim of her hat. He paused with his lips only a few inches from hers, looked into her eyes, and gave his own opinion on the matter. "I think you're luscious. I thought so the first moment I saw you."

Her eyes went wide at the savagery in his voice, and no wonder. He heard it, too.

"Luscious?" she repeated, and swayed a fraction of an inch closer to him. Her lips parted, and she moistened them with the tip of her tongue. "Truly?"

Rhys's anger evaporated at that tiny, feminine invitation, and arousal took its place, flooding through his body in an instant. He turned his hand, cupping her face, his thumb sliding back and forth over the soft skin of her cheek. "Truly."

His other hand slid beneath her arm and around her waist, and he pulled her close, crushing stiff silk and inhaling the scent of fresh, sweet lavender. He almost groaned aloud at the feel of her lush curves pressed against his body, and everything in him wanted to give her what she was so innocently asking for.

He couldn't do it.

He jerked back, letting her go with an abruptness that startled them both. He saw the disappointment cross her face, and it was a feeling he could fully appreciate. He was rather disappointed about it himself. But to win her, he had to court her, and it was too soon in that game for kissing. Anticipation and uncertainty were the essence of romantic courtship.

"I'd best escort you back to your cousin," he

said, and turned away, "before I forget I'm a gentleman."

He picked up his hat and started for the door. She followed him out of the room, and they did not speak as they retraced their steps down the corridor to the galleries.

They found Robert in the main foyer, looking around in a clueless fashion, but at the sight of him with Miss Abernathy, that expression changed at once to one of displeasure.

"St. Cyres," he greeted stiffly. "What are you doing here?"

"I fear I'm one of those bad pennies, Sir Robert," he answered cheerfully. "Just keep turning up, you know."

The other man recovered his poise with an effort. "Prudence, are you finished here?"

"Not yet. I'd like to see the Dutch exhibit. I believe they said there was a van Gogh. Will you accompany us, Your Grace?"

Sir Robert bristled at that, clearly displeased.

Rhys's smile widened. "Thank you," he answered her without taking his eyes from her cousin. "I should like that very much."

"Let's go, then," Robert snapped, and moved to Prudence's other side. Taking her arm, he began propelling her toward the Dutch gallery.

Rhys lingered behind, reaching into the inside breast pocket of his jacket for a lead pencil and one of his cards. He scrawled a few words on the back of the card and replaced the pencil in his pocket, but as he quickened his steps to catch up to Miss Abernathy and her cousin, he kept the card hidden in his palm, waiting for his chance.

Robert's patience with van Gogh and other Dutch masters lasted about a quarter of an hour before he pulled his watch from his pocket and said, "It's getting on for tea, Prudence, and I promised Edith most faithfully I'd have you back by five o'clock. We must be going."

"Tea time already?" Rhys asked. "My, how time does fly. I must be on my way as well." He turned to Prudence. "Forgive me?"

"Of course. It was a pleasure seeing you, as always, Your Grace. I hope—" She hesitated, then added in a rush, "I hope to see you again."

"I hope that as well, Miss Bosworth." He took up her hand, managing to tuck his scribbled note under her palm as he did so. Her eyes widened in surprise as she perceived what he'd done, and he gave her a wink just before he bent over her hand. "And I hope it will be soon."

The moment he let her go, her fingers closed into a fist around his card, then she thrust her hand into her skirt pocket. Satisfied, he bid them both farewell and departed.

His valet was waiting for him outside.

"Fetch my carriage, Fane, will you? Once you've done that," he added on impulse, bringing the other man's departure to a halt, "there's something else I want you to do for me."

"Sir?"

"Mr. Stephen Feathergill makes a practice of coming to town from Sussex the first of every month. Find out why, discreetly, of course. And I want you to follow him for the next few days as much as you are able. Note where he goes and what he does."

"Very good, sir."

Fane departed, and as Rhys waited for his carriage, he thought about the events of the afternoon. He was quite satisfied with his choice of heiress, for despite her denials, Prudence Abernathy was sweet. She had a trusting heart, a forgiving nature, and a secret taste for the devil. All of which could only work in his favor.

Yes, he decided as he stepped into his carriage, getting Miss Abernathy to the altar was going to be easy. He settled back against the seat, smiling to himself. Like taking candy from a baby.

Chapter 6

Miss Abernathy's second cousin, Sir Robert Oglivie, seems her favorite companion at present. He follows on her heels like an adoring suitor. Or like a watchdog. We are not sure which.

—Talk of the Town, *1894*

She was luscious. Prudence smiled to herself as she stared into space, oblivious to the luxurious surroundings of the Savoy tearoom, not hearing a word of the conversation going on around her. All she could think about was what had happened that afternoon. No man had ever called her luscious before.

And so emphatic he'd been about it, too, a frown drawing his brows together and a spark of anger in his eyes. She gave a little shiver and a sigh and closed her eyes, remembering the delicious feel of his hand touching her face. Oh, the thrill when he had wrapped his arm around her and pulled her close to him! It was the most romantic thing that had ever happened to her. Just thinking about his masculine frame pressed against her with such shocking intimacy made her feel flushed and tingly all over.

And as if that hadn't been exciting enough, there was the note. So daring of him to slip it into her hand right under Robert's nose, but though that happened over an hour ago, she still hadn't had the opportunity to read it, for she hadn't been out of Robert's sight a single minute. After leaving the National Gallery, they had come straight back to the Savoy, and he'd ushered her directly into the tearoom where Millicent, Edith, and Stephen had been waiting for them.

"You don't seem particularly enthused, Prudence, dear."

"Hmm? What?" At the mention of her name, she jerked upright in her chair. "I was woolgathering, I'm afraid, Cousin Millicent." She tried to look attentive. "What did you say?"

"I have obtained vouchers for us to attend Lady Amberly's charity ball two nights hence. Rather a coup, if I do say so myself," she added, trying and failing to appear modest about it. "This is one of the important events of the season, and most of the vouchers were given weeks ago. Yet, you seem uninterested."

She would have been very interested if the Duke of St. Cyres planned to attend, but she didn't suppose it would go over very well if she inquired about the matter. She thought again of the note and felt as if it were burning a hole in her pocket. The suspense became intolerable.

"I'm so sorry," she mumbled, and pressed a hand to her forehead. "But I've developed the most beastly headache. I think I shall go to my room and lie down for a bit, if you don't mind."

"Of course, dear." Edith put down her teacup, eyeing her with concern. "Yes, go have a lie-down. You don't want to miss the theater tonight."

Trying to look as if she were in genuine pain, Prudence gave everyone a wan smile and departed from the tearoom, forcing herself not to run for the elevator.

"Fourth floor, please," she told the boy attending the lift, and the iron grill of the door had barely slid across before Prudence was reaching into her pocket. The elevator jerked into motion, and as she read the words the duke had written, her heart gave a leap as well.

I must see you again. Meet me at Richmond Station. Noon tomorrow.

She gave a cry of delight, earning herself a curious look from the boy who attended the lift. She smothered her exuberance long enough to arrive at the fourth floor, but as the lift sank out of sight,

Prudence read his words once more and her delight came flooding back, stronger than ever.

He wanted to see her again.

She laughed out loud, and as she went down the corridor to her suite, she felt as if she were dancing on air.

Prudence's blissful mood was not lost on Nancy Woddell. "You seemed to enjoy your outing today, miss," the maid commented, her pretty freckled face breaking into a smile as she watched Prudence fall back onto her bed with a happy sigh.

"I had a wonderful day, Woddell. I hope you did as well?"

"I did, miss, thank you. Some of your new gowns arrived from Madame Marceau's showroom, and they are ever so nice. Would you like to see them?"

Prudence at once began to wonder which of her lovely new dresses she should wear for her rendezvous with the duke on the morrow. "Oh, yes, bring them out."

The maid vanished into the dressing room and returned moments later with two evening gowns. "One of these might be nice for the theater tonight," she said, holding up the ivory damask and the blue-black velvet.

They were both lovely, but at the moment she couldn't summon much interest in evening gowns. "What about the black and white outing dress? Did that come?"

"The stripe?" Woddell sounded surprised. "Yes, miss, that came as well."

"Excellent!" Prudence sat up. "Bring that one out, would you? And the hat. It's red straw, if I remember, with black, red, and white ribbons. It is red, isn't it?"

"Yes, miss, but—" The maid hesitated, looking uncertain. "It's to the theater you're going tonight, isn't that right?"

She didn't care about tonight. "What a pity I didn't order an outing dress in red," she murmured. "Well, the red hat will have to do."

"Miss?"

Prudence looked up and laughed at the maid's obvious bewilderment. "It's all right, Woddell. I haven't lost my senses. Yes, I'm going to the theater tonight. But tomorrow I'm going on a picnic, and I want to try on my new outing dress to be sure it fits. By the way, I'll be out all afternoon, so once you've finished your duties, you have my permission to take the remainder of the day for yourself."

"Thank you, miss," the maid said, and returned the evening gowns to the dressing room. A moment later she brought out the dress her mistress wanted.

A short while later Prudence stood before the long mirror in her pretty new outing dress and hat and gave a sigh of pure pleasure. The gown suited her figure perfectly, with its simple lines and vertical stripes. It was always wonderful to wear something she hadn't had to make herself, and there was such bliss in fine silk lingerie and sheer silk stockings. She had never felt prettier.

Satisfied, she had Woddell return the outfit to the dressing room. After changing into evening undergarments, she asked the maid to press the blue-black velvet, then she sat down at her dressing table.

Red's my favorite color.

Prudence smiled, but before she could do any more daydreaming about a certain duke, the door to her bedroom opened and Aunt Edith came in.

"My dear niece, I am so distraught."

That did not bode well. "Indeed," Prudence murmured, and pretended vast interest in the toiletry articles of her dressing table. "I'm sorry to hear it. I'm feeling much better after my . . . ahem . . . nap. Perhaps you should follow my example and lie down for a bit."

Edith did not seem enamored of that suggestion. She bustled across the crimson, cream, and gold carpet and came to a halt beside the dressing table. "Robert has told me that St. Cyres accosted you at the National Gallery this afternoon." One hand fluttered up to her heart. "To think that dreadful man dared to impose himself upon you again. Oh, what shall we do? Perhaps Stephen should speak with him."

"I should hardly describe the incident as an imposition, Aunt. I encountered the duke at the gallery, and we took a stroll together. Why would that cause you such distress?"

She should never have asked.

Edith reached for the nearest chair, an ornate, gilded affair with a straight back and a seat of emerald green velvet. She pulled it close to the dressing table and sat down beside Prudence.

"Millicent has been telling me more about him. After he paid such attention to you at the opera, she felt compelled to make inquiries, and her information confirms what we suspected, and worse. My dear, the man is notorious. His affairs with women, his gambling." She glanced toward the open door that led to Prudence's dressing room, then leaned closer and lowered her voice to a whisper. "Opium dens," she hissed.

Prudence pressed her lips together, ducking her head with a choked sound.

Edith sat back with an aggrieved sigh. "You are laughing at me. No, no, don't deny it," she added as Prudence felt compelled to protest. "You do not take what I say seriously. I am not a good chaperone for you, I fear. Everything is so difficult nowadays. When Beryl and Pearl were coming out, it was so much easier."

It was obvious Edith had forgotten all the fretting and fussing she had done when Beryl and Pearl began attending balls and parties. Prudence murmured an innocuous reply and reached for her hairbrush.

"Oh, let me do that, darling." Edith took the silver-backed brush from her hand, rose from her chair and moved to stand behind her. "We weren't in London when the girls came out," she explained, as if reading her niece's mind. She draped the dark strands of Prudence's long, straight hair behind the chair back and began to brush it out. "Country dances and parties among friends are so much safer, I feel. London is filled with all manner of decadent goings-on."

Prudence did not point out that Edith hadn't had any such misgivings about London when her niece had moved here, alone, to live unchaperoned in a lodging house and work for her own living. She had been quite relieved at the time. To remind her aunt of such things now, however, would only gain her that wounded spaniel look at which her aunt so excelled. So Prudence leaned back in her chair and closed her eyes, leaving Edith to chat unhappily on about the evils of London and the stresses of being a chaperone, while she indulged in the far more pleasurable pastime of imagining her rendezvous with the duke.

As she thought of it, anticipation rose within her like the effervescent bubbles in a glass of champagne. To spend an entire afternoon with him, to talk with him, to see him smile—

Edith stopped brushing her hair, interrupting these delightful speculations. "My dear niece, you are most distracted today. I don't believe you are listening to a word I say."

Prudence gave a guilty start and opened her eyes. "Of course I was listening, Aunt," she lied, straightening in her chair. "You are a most conscientious chaperone, I'm sure. Look what excellent marriages Beryl and Pearl made as a result of your efforts."

The older woman brightened at once. "That is true. Beryl's dear Winston is a barrister in London now, and although Pearl's husband is still only a bank clerk, he is most respected by his employer, I'm told."

"There, you see? You must stop worrying so much." She started to lean back in her chair again, but Edith's next words stopped her.

"Of course, my daughters didn't have the dowry to tempt fortune hunters like St. Cyres." She set aside the brush and put her hands on Prudence's shoulders, gazing at her earnestly in the mirror. "Your situation is different. I feel such a strong responsibility to safeguard you, yet I fear I am not up to the task of keeping wolves like St. Cyres at bay."

"He is not a wolf!" Aware that her blissful mood was once again diminishing, Prudence took a deep breath. "I like him. And should he choose to confer his attentions upon me, I see no reason to discourage him. Nor should you. He is a duke, after all, and a most courteous gentleman."

There was a long pause as the gazes of the two women locked in the mirror. She expected her aunt to exercise her authority as chaperone and forbid her to see St. Cyres. At which point she would have to openly defy her, and that would make everything during the coming two months terribly difficult.

But to her surprise, Edith gave a gentle nod and patted her shoulder. "I understand, dear."

Prudence was astonished at such easy capitulation. "You do?"

"Of course I do. Marrying a duke would be considered by many to be quite a coup, and of course, being a duchess is something every girl dreams of."

"That isn't the reason I would—"

"And the man is quite good-looking. Even I can appreciate that. Charming manners, too. His attentions would turn any girl's head, I am sure. But you have always been such a responsible young woman, and wise beyond your years. Prudent, you know, like your name, without the reckless, immoral nature of your mother."

Prudence tried very hard not to grind her teeth.

"I'm sure that when the time comes," Edith went on, "you will make a wise matrimonial choice."

"Of course."

Edith nodded, as if they were in complete agreement about everything. "You know as well as I that to abandon the sphere into which you were born and raised is seldom wise. We are simple gentry folk, Prudence, and your upbringing makes you wholly unprepared for and unsuited to the rigorous burdens of being a duchess. And marriage for the purpose of rising to a higher social position would be a grievous thing, and most unworthy of you. It is a course I cannot, in good conscience, approve."

Prudence bristled at that. "I believe it is the trustees, Aunt, who must give their approval."

A dull flush crept across Edith's cheeks. "They would hardly approve a fortune hunter."

"And Robert's interest is pure?" she countered before she could stop herself. "Even though he's never paid a jot of attention to me? Why, I might have been living in America, instead of a few miles away, for all the notice he has given me over the years."

At once, Edith's face crumpled into lines of distress. "Now I've made you cross," she said, a tremulous note entering her voice. She sank into her chair and pulled a handkerchief from her pocket. "I knew this would happen. I knew we would quarrel. It's just as it was when you were a girl. Oh, dear!"

She gave a sob and buried her face in the hand

kerchief. "I'm making such a mess of things. Perhaps you would be better chaperoned by Millicent."

And have Robert hovering over her at all hours of the day? Prudence felt a pang of alarm. "I don't believe that's necessary, Aunt."

Edith lifted her head with a sniff. "I only wish for you to make a match for the right reasons, Prudence, as my own daughters have done. For love, if that is possible. Or if not, then for shared affection and like minds. Which is why Robert would be a good match for you. He has been elevated to baronet, but that's not too high for a girl of your background. He has been brought up in the same social circle as we. He is family, someone we can trust, and it's perfectly acceptable for second cousins to marry. And he is fond of you. Oh, yes, he is," she added as Prudence started to protest. "He is, though you don't see it. He feels slighted by you, which is why he never called upon you in Little Russell Street. You criticize his inattention, yet you have made no effort in that regard, for not once have you called upon his mother here in London."

"Nor has she called upon me," Prudence shot back, stung. "I have at least written letters inquiring after them. Millicent has never reciprocated even that. Not once. Amazing that she is so attentive to me now! I wonder why."

She might have been talking to the wall.

"Your snub quite hurt Robert's feelings," Edith went on. "Yet you are ready to throw him over, and for a disreputable cad like St. Cyres. Oh, it pains me to think of it." She lowered her head with another sob.

Prudence pressed her fingers to her forehead, feeling a genuine headache coming on. Chaperones really were the most inconvenient thing ever invented, and Edith was impossible. "The duke has expressed a polite interest in me, nothing more," she said. "If he were to demonstrate a deeper regard . . . " She paused, a quiver of excitement replacing her aggravation as thoughts of tomorrow flashed through her mind. Would he touch her again as he had today? He might even kiss her. How wonderful that would be.

She took a deep, steadying breath, and told herself not to let her imagination run away with her. "Even if he were to demonstrate a deeper regard, it does not follow that I would be inclined to reciprocate his feelings."

But as she spoke those words, Prudence knew they were rot. She feared she was half in love with the duke already. Since she'd only known him a week, that put her rather in the suds. "You may rest assured, Aunt, that I intend to marry the man whose regard for me is genuine."

What a prig she sounded, but her aunt didn't seem to notice. "It relieves my mind to hear you say that, dearest." She dabbed at her eyes, lifted her head with a final sniff, and stood up. "My only wish, you know, is for your happiness."

After Edith had gone, Prudence breathed a sigh of relief and returned her thoughts to someone who was already providing her with far more happiness than Aunt Edith ever would.

I'd best escort you back to your cousin before I forget I'm a gentleman.

The memory of those words brought back her smile. Resting her elbow on the dressing table and her cheek in her hand, she began to imagine what the duke was like when he forgot to be a gentleman.

It was a bit tricky to arrange an afternoon away from the cloying attentions of her family, but she managed it, stating that she and several of her friends from Little Russell Street were going on a picnic in Hyde Park. She emphasized the damp ground and the presence of Mrs. Morris to act as chaperone, thereby convincing Edith there would be no harm in her remaining behind to spend the afternoon shopping with Millicent. She then left the Savoy and walked to Charing Cross Station.

The train to Richmond took less than sixty minutes, but it seemed a much longer journey than that, for she was in such a dither of excitement she couldn't sit still. She fidgeted and tapped her feet and drummed her fingers, firmly telling herself the entire time not to be nervous.

He was waiting for her on the platform. She

saw him through the window the moment the train pulled into Richmond Station. He wore no coat, for the day was fine, and he looked so devastatingly handsome in his shirtsleeves, dark brown trousers, and riding boots that her throat went dry. As her train stopped, she watched him give a nervous tug to his tweed waistcoat, adjust his necktie, and rake a hand through his hair, and those efforts made her smile. She wasn't the only one who was nervous, it seemed.

He saw her the moment she stepped down from the train. As he came forward to greet her, the pleasure in his face warmed her like sunlight, and all her nervousness slid away. "You came."

"Are you surprised?"

"I am," he admitted. "Most women wouldn't have, you know. It's not quite the thing to go picnicking alone with a man. I thought you either wouldn't come at all or that you'd bring a chaperone with you."

"I thought carting Aunt Edith along would put a damper on things."

"Rather," he agreed with feeling. His gaze lifted to the top of her head and his smile widened. "Nice hat."

She touched a hand to the red straw boater, feeling a little self-conscious that he knew she'd worn it for him, and yet ever so pleased he'd noticed at all. Most men wouldn't have. "Thank you."

"We'd best be on our way." He turned so she

might take his arm. "It's about five miles, so I have a carriage for us."

"Did you come down by carriage, then?" she asked as they left the tiny station. "Or did you hire one?"

"Neither. When I cabled last night to see if Cam was in residence, I learned that he's not. The house is let to some rich family from America. I've no idea who they are, but they sent me back an invitation at once to spend the weekend. Dukes always seem to impress Americans. There was such a to-do when I arrived this morning, I've never seen the like. I fear I quite let them down by provisioning my own picnic hamper, and they kindly lent me a carriage, even though I'm being quite secretive about the identity of my companion. Got to protect your reputation, you see. Here we are."

He brought her to a halt beside a carriage where a liveried driver stood waiting. The driver bowed to her and bent to roll out the steps as St. Cyres took her hand.

"Mind the basket," he warned her as he assisted her into the two-seated vehicle. "Had to put it in front. What with the blanket and the fishing rods and tackle, there's no room in the back."

She stepped over the enormous picnic basket on the floor of the carriage and sat down. "Rods and tackle?"

"I intend to teach you to fish," he explained,

following her into the carriage. "I hope you don't mind? I can't stand the thought of a country girl not knowing how."

"I don't mind at all. Fishing and a picnic sounds delightful." She bent forward for a look at the basket, and when she saw the monogram on its wicker surface, she gave a cry of delighted surprise. "Fortnum and Mason? Oh, how lovely!"

"I'm glad you think so." He glanced up at the driver. "Take us to Greenbriar's boathouse, Halston, will you?"

"Aye, sir." The driver released the brake and snapped the reins, sending the carriage into motion.

"Are we boating, too?" she asked.

"Well, we have to for a bit," he explained. "Rosalind's Pond is in rather a remote spot and there's no road, but there's a stream runs to it. I could have ordered horses instead, but I didn't know if you rode. Do you mind a boat?"

Prudence hesitated. "I don't know. I've never been in a boat."

"Never? Not even a punt?"

She shook her head. "I could never work up the nerve. I don't know how to swim."

"I'm an excellent swimmer, so you needn't worry. As long as you trust me?"

"Of course I trust you. I'd trust you with my life. After the way you saved Sally, how could I not?"

He gave her an odd look, one she couldn't quite define. "As long as you're not nervous about the boat," he muttered and looked away.

The carriage bypassed Richmond itself and turned off the main road, going down a lane lined with trees and shrubbery. After a few miles, he pointed to a manor house of gray stone in the distance, barely visible through the thick grove of trees. "That's Greenbriar," he told her. "It's a small place, but quite comfortable."

Small? It was at least three times the size of Uncle Stephen's house in Sussex and seemed huge to Prudence, but she supposed a duke might think it small.

"Americans are a strange lot," he went on. "They received Cam's permission to install gaslights in the house just because they're staying there through the year and find lamps and candles inconvenient. They probably regard it as an investment since they've made an offer to buy the place from Cam's family. Want to marry off their daughters to English nobility, I expect, and want a house near London."

"They have daughters?" Prudence didn't much care for the sound of that. No wonder St. Cyres's arrival had caused such a stir. "Are they pretty?" she asked before she could stop herself.

"No," he answered at once, but to her ears it sounded unconvincing. "Homely as can be, I swear."

She looked at him and made a sound of disbelief. "I think they must be very pretty."

He actually laughed, the wretch. "Are you jealous?"

"Not at all," she said with dignity.

"Good." He leaned close to her. "You've no reason to be jealous of any girl. I like you best."

Prudence's heart soared, but she immediately felt compelled to contain the happiness caused by his words, reminding herself it was foolish to harbor hopes of romantic attachment to a man so far above her. But despite her efforts, the exhilarating joy she felt would not be suppressed, and she was still smiling ten minutes later when the carriage halted beside a millpond.

There, a rather ramshackle boathouse stood beside a small dock where a rowboat was tied, motionless in the still water of the millpond. St. Cyres helped her step down from the carriage, grabbed the picnic hamper, and walked her to the edge of the dock, ordering the driver to bring the fishing gear and blanket from the carriage boot. The servant complied, putting the requested items in the bow of the boat, along with the picnic hamper. While Halston kept the rowboat steady, Rhys held out his hand to her. "Just step in slowly," he told her, "and have a seat aft."

She settled herself on the bench seat in the stern, and St. Cyres followed her in, taking the center seat, facing her. He reached into the bottom of the boat for the oars, locked them into place, and nodded to Halston. "Untie the lashings," he ordered, "then you may go. Return for us in about four hours."

"Very good, sir." The servant complied, then gave the boat a shove with one foot, and they were off. Making good use of the oars, St. Cyres guided the boat across the millpond and onto the river.

Prudence watched him, admiring the way his powerful arms and shoulders rowed against the river's current and kept the boat on a straight course. Still, after several minutes of watching him make all the effort, she felt compelled to offer some assistance. "You seem to be working much harder than I. Can I help you row?"

He grinned at her, leaning back as he once again pulled the oars through the water. "And have you sitting right beside me? I'd love it, but I'd still have to sit almost center or the boat won't trim, and that would be a bit uncomfortable for you."

She didn't know what he meant about the boat, but she did think sitting beside him would be wonderful. "I don't mind."

"All right, though if I were truly a gentleman, I'd refuse to let you. Rowing upstream's deuced hard work. But since we haven't that far to go, I'm going to be selfish, take you up on your suggestion, and squeeze you into half a seat."

"That's all right," she said shyly. "I'd like sitting beside you, so I'm being selfish, too."

"Are you, now?" He laughed. "I like a girl who's honest about her motives."

He stopped rowing, and she settled herself into the offered half a seat, moving carefully in the boat to avoid tipping it. He kept his hand on her oar, and she placed both her hands behind his.

"Ready?" he asked her, and when she nodded, he said, "On three. One and two and three."

They pulled back on the oars together, sending the boat shooting forward. "Am I doing this right?" she asked, feeling a bit awkward as she tried to lean forward and pull back in time with him.

"You're doing it perfectly," he assured her, and glanced over his shoulder to see if they were headed in the right direction. "We're straight as an arrow."

They rowed in silence for several strokes and soon developed a perfect rhythm. She liked the feel of his powerful body so close to her own, her shoulder and hip brushing his with each stroke. Following his instructions, she helped him guide the rowboat off the river and onto a smaller, more meandering stream, where immense weeping willows overhung the banks and dappled the water with sunlight and shade.

"I say, we do row together rather well, don't we?" he asked as they both leaned back.

"Yes, we do." She turned her head to look at him and smiled. "You'd think we'd been rowing together forever."

Then, for no reason she could define, both of them stopped at once. She watched his lashes lower as his gaze slid to her mouth, and everything in the world seemed to stop. He moved closer, ducking his head beneath her hat, and she realized he was going to kiss her.

Excitement flooded through her, and with it, a powerful happiness. This was what she had been daydreaming of yesterday, this moment, hardly daring to hope it would happen. She tilted her head back, and he leaned even closer, until his lips were only a fraction from hers. He went still, and the blissful excitement within her deepened and spread until it was an ache so acute she couldn't breathe.

"Prudence," he murmured, and his voice seemed to echo her own emotions. Her lips parted, her eyes began to close. But just before his lips touched hers, he pulled back, his movement so abrupt, the boat rocked in the water.

Disappointment pierced her, and she looked away.

"Hell," he muttered, the tone of his voice expressing just how she felt.

He started rowing again, and she helped him as before, reminding herself it was for the best that he hadn't kissed her. Such things were highly improper; only engaged couples ought to be kissing.

Neither of them spoke as they rowed along the stream, and as they pulled the boat through the water in perfect time, Prudence was certain his kiss would have been equally perfect. As a virtuous woman, painfully aware of the shame that could result when a woman behaved otherwise, she knew she ought to be relieved. But she wasn't. Instead, she felt a keen and profound regret that she hadn't thrown her arms around his neck and kissed him first. He was better at being a gentleman, it seemed, than she was at being a lady.

Chapter 7

Rumor has it the Duke of St. Cyres is spending several days at Richmond with wealthy American railway tycoon J. D. Hunter and his family. Mr. Hunter, a little bird informs us, has several beautiful daughters. Could Britain's most eligible and most notorious duke be considering an American to be his duchess?

—Talk of the Town, *1894*

Prudence and St. Cyres didn't speak as they rowed the short remaining distance to Rosalind's Pond, but to her, it was a companionable silence. When they scanned the grassy bank for a place to lay out their picnic, both of them pointed to the same spot beneath the willows at the exact same moment. By the time they settled themselves on the blanket and opened the picnic hamper, Prudence decided this day ranked as the most wonderful one of her life.

"Let's see what's in here, shall we?" he said, and lifted the lid of the basket.

"Don't you already know?"

He shook his head. "I haven't a clue."

She watched as he pulled out foodstuffs. "I'm amazed a duke isn't already well-acquainted with the picnic hampers of Fortnum and Mason."

"I've had no opportunity. I've been living on the Continent, remember?"

She laughed and sat back. "Yes, I know. Cavorting at the Moulin Rouge and bathing in Italian fountains."

"Bathing naked, if you please," he clarified as he set a box of chocolates on the blanket. "Though why every society paper in Europe seems to find that story perpetually entertaining is beyond my comprehension."

Prudence knew why. A picture of him rising naked from the water of a moonlit fountain flashed across her mind, and it was an image so vivid, she caught her breath. She'd never seen a real man unclothed in her entire life, but she had seen paintings and statues, and the immodest image conjured by her imagination made her face grow warm.

When she didn't reply, he glanced up from his task, and at the sight of her blushing, he smiled just as he had that night at the opera, as if he knew precisely what she was thinking.

Prudence ducked her head, studying the foodstuffs on the blanket. "Oh, look! Chocolates."

St. Cyres wouldn't let her get by with a diversion as transparent as that. He reached out and touched her, cupping her cheek and lifting her face so he could look into her eyes. "Sweets for the sweet," he murmured, his thumb brushing back and forth across her hot cheek in a lazy caress.

"I told you, I'm not sweet," she whispered.

He laughed low in his throat. "Ah, yes, that's right. I had forgotten you're hard as nails."

Letting go of her, he sat back and continued rooting through the picnic hamper. "Let's see . . . in addition to chocolate, we have pâté fois gras, pickles, mustard, smoked salmon, tongue, a wedge of Stilton and one of cheddar, savory biscuits, sweet biscuits . . . ah, and a bottle of very fine claret."

"It all looks wonderful," she said as they began unwrapping packages and opening jars. "I've always wanted to sample foods like these, but one can't afford such things on a seamstress's salary."

"I should imagine not. Pity there's no lemonade, though," he added, shaking his head in mock sorrow. "You're so fond of it."

She gave an exaggerated sigh. "I shall have to make do with the claret, I suppose."

"This time, perhaps, but I'll be sure to inform

Fortnum's that on our next picnic, you'll expect their sourest lemonade."

At the indication that there would be more outings with him, Prudence's happiness was complete. "Only if it's warm," she reminded him, laughing. "To be truly bad, lemonade has to be warm."

"All right, then. Their sourest, *warmest* lemonade." He reached for the bottle of wine and the corkscrew and nodded to the basket. "There's a pair of wineglasses in there. Pull them out, would you?"

She complied, bringing out plates as well as the glasses. She then closed the lid of the picnic hamper and put the glasses on top. As he opened and poured the wine, she removed her gloves, then began paring cheese, slicing ham, and arranging the various foods on the plates.

He set the bottle aside, helped himself to a piece of ham, then took one of the glasses and leaned back on his arm, staring at the tranquil scene spread out before them. "I'd forgotten how pretty an April day in England can be," he murmured.

Prudence paused in her task to glance out over the pond. It looked even more beautiful in reality than it had in the painting done by his friend, with the bright green of the newly unfurled willow leaves and the vivid yellow of the buttercups in the meadow beyond the water. "'Oh, to be in England,'" she quoted, "'now that April's there.'"

"You know that poem?"

The sharpness of his voice caused her to glance in his direction, and she found he was staring at her in surprise.

"'Home Thoughts, from Abroad,'" she answered. "Robert Browning. My mother read it to me as a girl. It's still one of my favorites."

"It's one of mine as well, though if you asked me why I like it so much, I couldn't really tell you. There are many poems more beautiful. All I know is that I found myself reading it quite often while I was away. Like Browning when he wrote it, I was living in Italy, so perhaps I felt rather a kinship with the fellow."

She leaned closer to him, smiling a little. "Or perhaps you were just homesick."

"Homesick?" He tilted his head as if considering it. "You know," he said after a moment, "I believe I was homesick." He gave a short laugh. "How extraordinary."

"Extraordinary?" she repeated, struck by that adjective. "How so? Living far away, anyone would feel homesick."

"I never thought I should." He resumed gazing out over the water. "I left England when I was twenty-one, and no young man could be happier to leave a place than I was. Sailing out of Dover, watching England fade into the distance, all I felt was a profound sense of relief."

"That sounds like escape." Prudence shifted her weight onto one hip and arm. "Why?" she asked, taking a sip of her wine. "What were you running from?"

"Running? Is that what it was? I thought I was just off to have adventures and see the world."

Prudence was not fooled by the lightness of his voice. "What were you running from?" she repeated.

He lifted his glass and swallowed the rest of his wine in one draught. "Everything," he answered without looking at her. "Especially myself."

Prudence studied his profile, the hard line of his mouth, and she knew there was a great deal more to this man than his good looks, chivalrous manners, and scandal-ridden past. "What is there in yourself to run away from?"

He gave a caustic chuckle and set his empty glass on the lid of the picnic hamper. "You've read the stories," he said as he refilled his glass. "I'm quite a shameless fellow, don't you know."

"I think you're wonderful," she blurted out, and could have bitten her tongue off for such a gauche remark.

He didn't seem to like it much either. Frowning a little, he reached out to slide his hand around the back of her neck, and he leaned closer. His gaze locked with hers, and there was a strange, silvery intensity in the depths of his green eyes.

"I'm not," he told her, sounding almost angry. "There's nothing wonderful about me, Prudence. Nothing."

She started to dispute his statement with a shake of her head, but his fingers tightened against the back of her neck, and his thumb pressed against the side of her jaw to keep her still. "I can appreciate that you would disagree. Given the night we met, I know you think I'm some sort of hero, but it happens you're wrong. I'm a bad apple. The De Winter family barrel's full of us." His gaze roamed her face and his frown deepened. "God knows, if you had any sense, you'd run from me as fast as you could."

Prudence stared at him in bafflement, wondering how he could speak of himself with such contempt. From the first, he'd shown nothing but consideration toward her. There was also the matter of how he'd saved Sally. Having worked as a seamstress for so long, she knew full well the vulnerability of women of her class to men of his. Faced with the situation St. Cyres had come across in that alley, most of his peers would have shrugged, walked away, and left the girl to be raped. Some might even have expected a turn. But St. Cyres was not the sort of man to think that way, nor would he stand by while a woman was assaulted against her will.

"I don't believe you," she said with quiet conviction. "Forgive me, Your Grace," she added, ignoring his exasperated sound, "but I think you are far too modest about yourself. Indeed, I have seen much in you to admire during our short acquaintance. I have certainly found nothing in you to condemn."

"But you will," he whispered, and pressed his thumb to her lips to stop her from further arguing the point. He closed his eyes, pulling her closer, so close his lips nearly brushed her cheek. "You will."

There was something in those few whispered words, something so raw that it hurt her to hear them. She said nothing more. Instead, she reached up to brush back a lock of hair from his brow.

At the touch of her hand, his eyes opened and he pulled back. Her hand fell to her side, and he let her go.

"Now that I know what you think of me," he said, "I might have to mend my wicked ways." He smiled at her, but it was a smile that did not reach his eyes, and she had the strange feeling a door had just been slammed shut between them. "You've such a good opinion of me, I fear I shall have to make the effort to live up to it."

His voice was careless and offhand, as if his strange mood had passed, but Prudence was not fooled. She could still feel the tension in him, though they were no longer touching. She wanted badly to know more, to open that door again and find out what was on the other side of his shuttered smile, but she sensed this was not the time for more questions.

"If you mean that," she said instead, "would you begin by passing that box of biscuits? I'm terribly hungry."

With those words, his tension seemed to ebb away, his smile widened into a genuine grin, and Prudence was glad she'd set her curiosity aside.

"So, you like Browning, do you?" he asked as he complied with her request.

"I do. But Tennyson's my favorite. I love 'Lady of Shalott.'"

He made a sound of derision. "Women always love 'Lady of Shalott.'"

She made a face at him. "So?"

"'Charge of the Light Brigade' is a deuced better poem."

"Better?" She paused long enough to eat a biscuit, then said, "I don't see how you can say it's better. It's about a tragic battle. Into the jaws of death, and all that."

"Exactly so. What could be more exciting?"

"But hundreds died."

"Bravely and well, as the poem says."

She began to laugh. "And you call me a romantic?"

He paused in the act of dunking a slice of cheese in the mustard pot. "What do you mean?"

"I mean, you are a romantic, too."

"That's absurd," he scoffed, and ate his bite of cheese. "I haven't a romantic bone in my body."

"So you say, but 'Charge of the Light Brigade' is all about the romantic ideal of honor and bravery. You're a romantic who just doesn't want to admit it."

He started to argue with her, then shook his head as if giving it up. "How did you develop such a love of poetry?"

"My mother." Prudence smiled, remembering. "She had a great passion for poetry. When I was a little girl, she and I would often go for picnics in summer. I would draw or sew, and she would read aloud to me. Keats was her favorite, but she would always read Tennyson because I liked Tennyson best."

"What about your father?"

Her smile faded. She swallowed painfully and looked away. She knew she ought to tell him the truth about the circumstances of her birth, but she just couldn't bear to see his manner toward her change, which it surely would when he learned she was born on the wrong side of the blankets. "I never knew my father."

Before he could ask any questions, she changed the course of the conversation. "But as many outings as my mother and I went on when I was a girl, she never taught me to fish."

He shook his head and sighed. "Your education is sadly lacking. Fishing is the greatest sport there is."

"I cannot fathom what is so exciting about standing by a stream, waiting to hook some poor helpless animal who's only swimming about his home, minding his own business."

He grinned at that. "Allow me to enlighten you

on the subject, then. Before the day is over, I will have taught you to appreciate the art of pulling in a nice fat trout. That, my dear Miss Bosworth, is the true stuff of poetry."

"Hmm," she said with skepticism, and drank her last swallow of wine. "We'll have to see about that."

Rhys knew he had done some very stupid things in his life. Dosing himself with absinthe during those months he'd spent in Paris, for example, had been very stupid. Becoming utterly besotted with his third mistress the year he was twenty-one also ranked high on his list of idiotic moments. And of course there was the fact that he'd spent his entire inheritance, a particularly stupid endeavor since a considerable portion of that money had gone to the absinthe and the mistress.

But by the time he had assembled a fishing rod and threaded the line, Rhys decided blurting out to the heiress he intended to marry what a sod he truly was had to be the stupidest thing he'd ever done. What the hell had he been thinking? This was romantic seduction, and therefore not the time for honesty. Rhys wanted to give himself a kick in the head.

He shot a swift glance at her as he tied the fishing hook to the line, watching as she put the remainder of their lunch back in the picnic hamper. The sight of those big brown eyes looking up at him with utter disbelief in his idiotic confessional was a picture still quite vivid in his mind. Being one of those naive innocents who abounded in this world just waiting to be taken advantage of, she hadn't believed him. Thank God. He vowed that from now on he was keeping mum about his flaws.

By the time he'd baited the hook with some pickled corn kernels from their picnic hamper, she had finished packing up lunch. "So how does one do this?" she asked, moving to stand beside him.

"The first thing I'm going to teach you is how to cast." He handed her the rod and showed her how to grip the handle, then moved into position behind her, all sorts of wicked possibilities running through his mind. He reached around her to place his hands over hers on the rod so they could cast the line together, but the moment he did so, he realized this was not going to work. The brim of her hat kept him much too far away. If she kept it on, he wouldn't be able to pull her back against him and hold her and smell the wonderful lavender fragrance of her hair. And he wanted those things a lot more than he wanted to fish.

"As much as I adore your hat," he said, "I think you need to remove it."

"I do? Why?"

Because I want your body as close to mine as possible.

"Because I can't teach you to cast if you're wearing it. The brim's so wide, I fear it will hamper our efforts."

Prudence accepted his reason without question, bless her trusting heart. She pulled out her hat pin, removed the confection of red straw, ribbons, and bows, and wove the hat pin through one side of the crown before tossing the hat onto the grassy bank near their feet.

"I'll cast it," he told her, once again bringing his arms up around her shoulders and placing his hands over hers on the rod. "All you have to do is follow my move."

"I see." She nodded. "A bit like dancing, isn't it?"

"Exactly." Hooking the line with one finger, he opened the bail and pulled her arm back along with his, then flipped the rod forward. She moved with him, and together they sent the baited hook and its accompanying weights flying out over the lake. The weights landed with a tiny splash and sank, taking the bait down. When he sensed the weights had hit bottom, he closed the bail.

She turned her head to look at him over her shoulder. "Now what do we do?"

"We wait," he answered, and as they stood there, he wondered how long he could get by with embracing her this way in the cause of catching trout. He breathed in the scent of lavender and decided he'd get by with it for as long as she let him.

Slowly, trying to be subtle about it, he let go of the fishing rod to ease his arms beneath hers and slide them around her waist. Despite the generous curves of her figure, she was so much smaller than he, and so soft, that he decided heaven wasn't up on high somewhere, it was right here.

After a moment she stirred, as if to remind him this wasn't a proper position for them to be in. Rhys, however, had no intention of letting propriety get in the way of something that felt this good, and he tightened his arms around her.

She capitulated at once, relaxing in his hold. Her token resistance gone, she leaned against him, her back against his chest and her shapely bum nestled against his thighs. The pleasure of it was so sweet, he actually had to bite his lip to keep from groaning aloud, and he hoped like hell the trout weren't particularly hungry.

"Do you fish often?" she asked.

"Yes, actually, I do," he answered, valiantly forcing himself to make mundane conversation even as the thick, aching heaviness of lust flowed through his body. "I have . . . " He paused and swallowed hard. "I have quite a passion for it."

"Indeed? I wouldn't have thought a man such as you would enjoy a sport such as this."

"No?" He closed his eyes, savoring the feel of her breasts against his forearms and the softness of her hair against the side of his neck. "Why not?"

"Well, Your Grace, by your own admission, you have had rather a wild past, and this sport seems a bit sedate for your taste."

There was nothing sedate about what he felt right now. "The pleasure of it is indescribable," he murmured as he began to imagine taking off her clothes. "The tension, the waiting, and then, at last, the victory. It's exquisite."

"Really?"

The image of her naked was becoming quite vivid in his mind. "Really," he said with reverent appreciation.

During the remainder of the afternoon, it took everything he had to keep his desire in check, but it was a torture for which he had only himself to blame. Knowing full well how his desire seemed to flare up every time he so much as looked at her, knowing he couldn't give in to that desire this early in the game, he'd still brought her here, where they could be alone, where he could put his arms around her and pretend it was for perfectly innocent reasons, where he could taunt himself with the shape of her body and the scent of her hair and no possibility of relief in sight.

After two hours of holding her without being able to kiss her or touch her soft skin or slide his hands beneath her skirts, Rhys was in such agony that he decided teaching Prudence to fish now took pride of place as the stupidest thing he'd ever done. But he relished every agonizing second of it.

Chapter 8

London's Newest Heiress has confirmed she will attend Lady Amberly's charity ball tonight. This bodes well for the event's success, for balls often fail from the presence of more ladies than gentlemen to partner them, and the presence of wealthy heiresses always prevents that particular calamity.

—The Social Gazette, *1894*

Instead of remaining in Richmond another night as he had originally arranged with his host, Rhys decided to accompany Prudence on the train back to London. During the journey, they were no longer alone, for the train was full, and because of that, he was forced to behave with absolute propriety. Propriety, however, did little to stop the naughty thoughts going through his mind, thoughts that lingered even after he parted company with her at Victoria Station.

He hailed a hansom, and as the cab crawled through the heavy London traffic, Rhys tortured himself with thoughts of her all the way to Mayfair, letting his imagination once again explore all the curves and valleys of her bountiful figure—the undulating dip of her waist and the plump roundness of her breasts and buttocks. He relived the afternoon again and again, even managing to laugh at his own frustration on the rare occasions when an actual fish had dared to interrupt the delicious pleasure of holding her.

When he arrived home, however, his good mood was snuffed out at once by Hollister, who met him at the front door.

"Mr. Roth and Mr. Silverstein are here, Your Grace," the butler informed him. "Since I assume the matter is business, I put the two gentlemen in the study."

When bankers called in person, in the evening, the news could not be good. Rhys mounted the stairs, passed the drawing room, and entered the study at the end of the corridor, bracing himself for the worst. The grave faces of the two bankers, who stood up when he entered, told him he was about to receive it.

First, the proper condolences were expressed over the demise of the previous duke.

"Thank you," Rhys answered, trying to look

appropriately grief-stricken for old Evelyn. "My uncle's death has taken a great toll on my entire family." He gestured to the pair of chairs facing the desk where they had been sitting. "Please, gentlemen, resume your seats."

They complied, and Rhys circled around Milbray's ornately carved mahogany desk to take the chair behind it.

"To what do I owe the pleasure?" he asked with an easy smile.

"We have come in response to your letter of yesterday," Mr. Roth explained, "in which you applied for additional funds."

"Yes. What of it?" He paused, seeming suddenly perplexed. "Is there a problem, gentlemen? Surely not."

The two men exchanged glances, and there was a long, painful silence before Mr. Silverstein gave him the bad, not at all surprising news. "With regret, Your Grace, we must decline your application."

Rhys looked down his ducal nose. "My family has been banking with your firm since the time of Queen Anne."

"Quite so," Mr. Roth put in. "Quite so, yes. And because of that history, it pains us to refuse any loan to the Duke of St. Cyres, but in this case, alas, we must. Begging Your Grace's pardon, we must speak frankly. Your family's financial situation is . . . precarious. Your uncle was liberal in his spending, a fact that has concerned us for quite some time."

Rhys locked gazes with Mr. Roth, who was the senior partner. "These are new times, and I am not my uncle."

"Of course. But what guarantee do we have that you will improve your family's financial situation?"

Rhys did not answer that question directly. Instead, he opened the right-hand drawer of his desk and pulled out a recent copy of *Talk of the Town*. He tossed it down so its headline faced the two men opposite.

Is Love in Bloom in Covent Garden?

Mr. Roth and Mr. Silverstein did not seem as impressed as he'd hoped. The two men exchanged glances, but again it was Mr. Roth who spoke. "With all due respect, Your Grace, you are asking for additional credit of three hundred thousand pounds. That is an enormous sum."

"It's not as if the money is for *me*, gentlemen," Rhys said, flattening his hand against his chest. "It's for Her Majesty's government." He heaved a sigh. "Beastly thing, death duties."

"We do appreciate your reasons for needing such a large amount of ready money," Mr. Silverstein hastened to say. "It is not uncommon for families of esteemed rank to be in such circumstances."

"I'm so glad you understand."

"But," Mr. Roth put in, making Rhys grimace,

"we cannot possibly loan such a sum simply because your name has been linked with Miss Abernathy in a newspaper." He smiled in a deprecating fashion. "Banking decisions of this magnitude cannot be made based upon society gossip."

"I see." Rhys leaned back in his chair, staring at the ceiling, deceptively relaxed. He waited a good thirty seconds before he replied. When he did speak, his voice was reflective, thoughtful. "Were a duke to marry one of the world's wealthiest heiresses, thereby claiming an income in the millions and ownership of an enormous mercantile empire in America, he would become one of the most powerful and influential men in the world, wouldn't you say? There would be so many bankers such a man could choose among to manage his assets." He let that sink in, then added, "I have such a long memory, gentlemen, and, I fear, a very unforgiving nature."

He gave them a look of apology for these flaws in his character.

There was a delicate pause, then Mr. Roth cleared his throat. "If said duke were officially engaged to this wealthy heiress, we might see our way clear to issue credit for the sum His Grace desired, and more, if it were needed. Such loans would be perfectly acceptable on note of hand alone, I think. What do you say, Mr. Silverstein?"

"I quite agree," the other man said with a nod. "An official engagement would not be gossip. It would be borrowing against one's expectations, and that is a different matter entirely."

"Excellent." Rhys rose to his feet, smiling. "I think we understand each other, gentlemen. And might I be so bold as to recommend that you make a practice of reading the society pages from now on? Gossip, you see, is so often the prelude to fact. Good evening."

He rang for Milbray's butler to show the bankers out, also asking Hollister to send for his valet. As he waited for Fane, he considered this new development and how it affected his plans. Because of Miss Abernathy's romantic nature, he had assumed a somewhat lengthy courtship would be required, but this visit by Mr. Roth and Mr. Silverstein made such a plan untenable. His circumstances demanded haste.

That suited him down to the ground. As delicious as this afternoon had been, it had been a deuced hard thing to arrange. When a couple was engaged, privacy was easier to obtain, giving a man far more opportunity to take liberties. And he intended to take as many liberties with Prudence Abernathy as he could, for she was the softest, sweetest thing he'd come across in a long, long time.

He liked things that were soft and sweet, perhaps because life was so full of things that were neither, including him. And she was such an innocent. He'd never understood the appeal of a virgin before, and yet he was beginning to find this particular virgin seductive as hell. The hero worship he saw in her eyes and her insistence on believing the best of him and everyone else were hopelessly naive qualities, of course. And yet, her sweet, placid nature was like a balm to all that was corrupt and cynical within him.

Romantic, she'd called him. So absurd. If she'd known what thoughts were going through his mind all afternoon, his virginal little heiress would probably have been shocked. And if she became aware of even a fraction of the things he'd experienced in his life, of all the self-destructive excesses in which he'd engaged, of all the ugliness of his youth and the corrupt skeletons in his family closet, she'd have been disgusted by just how unromantic and empty he truly was.

Rhys opened his eyes and once again pulled out the top drawer of the desk. Pushing aside some letters, he removed a small book with a gray-fabric cover, a book tattered and stained from its many years in his keeping. When he opened it, the pages came apart at once to an oft-read page.

Oh, to be in England, now that April's there.

As always when he read that line, a wave of longing swept over him, a longing for the England of Browning's brushwood sheaf and singing chaffinch, a longing for the ideals of his country, for the ideals of his position, for any ideals at all. A longing for home.

Perhaps you were just homesick.

No perhaps about it. He'd been homesick for as long as he could remember.

"You sent for me, sir?"

He looked up to find his valet standing in the doorway, and he shut the book with a snap. "I did, yes," he answered as he dropped the volume of Browning's poetry into the drawer. "What are Miss Abernathy's plans for tomorrow?" he asked, shoving the drawer closed.

"I believe she is attending Lady Amberly's Charity Ball for the Benefit of Widows and Orphans tomorrow night."

"Ah, a public ball. Did I receive a voucher?"

"Of course, sir, but you had declined the invitation."

"Inform Lady Amberly at once that I've changed my mind. I will attend after all."

"Very good, sir." The valet started to turn away, but Rhys's voice stopped him.

"And Fane?"

"Sir?"

Rhys paused for a moment, considering ramifications before he spoke. "Make certain Lady Alberta Denville learns of my plans."

"That should make for some interesting developments, sir."

"I hope so, Fane. In fact, I'm counting on it."

* * *

Prudence grabbed one post of the immense four-poster bed in her room at the Savoy and sucked in as deep a breath as she could manage. She grimaced as Woddell gave her corset stays a hard pull and vowed she wasn't eating any more of the Savoy's cream tarts at tea.

The maid tied off her stays and slid a tape measure around her waist. "Twenty-eight and one-half inches, miss," she announced a moment later.

Prudence groaned. "That's not enough. I want to wear the pink damask ball gown, and for it to fit just right, I need you to bring me in another half inch."

"The pink does look ever so nice on you, miss, but you'll want to be able to dance, remember."

Prudence wasn't worried about that. The duke was attending Lady Amberly's ball, and that fact meant she'd be floating on air all evening. "I'll be quite capable of dancing," she assured her maid with a laugh. "Try again."

Woddell finally managed to whittle Prudence's waist size down to the required measurement, and the moment the maid had fitted her into the confection of pink silk before the mirror, she knew their combined efforts had been worthwhile. She might not possess a fashionable hourglass figure, but this gown's low neckline, puffed sleeves, and gored skirt made her look as if she did. Prudence inhaled as deep a breath as she could manage and let it out on a satisfied sigh.

"You are certain the duke will be at the ball, Woddell?" she asked for perhaps the tenth time as the maid bent to adjust the ruched and embroidered hem of her skirt.

"Yes, miss. My young man is valet to Count Roselli, as I told you already, and he says the count knows His Grace very well. I saw Mr. Fane only this morning in the laundry rooms belowstairs, and he swore to me the duke will be there."

"It's so nice that you have a young man. Is he handsome?"

"Oh, yes, miss." The maid straightened and gave a laugh as she began to adjust the gown's sleeves. "Quite takes my breath away, he does, when he smiles."

Prudence laughed with her, a rather shaky laugh as she thought of St. Cyres's devastating smile. "I know just what you mean, Woddell."

At that moment Edith came bustling in, putting an end to their amusement at once. "Prudence, dear, is that as far as you've got?" she asked, glancing over her niece in obvious dismay. "Heavens, your hair isn't even finished yet. Stop dawdling, dear. Robert and Millicent will be arriving at any moment."

"We've plenty of time," Prudence pointed out. "Why, most of the aristocrats never even arrive at a fashionable ball before midnight."

"I daresay, but we are simple gentry folk when all's said and done. We hardly need to assume the pretensions of the aristocracy." She crossed the room to Prudence's side and gave her a long up-and-down glance. "You look lovely, dear," she said at last. "Robert will be so pleased to partner you. How many dances have you promised him?"

"Two. A quadrille and a galop."

Edith gave a cry of dismay. "No waltzes?"

"No." Prudence turned away as Woddell presented a shallow box of hair ornaments for her inspection, glad of the distraction. "Help me decide how to dress my hair, will you, Aunt?"

Edith, of course, would not be dismissed so easily. "Robert asked you most particularly to reserve three of your waltzes for him."

Prudence pretended to give the aigrette of feathers her maid held up her full consideration, hoping Edith would let the matter drop. "No, Woddell," she finally said. "I think something simpler would be best. Perhaps just these pearl combs," she added, removing them from the box, "and a spray of fresh gardenias or lily of the valley from the florist downstairs. That will do nicely."

"Prudence?"

Her aunt's sharp voice told her that avoidance had not worked, so she tried diplomacy as Woddell returned the other hair ornaments to the dressing room. "I told Robert earlier today which dances on the *programme* I shall give him," she said as she walked to her dressing table. "He seemed perfectly amenable to my decision. If he is content, why should you not be?"

"There are nine waltzes on the *programme*, and I insist you reserve at least three for the man whose admiration for you is genuine."

Prudence already knew which man's admiration was genuine. "Three waltzes in one evening would imply an engagement. Robert and I are not engaged." She turned and met her aunt's resentful stare with a determined one of her own. "Nor do I see us as ever being so."

"But—"

"Besides," she interrupted, "I do not believe in this idea of reserving waltzes for one particular man before the ball even begins. Such a practice makes men far too complacent. I shall give my waltzes to the men who ask me at the ball."

"You mean you are saving them for St. Cyres."

Prudence pulled out the chair in front of her dressing table and sat down. "I shall certainly waltz with him if he asks me. How could I refuse a duke?" At those words, anticipation bubbled up in her, but she felt impelled to add, "It is by no means certain he will ask me to dance."

"Oh, yes, it is," Edith snapped, crossing the room to stand beside her chair. "I think it is safe to say he will ask you for at least three waltzes."

Recalling their outing the day before, Prudence thought it was a fair certainty he would ask her to waltz at least once. Perhaps twice. And if there were three? She could hardly dare to hope for that.

"As you said yourself, three waltzes imply engagement," Edith went on. "Such implications suit him down to the ground, I daresay. And you as well, from the sound of it."

Prudence had no intention of allowing Edith to ruin her lovely mood with an argument. "As I said, Aunt, other than the two dances I have already promised Robert, I will reserve the places on my dance card for those men who ask me at the ball."

Edith made a sound of utter exasperation. "Time will tell if I'm not right about that man," she said, and started for the door. "Until then, I wash my hands of it!"

She walked out, and the moment the door slammed behind her, Prudence forgot about her entirely. Thinking about waltzing with St. Cyres was a much more enjoyable subject for contemplation.

Lady Amberly was a popular patroness of charities, and her ball was a prominent and fashionable one. The subscription rooms in Mayfair where the ball was held were filled to overflowing by the time Prudence arrived. It was so crowded, in fact, that it took her party an hour to hand over their wraps and accept dance cards at the cloak room, mount the stairs, and be announced into the ballroom.

The entire time, her gaze searched the crowd

for St. Cyres, but as it was barely eleven, she knew such efforts were probably in vain. As she had pointed out to Aunt Edith, aristocrats were always terribly late to the fashionable balls, and St. Cyres, being a duke, was bound to be among the last to arrive.

Though the duke had not yet made his appearance, Lady Alberta Denville was present. As much as Prudence hated to admit it, the girl was beautiful, tall and slender as a willow, with features of classic, perfect proportion. She also looked quite angelic, with her pale gold hair and ciel-blue satin gown. Prudence, however, couldn't help indulging in a bit of speculation about which poor seamstress Lady Alberta intended to abuse this evening.

As she had promised, she gave two dances to Robert, and did not lack for other partners. Many young men approached Robert and Uncle Stephen for introductions to her, and most of those gentlemen asked her to dance, but Prudence had only one man on her mind. She sidestepped the requests of those gentlemen who wanted to reserve waltzes with her for later in the evening, though she tried to do it diplomatically so as not to hurt their feelings. All the while, she could not stop glancing at the door, her tension mounting as each new group of guests appeared.

She had just finished an exuberant galop with a most enthusiastic partner when his name was announced. Out of breath, flushed and a bit damp, she fussed with the loose tendrils of her hair, smoothed her wrinkled gown, and bemoaned her disheveled appearance as he paused in the doorway and glanced about the room.

But her efforts proved to be in vain. His gaze skimmed right past her, then he turned and made his way toward the opposite side of the ballroom.

He must not have seen her. Disappointment shot through Prudence as she watched him make his way across the room, and that disappointment only deepened when she realized who he had seen.

Lady Alberta's beautiful face lit up at the sight of him, and within moments the pair were engaged in an animated conversation. Prudence watched them, her disappointment deepening as they smiled and laughed, their heads intimately close together.

When a certain Lord Weston approached her uncle asking for an introduction to her, she tried to be glad of the distraction. But when a waltz began and he asked her to dance, she hesitated and glanced across the room, only to find that the duke was leading Lady Alberta onto the ballroom floor. Her disappointment settled into a heavy weight in her tummy, but pride enabled her to accept Lord Weston's invitation. As they waltzed, he attempted to make conversation and she did her best to pay attention, but whenever she glanced at the other couple, it seemed as if St. Cyres was smiling at his partner as if thoroughly enamored, and she couldn't help the horrid sting of jealousy.

"I can see I am put in my usual position of playing second fiddle to my friend."

With an effort, Prudence returned her gaze to her partner. "I beg your pardon?"

Lord Weston inclined his head in the direction of the other couple. "The Duke of St. Cyres is a friend of mine, and I know the ladies are much more inclined to stare at him than at me. I tell myself it's his superior rank, not my lack of charm and good looks, that garners him more feminine attention."

Ashamed, Prudence endeavored to make up for her faux pas. She scanned his face, not a homely countenance by any means, and said, "You should not speak so disparagingly of yourself. You are every bit as handsome as the duke."

"Thank you, but since you've been staring at him since we began, I know that's a false opinion on your part. Still, it's a kind thing to say."

She bit her lip, feeling terrible. "I'm so sorry."

"Quite all right," he assured her with a good-natured smile that marked laugh lines at the corners of his blue eyes. "If there's anything about Rhys you'd like to know, I'd be happy to oblige."

"You know him well?"

"I suppose I do, yes. At least, as well as anyone can ever know Rhys."

That enigmatic answer only heightened her curiosity. "What do you mean?"

"For all that careless surface charm he displays, he's a deep one. There's a bit of a wall around him. Try getting past that wall, and you'll find the gates slammed in your face."

Prudence was struck by the choice of words, for she remembered the day before when she'd had a similar feeling. "I think I know what you mean. Not letting anyone get too close."

"Exactly so, yes. I visited him several times when he lived in Paris, and I stayed with him in Florence for a year, but I've actually known him since we were boys. Despite all that, every time I see him, I have the odd feeling I'm talking to a stranger. Still, I'd love to tell you anything I do know. Only fair, I say, after all the scrapes he led me into when we were boys."

"Did you attend the same schools, then?"

"No, we went to different schools—he's Eton and Oxford, I'm Harrow and Cambridge—but both our families possess lands in Derbyshire, and he stayed with my family once or twice during summer holidays. After his brother's death, he never stayed with any of his own relations, though I don't know quite why. He and his mother don't get on, I know that much."

"His Grace had a brother?"

"Thomas, yes. He died when he was twelve. Rhys was thirteen at the time."

"How did the boy die?"

An evasive look came into Weston's face. "Do you know, I'm not sure," he murmured, but Prudence was certain he was lying. "Accident of some kind, I expect," he went on. "It happened when the boy was at school, I remember. Rhys has never spoken of it to me, and I highly doubt he's spoken of it to anyone else."

"It must have hit him very hard."

"It shattered him. That I do know. They were very close. Their father had passed away one or two years earlier, and Rhys, being older, felt it was up to him to watch out for his brother. He blamed himself for not being there when Thomas died. But he could hardly be expected to be there. They were at different schools by then. Being thirteen, Rhys was already at Eton when Thomas died."

She wanted to ask more questions, but the waltz was coming to an end. When the music stopped, Weston escorted her back to her place beside her family. "I should very much like to linger here, Miss Abernathy, in the hope that my friend would become less interesting and myself more so," he told her with a rueful smile, "but I promised my sister most faithfully I would make an appearance at the ball of her friend Lady Harbury, and since it's getting on for midnight, I had best be on my way."

"Thank you, and I am sorry if my attentions were engaged elsewhere during our dance."

"Pray do not apologize. A waltz with a lovely woman is always a pleasure." With that, he bowed and departed, exiting the ballroom.

The moment he was gone, Robert appeared beside her, asking if she would grant him the next dance.

"Not this one, Robert," she said, her gaze moving to the other side of the room, and lighting at once on the duke. He had escorted Lady Alberta back to her place and they stood side by side, observing the crowd and talking.

She told herself perhaps he did not know she was there. Once he saw her, surely he would ask her to dance. She gazed at him, waiting, hoping, almost willing him to find her. And then, just as she was sure she must have inexplicably become invisible, his gaze caught on her.

He bowed to her in acknowledgment, and Prudence once again felt that delicious sense of anticipation, along with an overwhelming relief. A waltz was next on the *programme.* Any moment now he would come to her and ask her to dance it with him. Surely he would.

She smiled at him. He did not smile back. Instead, to her utter astonishment, he returned his attention to the woman beside him.

She stared at him, unable to believe he had just snubbed her. When the band began to tune for the waltz and St. Cyres once again led Lady Alberta toward the ballroom floor, her disbelief deepened into a bruising, aching hurt. Why? she wondered in bewilderment. Why would he behave this way?

"Will you grant me at least this one waltz, Prudence?" Robert asked, breaking into her thoughts.

Pride came to her rescue. "Yes, Robert," she answered. "I will."

She danced with Robert, and though she tried to keep her attention fixed on her partner, she could not resist an occasional glance at the other couples around them. Every time she spied St. Cyres and Lady Alberta, it was like an arrow piercing her heart.

Only yesterday, they had spent such a wonderful day together.

I like you best.

If those words were true, why was he dancing with Lady Alberta and not with her? As often as she asked herself that question, she could find no answer, and by the time Robert escorted her back to her place at the end of the dance, all she wanted was to vanish into the pale gold wallpaper. But despite his actions, she could not abandon all hope. Perhaps he was only fulfilling an obligation to the girl. She knew from the night she'd met him that he had promised Alberta at least one waltz. Perhaps he had also promised her a second one and had to make good on that promise.

Heartsick, yet hoping for a miracle, Prudence

watched him as he hovered by Lady Alberta's side. She danced with those partners who asked her and kept her head held high. But when she saw him take Lady Alberta out onto the dance floor for a third waltz, her hurt became unbearable. She knew full well what three waltzes meant. An engagement was sure to follow.

Anger, an emotion Prudence seldom felt toward anyone, began to smolder deep within her as she thought of what he had done. Only yesterday he'd taken her for an outing, acted as if she was the one he wanted, said she was the one he liked best. He had sat beside her, laughed with her, touched her, almost kissed her. Only yesterday he had embraced her, using that transparent excuse about fishing to do so. He had led her on and encouraged her hopes. Clearly he had only been toying with her, because Alberta was the one he intended to marry. Alberta was obviously the one he loved.

Anger bolstered her pride, smothered any vestige of her hope, and extinguished any tears that might threaten to fall. He wasn't worth crying over, and she vowed she was never, ever going to waste a tear on him. She lifted her chin, turned away from the pair on the dance floor and walked around Robert to where her aunt and uncle were standing. She informed them that she had a headache and wished to leave. Without waiting for an answer, she turned on her heel and departed from the ballroom.

Her aunt and uncle seemed quite pleased to go, she noted as they waited downstairs for their carriage to be brought around. They were no doubt relieved that the unwanted duke wouldn't be conferring his attentions on their niece tonight, or any night in the future now that he had made his intentions clear to all of London society.

Thinking it over as the carriage took them back to the Savoy, Prudence decided it was quite a suitable match. The hell Lady Alberta would put him through once they were wed was just what he deserved, the scoundrel.

As she prepared for bed, her anger stayed at a slow, steady simmer, controlled and contained beneath the smooth surface of her usual placid nature. She was even able to assure Woddell that her evening had been delightful until this beastly headache forced her to leave.

She refused the maid's offer to order an ice poultice for her head, assuring the other woman all she needed was a good night's sleep. After dismissing Woddell, she crawled into bed, but did not sleep.

Instead, she lay there in the dark, unable to stop thinking of the events of yesterday and today, and as she did so, her anger continued to rise.

How dare he toy with her? Pay her his attentions and engage her affections to no purpose? He'd been telling her the truth, obviously, when he'd said there was nothing wonderful about him. If

Lady Alberta was the one he wanted, why hadn't he taken *her* on a picnic?

Prudence tossed aside the sheets and got out of bed. She crossed to her dressing table, yanked open the drawer, and pulled out the card he'd slipped to her that day at the National Gallery, along with the note he'd given her at the opera. She stared at them for a long moment, and then, her hands shaking, she ripped both missives into pieces and tossed them into the wastepaper basket.

I like you best.

Suddenly, all the anger went out of her, and Prudence sank down in the chair of her dressing table. She stared at the notes that were now as shredded as all her hopes, and broke her resolution. She burst into tears.

Chapter 9

Though he has only been home a fortnight, it appears that Britain's most scandalous duke has chosen his duchess. We can only commend him as a most expeditious suitor.

—The Social Gazette, *1894*

By morning Prudence had shed all the tears she ever intended to shed over the Duke of St. Cyres. Assisted by Woddell, she applied compresses of cold tea leaves to her eyes, dabbed a bit of face powder to her nose, and by the time she attended second church service with her aunt and uncle, she was optimistic that her appearance showed none of the ill-effects of a night spent crying. She appreciated full well that her own unrealistic expectations were partly to blame for the hurt she felt now, and she had no intention of allowing herself to be so silly over a man again, even if he was handsome as sin.

After church, she overrode her aunt's plan to spend the remainder of the day at Millicent's, saying she intended keep to her usual custom and have Sunday-afternoon tea in Little Russell Street.

Her richly appointed brougham, open to the fine spring day, drew some interested stares from passersby as it stopped in front of the lodging house and her driver rolled out the steps for her. Prudence exited the carriage and paused on the sidewalk for a moment, studying the prim brick lodging house with its green door and lace curtains, and she felt overcome by a wave of homesickness. The Savoy was a luxurious place, to be sure, but it wasn't Little Russell Street.

Only a week had passed since she'd last been here, and yet her entire life had changed. For the better, she'd thought, but now, staring at the building that had been her home for eleven years, still a bit raw from the heart-bruising events of last night, she was not so sure.

She didn't ring the bell. Though she might not live here any longer, she wasn't going to stand on ceremony with her friends. She opened the door and walked right in. "Hullo, everyone," she called out with forced cheerfulness as she stepped over the threshold. "Kettle's on, I hope?"

A round of delighted cries answered her from

the parlor, and within moments her friends were pouring into the foyer.

Mrs. Morris was the first to greet her. "Prudence, dear, what a lovely surprise!" the landlady cried, giving her a wide smile. "We didn't expect to see you today."

"I can't imagine why not," she answered as she unbuttoned her cloak and hung it up. "You know I never miss Sunday tea."

"We didn't think you'd want to associate with our lot anymore," Maria told her with a breezy offhandedness Prudence knew was a pose. "You being an heiress now and all, you might be too grand for the likes of us."

Prudence looked at the smiling faces around her, and her heart tightened at the sight of all her friends. Dear, silly Mrs. Morris, who began fluttering and fussing, sure that afternoon tea at the Savoy must be far superior to anything served here. Rotund, cheery Mrs. Inkberry, Mrs. Morris's oldest friend, who hadn't lived in the lodging house since her marriage over two decades earlier but still came for tea every Sunday. And her fellow girl-bachelors—Miranda, Daisy, Lucy, and, of course, Maria, who gave her a warm hug and a cheeky grin and asked if she was engaged yet.

At that question, Prudence's smile faltered. Her reaction did not go unnoticed. Questions were immediately asked, and moments later she found herself ensconced in her usual place on the horsehair settee, pouring out the humiliating events of last night to a very sympathetic audience.

"Oh, my dear, how awful," Mrs. Inkberry murmured when she had finished, patting her shoulder in a comforting way and handing her a handkerchief. "What you need is a cup of tea, hot and strong, and a bite to eat." She looked across the tea table. "Abigail?"

"Tea?" Mrs. Morris shook her head and rose from her chair. "Oh, no, Josephine, tea's of no use at all to a girl at a time like this. A small glass of my damson gin's what she needs to put her right again."

There was an uncomfortable silence and a surreptitious exchange of glances around the room. No one had ever had the heart to tell Mrs. Morris that her damson gin was vile.

"No, no, please," Prudence demurred. "I'd prefer not to drink spirits during the day, even for medicinal purposes. Tea would be ever so lovely, thank you."

Mrs. Morris looked a bit doubtful, but resumed her seat. Prudence's cup of tea was duly poured and passed around to her, a fragrant, steaming cup of Earl Grey, the tea most favored by the Queen, and therefore the only tea served on Sunday afternoons in Little Russell Street.

Mrs. Inkberry gave her shoulder another motherly pat. "Now, you down that, Prudence, and you'll feel much better."

Prudence took several sips and found that her mood was lighter, though she suspected pouring out her feeling to her friends had more to do with it than Earl Grey.

"He did not even speak to you?" Lucy asked, returning to the subject as if she couldn't quite believe it. "Not once? Not after spending an entire afternoon in your company the day before?"

Prudence shook her head and took another gulp of tea. "Not even once."

"Mind you, Prudence, you never should have spent an afternoon alone with him," Mrs. Inkberry pointed out with gentle, motherly censure.

Prudence shifted guiltily in her seat. "I know, I know," she mumbled, "and I suppose you'll say I deserve what I got after such a lack of propriety, but—"

"Nonsense," Mrs. Inkberry interrupted. "You are a good girl, Prudence, and your romantic impulsiveness does not excuse his rudeness. For him to cut you directly—"

"No, no," Prudence hastened to correct her, "he was not so rude as that. He did acknowledge me. He bowed to me most politely."

"Well, now that's not so bad, then, is it?" Miranda asked with a cheerfulness that sounded terribly forced. "At least he did acknowledge you."

"He bowed from the other side of the room," Prudence told her. "With Lady Alberta standing right beside him, looking like a cat swimming in cream."

Lucy set down her cup and saucer with a decisive clatter. "I cannot believe he snubbed our Prudence to waste his affections on someone like this Lady Alberta. She sounds a horrible person."

"I agree," Daisy put in, "and I think if this Lady Alberta is the sort of woman he wants, then he's too dim for words and not worth crying over. And he's certainly not worthy of you, duke or not."

There was hearty agreement on that point, but somehow Prudence didn't find this collective opinion of much consolation.

Miranda spoke again. "Perhaps there was a reason for his actions," she said with her usual hopeful optimism. "Something that we know nothing of."

There was a round of groans over such a naive assumption, but Lucy, usually one to assume the worst, actually agreed with it. "That might be true. Prudence, you mentioned that he danced with this Lady Alberta, but perhaps he felt obligated to do so. You know how these things happen. Well-meaning friends shove two people together and suggest they have a go, and there you are, feeling you must dance with someone you're not the least bit interested in."

As much as Prudence wanted to believe that explanation, she knew it wasn't viable. "They danced three times," she clarified glumly. "Three waltzes."

"Ohhhhhh," came the chorus of dismay that followed this news, for all of them understood the implications of it.

"The oddest part," she said, "is that I hardly know him, and yet from the first I felt such a strong attraction to him. I know it was foolish of me to entertain hope he returned my affections, but—"

"It wasn't foolish at all!" Maria burst out. "He invited you out that day because he wanted to be with you, that's what I say. I saw how he helped you that night at the ball. Men don't do things like that just to be kind. He couldn't take his eyes off of you that night. From the start, it was plain as a pikestaff he wanted you."

"I thought so, too. I was wrong, it seems." Prudence stared down at her teacup, watching the pink roses of the Royal Doulton pattern on the saucer blend and blur. She dabbed savagely at her eyes before any tears could fall. "It doesn't matter," she lied, and shoved the handkerchief in her pocket. "I don't care."

Feeling in need of some gastronomic fortification, she reached for one of the tiny chocolate éclairs on the tea tray as her loyal and indignant friends pronounced their opinions of the Duke of St. Cyres.

He was a cad.

He was a brute.

He might simply be dense. Men so often were.

Or perhaps he was in love with Lady Alberta.

That made him a cad with bad taste.

Prudence ate another éclair, and then another, as her friends continued their attempts to interpret the inexplicable actions of gentlemen in general and the duke in particular.

Just as consensus had been reached that gentlemen could not be relied upon for anything remotely approaching good sense, and that their behavior often proved a test of even the keenest feminine intellect, the doorbell rang. As Dorcas bustled past the parlor to the front of the lodging house, conversation turned to speculation about who the new arrival might be. Prudence wasn't much interested, but when the sound of a well-bred, distinctly masculine voice floated through the parlor doorway, she gave a gasp of astonishment.

"It's him," she whispered, feeling a wave of panic. "The duke is here."

Surprised murmurs rippled through the room at this announcement, but Prudence scarcely heard. Struggling to be calm, she set aside her tea, brushed crumbs from her skirt, verified with a hasty touch of her fingers that she had no sticky trace of chocolate icing on her face. "Do I look like I spent the night crying?" she asked Maria, who could always be counted upon for an honest opinion.

"Yes," her friend answered, and Prudence wished she'd asked Miranda instead.

"The Duke of St. Cyres," Dorcas announced.

All the women in the parlor stood up as he entered. He paused just inside the door, and even though she was still stinging from the snub he'd given her the night before, she couldn't help feeling that quixotic rush of pleasure and longing at the sight of him.

No other woman alive could blame her for that. Standing in this wholly feminine enclave of cabbage-rose wallpaper, bobbin lace curtains, and shabby gentility, his powerful masculine presence dominated. He seemed larger than life.

Prudence was not the only woman in the room feeling the heady affects of his presence, for there was a rustling of petticoats and a great deal of furtive primping going on. The duke didn't seem to notice all these feminine flutterings, however, for his gaze was riveted on Prudence alone.

"Miss Bosworth," he said, removing his hat with a bow.

Prudence curtsied in deference to his rank, but she did it grudgingly, and when he started toward her, she lifted her chin, determined to be self-possessed and aloof, despite a puffy face and a tummy full of éclairs. "Your Grace."

She must have succeeded to some extent, for he came to a halt halfway across the room, and a hint of what might have been guilt shadowed his face. "Miss Bosworth, I know you must think me the most callous of men, but I beg you to believe I had reasons for my actions last night, reasons which I feel impelled to explain to you, if only you will be so good as to allow me the oppor—" He stopped and looked around, suddenly seeming to realize they were not alone. "Forgive me. I fear I have interrupted a party."

Mrs. Morris gestured to the tea things. "No, no, just afternoon tea as usual. Prudence, shall you introduce us to your friend?"

She complied, but as she performed introductions, her thoughts were preoccupied with the crucial effort to appear unimpressed by his surprising arrival. She was so engaged in this attempt at indifference, in fact, that it took her a moment to realize the room had gone completely silent and everyone was looking at her.

She forced herself to speak. "Will you take tea with us, Your Grace?" she found herself saying, and then wanted to bite her tongue off, for what she should have done was ordered him to leave, told him to save his explanations and go take tea with Lady Alberta.

"Yes, Your Grace," Mrs. Morris put in, "please do take tea with us." She picked up the teapot, gave it a little shake, then laughed. "Oh, dear, I don't believe we've any tea left. I shall have to make a fresh pot."

"I do not wish to give any trouble," the duke said, but the landlady overrode this polite protest with an airy wave of her hand.

"It's no trouble at all," she assured him, and bustled toward the door. "We could all do with a second cuppa, I daresay, and a few more sandwiches. And some nice hot scones would be lovely, too, I think. Oh, but—" She paused at the door. "I fear I cannot manage all of that by myself. Will some of you ladies assist me?"

Prudence felt her panic rising as the other women in the room immediately volunteered to help, rose to their feet and began moving toward the door.

"Prudence, you stay here," Mrs. Morris ordered as she ushered the other ladies out of the room, "and converse with your friend. We will return in ten minutes. Forgive us, Your Grace?"

Without waiting for an answer, she followed the other women out of the room, and in the wake of their departure, the silence seemed deafening. Prudence felt compelled to say something. "How did you know where to find me?"

"I called at Madame Marceau's to gain your address. She wasn't in, but a certain Miss Clark asked me to give you her best regards."

"I see."

There was another long, awkward pause. She wondered if she should talk about the weather.

"Miss Bosworth," he said, saving her from a mention of the lovely day, "I must speak candidly to you."

As if his arrival wasn't enough cause for surprise, he proceeded to surprise her further by closing the door, a shocking action, the sort of thing only done when a man intended to propose marriage, and since he was for all intents and purposes engaged to Lady Alberta, the possibility that he was about to propose to her seemed as likely as Jules Verne's rocket ships to the moon. He turned toward her, flattening his back against the door. "Miss Bosworth, that day in the National Gallery, you said you believed in marrying for love."

The introduction of the topic of marriage might have been cause for hope, she supposed, but she suspected those words were simply a prelude to giving her the news about his engagement to Alberta. Prudence swallowed hard. "You said the same, I believe," she reminded him.

"Yes, quite. I—" He stopped and shifted his weight, then gave an awkward laugh. "This is more difficult than I thought it would be."

With those words, he proceeded to increase her suspense even further by walking to the window. Seconds passed that seemed like hours as she waited, watching him. The afternoon sunlight poured over him, glinting off the silver stick pin in his lapel and making his hair seem like burnished gold. Finally, she could stand it no longer, and gave a little cough.

He glanced at her, then away. "I also believe marrying for love is the most desirable course," he said. "To choose a partner for marital life who is also one's true love would be a happy thing indeed." He turned toward her, his wide shoulders square, his jaw set. "For me, such a choice has never been possible."

Her spirits sank another notch. "I don't quite understand."

"Of course you don't. How could you understand the sordid realities of the aristocracy? For those of my class, love is never a consideration in choosing one's spouse." He drew a deep breath, his gaze locked with hers. "I am a duke. Position and duty, not love, must dictate my course."

She swallowed painfully, well aware of the difference in station between them. "You mean that in choosing a wife, it is her background and breeding you must consider?"

"Breeding? God, no. That doesn't signify at all nowadays. In these times of agricultural depression, it is money that matters, Miss Bosworth. Yes," he added, making a sound of disdain through his teeth, "as crude as it is, I must marry a woman with a dowry. A very substantial dowry, for a dukedom is an expensive responsibility. I simply haven't the blunt to maintain it all myself. Believe me when I say I wish it were otherwise."

"So, Lady Alberta . . . "

"Has money. It is as simple as that. She has an enormous dowry."

"You do not love her?"

"I've known her since she was a child, our families have long been connected through friendship. It would be a perfect alliance."

Prudence persisted. "But do you love her?"

His lips pressed together, and for a moment she thought he was not going to answer her question. "No," he finally said. "I do not love her. If I could follow my own inclinations in matrimony, I would never consider making Lady Alberta my duchess and the mother of my children." He paused, and his expression softened as he looked at her. "If I were free to love, I would make a different choice."

Pleasure bloomed inside her with those words, and hope rekindled. "Then—"

"But I am not free!" He raked a hand through his hair. "The day of our picnic, I forgot that fact. For one day I chose to forget my situation and my responsibilities. I thought only of my own yearnings and desires. And though it was one of the most pleasurable afternoons of my life, I fear it led you to believe I could offer you more than mere friendship, led you to hope for more than I can give. Indeed, I can see by your face today that my selfish actions have wounded you, and I deeply regret that."

Despite this confirmation of her puffy face, her spirits were soaring higher with each word he spoke, and she knew she had to tell him about her inheritance. "Your Grace—"

"Please indulge me a moment longer," he interrupted. "I must say these things now, for I fear there will never be another opportunity. I come from a family of ne'er-do-wells and spendthrifts, Miss Bosworth, and I confess, to my shame, that I am no exception. When I went abroad, I was young, wild, and damnably irresponsible. I spent my inheritance in the pursuit of my own pleasure, and when that was gone I accumulated debts, never caring about the future, or even thinking about it. But when I came home, when I assumed the title, I finally appreciated just what an enormous burden it is to be the duke. I also found that I was not the only one in my family with debts. My uncle was bankrupt when he died. They called his death a hunting accident, but it was suicide, for his creditors were about to take what little there was. My mother is nearly destitute, for he hadn't paid her jointure for years. I have aunts, uncles, cousins, all in the same situation, and they are all looking to me. I am the duke, the head of the family, I must take care of them."

"Of course," she said, eager to share her news now, berating herself for not having told him straightaway. Of course, a duke would need to wed a woman of means. If she'd thought it through, she would have concluded that for herself. She had to tell him the truth.

He didn't give her the chance. "My uncle allowed the seven ducal estates to go to rack and ruin," he went on. "Some of those estates have been in the De Winter family since the time of Edward I. Those lands supported their nearby villages for centuries, but now cannot even honor their debts to the local tradesmen. There are hundreds of people to whom I owe debts on behalf of the estates, debts I cannot honor. There are servants and former servants owed back wages, village tradesmen owed money on account. These people have their own families to support, and since I cannot pay them, they suffer terribly. Then there are the tenant farmers who can't pay their land rents, yet have nowhere else to go. All of these people are looking to me, waiting and hoping I can save them from these times of agricultural calamity. I cannot save them unless I marry a woman of wealth."

It was destiny, she realized. She had all this money coming to her, money she could only claim upon marriage, money she yearned to use for some useful purpose. All her life she had longed for a place to belong. And here before her was the most extraordinary man she had ever met, a man who only had to smile to gladden her heart, a man whose touch filled her with longing, a man who had made it clear to her that were he free to follow his heart, he would love her and give her the honor of his name.

"So," he said, bringing her out of these romantic speculations, "now you have the ugly truth about me." He shook back his hair with a trace of defiance. "How you must despise me for it."

"No, no, I don't despise you," she assured him, dismayed that he would think such a thing. She crossed the room and laid her hand on his arm. "I—"

He jerked away as if her touch burned him. "I must take my leave. I am expected at Lord Denville's for dinner." He stepped away from the window, walked around her and started for the door.

"Wait!" Prudence cried, turning. "Please, don't go."

He stopped, one hand on the handle of the closed door, his back to her. "Tarrying here only tortures me further, Miss Bosworth. Let me go."

"No, please, stay," she said, and once again walked to his side. "This is a day for confessions, it seems, for there is something I must tell you. I ask you to remain a few moments longer."

"Very well." He did not look at her. Instead, he kept his gaze fixed on the oak panels of the door. "What is it you wish to tell me?"

She once again laid her hand on his arm, and this time he did not pull away. He remained perfectly still, the muscles of his arm hard and tense beneath her fingers. "Your Grace, when we saw each other at the opera, I told you I'd had a change in my circumstances, but I did not explain precisely what that change was."

"Yes, you did. I remember. You were reconciling with your mother's family, you said." He stirred beneath her touch. "Is this important?"

"What I failed to tell you was that I have money."

He gave a short laugh, tilting his head back to stare at the ceiling. "Prudence, while I'm sure your uncle has managed to scrape together an allowance for you so that you might have some pretty dresses and a season in town, and though he may even be able to provide you with a dowry, it couldn't possibly make a dent in the De Winter family debts. We are drowning. We owe money everywhere." He shook his head violently and once again tore his arm from her grasp as if to leave.

"I have millions," she burst out, not knowing how else to say it.

St. Cyres turned to stare at her, looking blank and a bit stunned. She completely understood what he must be feeling. This sort of news was rather shattering. "Prudence, what are you talking about?"

"My father was Henry Abernathy, the American millionaire. He died recently, and in his will he left his entire fortune to me. I'm surprised you haven't heard about me already. The news has been in all the papers, and I'm sure people have been talking about it."

"I've been shut up in my study most days with matters of business," he murmured, sounding dazed. "There's been so much to do since I arrived home, and I haven't had much time for reading the papers, or for gossip either." He frowned, looking thoughtful. "I did hear something about the Abernathy heiress at the ball last night. That woman is you?" Even when she confirmed it with a nod, he still didn't seem to believe her. "You are the Abernathy heiress?"

"Yes. When I marry, I shall receive an income of about one million pounds per annum." Anxious, she stared at him, waiting, hardly daring to hope. "Is it enough to save you?"

"Enough?" He laughed at that. "Enough? Woman, it's enormous."

"It is rather."

"But—" He paused, frowning at her. "Why didn't you tell me this sooner, Prudence? You had plenty of opportunity." He sounded quite nettled all of a sudden.

Prudence swallowed hard. "I didn't want you to know because I was ashamed."

"Ashamed of what, in heaven's name? Being rich?"

"I was afraid that if you knew the truth, you would not . . . that I could never be the sort of woman you would . . . that you couldn't possibly want to . . . " She took a deep breath amid the tangle of awkward attempts and just said it. "My father never married my mother. I am illegitimate."

"And you thought I would condemn you for that?"

"Most people would. Besides, you're a duke. You

could hardly wish a woman born on the . . . on the wrong side of the blankets to be your duchess."

He shook his head and began to laugh. "Of all the absurd—" He broke off, tossed aside his hat and lifted his hands to cup her face. "If you knew how many peers are not the true sons of the men whose titles they claim," he said, smiling at her, "it would shock you right out of your middle-class sensibilities, Prudence."

Disbelieving, she started to shake her head, but his hands held her still. "It's true," he assured her. "Rumors have been floating around our family tree for years as to who my father really was."

"What?" Despite his warning, she was shocked. "Do you mean—"

"My mother had so many lovers, there was no way to be certain. So you see? I've no cause to disparage anyone's paternity. The man I knew as my father claimed me, but there was no way he could ever be sure."

"So you don't care?"

"I don't give a tinker's damn. The only thing that matters to me is what can now happen for us. Your news means we can marry. That's the only thing I care about."

This had to be a dream. He was a duke, so far above her that he might as well be the golden sun in the sky, so handsome it almost hurt her eyes to look at him. She was only a seamstress when all was said and done, a plump girl-bachelor of unremarkable looks and no consequence whatsoever, born of parents who hadn't even had their marriage lines. He was everything she could ever want, but that he could want her seemed impossible. "You really want to marry me? Really?"

His smile vanished. His fingers slid into the hair at her temples and he tilted her head back. His thumbs brushed across her cheeks. "I can think of nothing that would bring me greater happiness."

She gazed up at him, at his silvery-green eyes and beautiful, smiling mouth, and her heart ached in her breast with a happiness so strong, she could hardly breathe.

He bent his head, and when his lips touched her own, the pleasure was so acute, she made a wordless sob of pure joy against his mouth. The sweetness of it was like nothing she had ever experienced before.

Like a butterfly breaking free of its chrysalis, she felt as if she were suddenly coming to life, as if she had spent all the days before this one waiting to emerge, waiting for this feeling and this moment. Waiting for him.

With his warm mouth against her own and his fingertips caressing her face, she was lost. Her arms wrapped around his neck, her heart tumbled into his hands, and her fate became inexorably entwined with his. For the first time in her life, Prudence Bosworth fell in love.

Chapter 10

Abernathy Heiress Engaged! But Is It Love?

—The Social Gazette, *1894*

She was his. Rhys could feel it in the parting of her lips, in the twining of her arms around his neck, in the soft yielding of her body against his. He savored the sweetness of victory along with the hot, hungry arousal coursing through his body, but even that potent combination wasn't enough. He wanted more.

Though he knew a woman's surrender when he felt it, he wanted her to give her consent to be his wife out loud. He broke the kiss and tilted his head, touching his lips to the side of her neck. "Was that a yes?" he asked, tasting her skin with his tongue.

In reply, she made a soft, moaning sound that

was definitely affirmative, but he wasn't satisfied. He wanted to hear her say it.

He pressed kisses upward along her throat. "I didn't quite understand that," he murmured against her ear. He took her earlobe into his mouth and raked his teeth gently against her velvety soft skin, feeling her entire body shiver in response. "Could you say it again?"

"Mm," she answered, arms tightening around his neck, her breath quickening. "Umm-hmm."

That was still not enough for him. He had to have more. Suckling her earlobe, Rhys left off caressing her face and slid his hands down between them. When his palms embraced the fullness of her breasts, the pleasure was exquisite, but he didn't linger there. Instead, he lowered his hands still farther, savoring the deep dip of her waist and the wider flare of her hips. Even through the layers of her clothing and the whalebone stiffness of her corset, he could discern the true shape of her, and it was a shape so perfect, he gave a low groan of pure masculine appreciation.

"You're lovely," he muttered, and immediately cursed himself for not coming up with something more original to say than that. But for the life of him, he was unable to make his mind fashion a more sophisticated compliment. He kissed her ear, her cheek, her hair. "Luscious."

He cupped her buttocks in his hands, and the

move shocked her, he could tell. Her hands slid down from his neck and her palms flattened against his chest. He was shocked as well, for he could hear his own breath harsh and quick against her ear as he shaped the contours of her lush and lovely bum, and realized with chagrin that his control was slipping.

He reminded himself that they were in the parlor of a respectable ladies' lodging house and the respectable ladies would return at any moment. Yet even as he ordered himself to stop, he lifted her in his hands, and her arms tightened around his neck again as he brought her hips up hard against his. The pleasure was so great, it almost knocked him off his feet, but he reminded himself again that this wasn't the time for amorous explorations. He had to let her go, but not before he had her pledge. "Say you'll marry me, Prudence. Say it."

"Yes." The word was a gasp. "Yes, I'll marry you."

With that promise, relief washed over him, mingling with unrequited lust. Rhys drew a long, deep breath and reluctantly eased her down onto her feet. Then, with one more kiss, he let her go, clasped his hands firmly behind him, and took a long—a very long—step back.

"I shall have to speak with your uncle," he said, his voice a bit unsteady.

She nodded but didn't answer. Instead, she

lifted her hand to touch her mouth with the tips of her fingers and stared at him with amazement.

Rhys appreciated the reason. "You've never been kissed before, have you?"

She lowered her hand. "Yes, I have," she answered, to his surprise. "Once, in Sussex. John Chilton, the baker's son. We were both fourteen. It—" She broke off, spread her palm across her rib cage and drew a deep breath. "It wasn't at all the same."

That made him laugh, and before he knew what he was doing, he broke his own resolution. Stepping forward, he cupped her cheek, tilted her head back and kissed her again, hard and quick. "Do you know where Mr. Feathergill is this afternoon?"

"He is a member at White's. He might be there."

Rhys nodded. "And I shall have to meet with the trustees of your estate—you have trustees, I assume?"

"Yes, Mr. Elliot Whitfield, and two other solicitors. They must approve the engagement."

"I can't see how they could do otherwise. I am a duke, after all. And, as baffling as it is, you want to marry me. If you're willing to take me on, they can hardly object. Though they might question your sanity." He slid his arms around her waist and kissed her nose. "Shall I dine with you tonight?"

"If you wish to."

"Why shouldn't I?"

"It's not likely to be a friendly meal. Uncle Stephen and Aunt Edith aren't very fond of you."

Rhys thought of her situation when they had met, of her down on her knees taking abuse from Alberta, working grueling hours as a seamstress and living in a lodging house, alone and on her own without even her own relations looking out for her, and he decided he wasn't fond of them either.

"Then let's talk of something more pleasant. Where shall I take you for our honeymoon, hmm? Would you like to see Italy? Paris?"

She shook her head. "I want to see your estates."

"What?" Rhys was astonished. "Whatever for?"

She seemed more surprised by his question than he had been by hers. "I am to be your wife. Is it so surprising I should want to see your estates?"

"Of course not," he said hastily, cursing himself for not having anticipated this. "Of course you want to see everything. It's just that the houses aren't—" He broke off, trying to think of a way to avoid it. "They aren't furnished. There's not much . . . that is . . . the roofs leak, and the drains are bad, and the gardens are shabby. The estates aren't in any sort of shape for visitors."

"But that's exactly why I want to see them," she

explained. "I want to see what is needed. I want to meet the people, I want to show them we intend to be a responsible duke and duchess."

He looked into her earnest face and realized with dismay that he'd overdone the heroic, ducal responsibility business.

"In fact," she went on, "I don't think we should wait. We should go at once."

"You want to go before the wedding?"

"Yes. Things sound so dire, we have to go immediately and see what needs to be done. And if the drains are bad, there is always the risk of typhoid."

"Prudence, it's not possible. Except at Winter Park, we'd have to board at local inns in the villages."

"I don't mind. Besides, if we go now, all the work can be done while we're on our honeymoon."

She had every right to see the estates, she'd have to see them eventually, and arranging the repairs before they went on their honeymoon made perfect sense. Try as he might, he couldn't think of a single logical reason to refuse. He thought of his boyhood, of Winter Park, of all the things he'd buried two decades ago, and his dismay deepened into dread. "Prudence, you're not serious?"

"If I'm to be your duchess, I should see what our homes need, don't you think?"

He gave a violent start, fear shuddering deep

within him like a slumbering giant about to wake up. "Some of those places will never be our homes," he said through clenched teeth, thinking of Winter Park. "Never."

A bewildered frown knit her brows at his vehemence, and he worked to recover his poise. She wanted to use her money to repair those places and turn them into homes, sweet, naive dumpling that she was. She didn't know some things could never be repaired. He pulled her hard against him and buried his face in the lavender-scented sweetness of her hair.

Her fingers caressed his cheek. "If you don't want to go—"

"No." He took a deep breath and lifted his head. It had been twenty years since he'd been to any of the estates. Surely that was long enough. Perhaps Prudence's presence could wash it all away. Perhaps he could finally lay the ghosts to rest for good.

Rhys looked at her and pasted on a reassuring smile. "You're right, of course. We'll have a quick tour of the lands and the houses, then we'll return to London for the wedding. We'll go on our honeymoon, and all the work can be done while we're gone. Does that make you happy?"

"Yes." She smiled back at him, her face shining with such pleasure, Rhys felt as if he were sliding sideways. "You realize my aunt and uncle will have to go as well?"

"On our honeymoon?" he quipped, trying to ignore the sick feeling in his guts.

She laughed. "No, silly, to tour your estates! I can't go unchaperoned, so they must accompany us."

He groaned. "Lord, we wouldn't want anything to be easy, would we? I'm not yet acquainted with your uncle, but your aunt despises me."

She gave him an apologetic look. "She doesn't despise you. It's just that she and my uncle wanted me to marry Robert."

With Sir Robert's milquetoast temperament, Rhys was not surprised. If Robert had control of her money legally, Mr. and Mrs. Feathergill would have had control of her money in reality. "You are past the age of consent. Do the stipulations of your inheritance demand your uncle's permission for you to wed?"

"No, but the trustees have to approve, and my family could influence them against you."

"Let them try." He lifted one hand to gently caress her cheek. "I was forged in the fires of hell, my darling. If anyone tries to prevent our marriage, I'll burn them alive."

When Rhys departed to search for her uncle, Prudence watched him from the window of the parlor, peeking from behind bobbin lace curtains as he left the lodging house and walked to his carriage. As always, her heart gave a leap of pleasure at the sight of his handsome profile, tall frame, and tawny hair. She was to be his wife, his duchess. He wanted her and no other.

With a dreamy sigh she turned away from the window, smiling. Never in her life had she been this happy. Now she understood why poets wrote sonnets about love and why people said it was the most wonderful thing in the world.

"Well?"

She turned to the parlor doorway, where Maria was standing. The other girl-bachelors, Mrs. Morris, and Mrs. Inkberry were gathered behind her, all of them looking at Prudence with anxious faces.

"The duke proposed," she told them, and with those words, she began to laugh in amazement, still not quite believing it. "He proposed to me."

Exclamations of delight greeted this news, and the other women gathered around her at once to offer their congratulations.

"He said I was the one he wanted all the time, but that he felt obligated to marry Lady Alberta," she went on, her voice muffled as she hugged her friends.

Lucy, always shrewd, was the first to comprehend. "To clear his debts?"

"Yes. Does that make him sound terrible?"

"Not at all," Miranda said stoutly. "All the peers have to marry girls with dowries, especially nowadays. Look how many are having to marry

American girls because our English girls don't have a dowry to offer."

"So true," Mrs. Inkberry agreed. "Why, without a dowry, a girl can't expect to marry a man of any position at all. That was the way of things even in my courting days."

"It's more true now than ever," Lucy said dryly. "What with the agricultural depression, most peers are broke. And an heiress like Prudence has to marry a peer."

"Do I?" Prudence said with a chuckle. "Then it's fortunate I fell in love with a duke, not a bank clerk or a land agent!"

"And being a duke, he could have his pick, couldn't he?" Daisy said. "He could have had any heiress he wanted. But he's marrying our Pru. Well," she added, giving Prudence a hug, "Maria said it was plain how much he wanted you from the very start."

"So all's well that ends well." Mrs. Morris gave Prudence a kiss on the cheek. "We must celebrate. A bit of my damson gin, I think, to toast the engagement."

Wry glances were exchanged by the others, but they all sat down again as the landlady brought out tiny crystal goblets and a bottle of her plum liqueur from the corner cupboard.

"This is so exciting," she said as she began to pour damson gin into the glasses. "First Emma marries a viscount, and now Prudence is to marry a duke. Why, I don't think we've ever had this much to celebrate at Little Russell Street in all the years I've owned this lodging house. I can't help wondering what's next."

"A duke," Miranda repeated dreamily, falling back in her chair. "Think of it. Our Pru a duchess."

"A very rich duchess," Daisy reminded them, making everyone laugh. Everyone except Maria.

Prudence cast a sideways glance at the woman beside her on the horsehair settee. Her friend hadn't spoken, and her pensive profile reminded Prudence of their conversation just one week ago.

"There's something I want to discuss with all of you," she said, raising her voice a bit to be heard above the laughter. When her friends turned to give her their full attention, she continued, "Once I marry, I will receive my inheritance, and I want each of you to have a share."

Silence followed this announcement, and she hastened on, "I realize it's a bit awkward, but I'm going to be so rich, and have so much, and I want to share my good fortune with my friends."

There was another long pause as the other women in the room exchanged glances.

Lucy pushed back a lock of her auburn hair and cleared her throat. "Pru, we don't need your money," she said, echoing Maria's words from the week before. "You'll be needing it, surely, to help the duke. All those estates need to be supported.

And there are charities to which you'll want to contribute, people you'll want to help . . ."

Her voice trailed off, leaving the room silent once again. Prudence looked around at the proud faces of all her dear friends with a sinking feeling. They weren't going to accept her help, even though they lived just a hair's breadth from destitution and she was to receive millions. They thought it charity, even though they were her dearest friends and wouldn't hesitate to do the same for her. Prudence knew she had to find a way to help them without hurting their pride. "We can talk about it again some other time."

"After you're married," Mrs. Inkberry said, and leaned over from her chair to give Prudence's knee an affectionate pat. "Then we'll see. Abigail," she added, raising her voice and looking at Mrs. Morris, "aren't we supposed to be having a celebration toast? How slow you're being."

Prudence couldn't help noticing the relief of the others as the subject of the money was dropped, but as far as she was concerned, the matter was far from over.

"I'm just coming, Josephine," Mrs. Morris said, answering Mrs. Inkberry's question. She began to hand the glasses of ruby-colored liqueur around, and when each of them had one of the tiny crystal goblets in hand, she took her own seat and raised her glass.

"To our Prudence," she said, smiling. "Who fell

in love with a duke. And to His Grace, who had the good sense to fall in love with her."

Prudence laughed and lifted her glass along with the others. When she took a sip, she knew love was indeed a wonderful thing, for it could make even Mrs. Morris's damson gin taste good.

Chapter 11

Will the trustees of the Abernathy estate accept the Duke of St. Cyres? Or will the duke's wicked past prevent the match? We can only wait and see.

—Talk of the Town, *1894*

Rhys went home to meet with Fane, who proceeded to outline in detail all that he had learned of Mr. Feathergill during the past week. Upon hearing just what fascinating tidbits his valet had uncovered, he gave a low whistle. "Well done, Fane. Very well done. When I'm wed to Miss Abernathy, I'm tripling your wages."

Fane, who had finally been paid his back wages due to Rhys's meeting with the bankers and his subsequent loan, looked at him with gratitude at the promise of such a large increase in pay. "Thank you, sir."

"Where is Feathergill this afternoon?"

The valet confirmed that the squire was spending the afternoon at White's, but etiquette forbade even speaking to the other man without a formal introduction. Rhys dismissed Fane and left the house to call on Lord Weston for the purpose of enlisting his aid. Wes had some lands in Sussex and was already acquainted with Squire Feathergill, he had danced with Prudence at the ball the previous evening, and he was also a member of White's.

In Rhys's opinion, White's was a hoary old chestnut and boring as hell, but he was glad Uncle Evelyn had kept the dues current. Damned awkward for a duke to be told at the door he couldn't come in without paying up.

He and Weston found Feathergill in one of the reading rooms of the club, scanning that day's issue of the *Times*, a bottle of port on the table beside his chair and a glass of the wine in his hand. Wes paused beside the chair and made a surprised exclamation. "By Jove, it's Feathergill! Haven't seen you in ages."

"Lord Weston." Feathergill, a portly man of middle age, set aside his port and stood up, folding his newspaper into one hand so he might shake hands with the other. "Last we met, my lord, I believe we were both at that horse auction in Haywards Heath."

"Ah, yes, looking at that chestnut filly. Did you buy her?"

Feathergill shook his head. "She went far too high for my purse."

"Pity. She was a pretty thing." He turned, gesturing to Rhys. "Do you know my friend, the Duke of St. Cyres?"

All the friendliness went out of the older man's face, and his expression became a mask of frozen civility. "How do you do," he murmured with a stiff bow.

Rhys reciprocated, though his bow was much more relaxed. "It is a pleasure to make your acquaintance at last, Mr. Feathergill," he said as he straightened.

"At last, Your Grace?"

"I met your niece, your wife, and your cousins at the opera not long ago, but I did not have the pleasure of seeing you there."

"Yes, yes, I . . . um . . . my wife told me. I believe it was during intermission. I was in the smoking room, I think."

An awkward silence fell over the circle for a moment, then Rhys spoke again. "Did you enjoy the champagne?"

"Er . . . yes, yes, we did. Deuced fine, it was."

"I'm glad to hear it." He paused, then said, "It's such a fortuitous thing, encountering you here, Mr. Feathergill. I've been meaning to make your acquaintance, for there is a matter of business I should like to discuss with you."

The frozen mask became even stiffer, if that

was possible. "I cannot imagine what you and I would have to discuss, Your Grace."

"It is a matter of great concern to us both, I assure you."

In the pause that followed, Weston cleared his throat. "Well, I must be off," he said, clapping Rhys on the shoulder. "My whist game is about to begin. Gentlemen, forgive me?"

His task accomplished, Weston bowed and departed, leaving the two men alone.

Rhys gestured to the chairs nearby. "Shall we?"

Feathergill sat down again with obvious reluctance. Rhys took the chair opposite, but before he could bring up the issue of Prudence, Feathergill did it for him.

"I can guess what it is you wish to discuss with me, Your Grace," the older man said, dropping his newspaper to the floor beside his chair.

"Indeed? How perspicacious you are."

"You wish to court my niece."

"Court her?" Rhys gave a pleasant laugh. "My dear fellow, you are rather behind the times. The courtship is over, and we are engaged to be married."

"What?"

Feathergill's outraged exclamation caused several other men in the club to turn their heads in disapproving surprise, and some made hushing sounds of admonishment.

The squire swallowed hard and lowered his voice. "You cannot possibly be engaged to her. You are already engaged to Lady Alberta Denville."

"I don't believe any such engagement has been officially announced."

"Yes, but . . . but Prudence is to marry her cousin, Sir Robert Ogilvie."

"Oh, dear." Rhys donned an air of perplexity. "I fear you, and possibly Sir Robert as well, are under a misapprehension. Miss Abernathy gave her consent to marry me not two hours ago. I suppose I should have asked your permission to court her first and all that, old chap," he said, giving the old man a look of apology, "but I fear that she and I were carried away by the spontaneity of the moment."

"Spontaneity, my eye! You're after her money, but if you think you will receive one penny of my niece's inheritance, you are the one laboring under a misapprehension!" Feathergill was growing quite red in the face, though he did manage to keep his voice down. "You are a fortune hunter, sir, and your past conduct demonstrates a disgusting lack of moral restraint. I know all about you, and I will be sure Prudence knows all about you as well. Once I have made your notorious exploits clear to her, she will certainly change her mind and break the engagement."

"My exploits?" Rhys leaned back in his chair, smiling, pretending to be relaxed, though his entire future hung in the balance. "And which of them shall you reveal? That I am in need of money? She knows that. That I have had numerous liaisons with women? She knows that, too. That I am a scoundrel? I have admitted that to her myself. She knows all those things, and yet, she still wants to marry me. Astonishing, but there it is. Love is blind, they say."

"No, no, no." Feathergill shook his head back and forth in violent denial. "Even if what you say is true, it hardly signifies, for I refuse to give my consent."

"I'm sorry you oppose the match, but fortunately, your niece is past twenty-one. We do not require your consent."

The older man stirred in his chair, keeping his emotions in check with an effort. Rhys waited with an air of patient gravity as Feathergill worked to suppress his anger and think of how to proceed.

"My consent may not be necessary," he said after a moment, "but to marry her and gain her inheritance, you do need the consent of the trustees." He nodded several times and his expression became more confident. "They will never approve the match."

Rhys made a derisive sound. "Do you really think they would dare oppose a duke?"

"Your rank will not impress them overmuch once they are informed of your sordid family skeletons."

Rhys was glad he'd learned long ago how to act as if he didn't give a damn. He tensed, but his smile stayed in place. "God, man, if every marriage were opposed because of family skeletons, no peer would ever wed, and the entire British aristocracy would die out. The trustees of Miss Abernathy's estate could hardly oppose our marriage on such trivial grounds."

"Trivial, you say? Is it trivial, sir, that your uncle shot himself to avoid financial ruin and your brother hanged himself at school? That your mother has had more lovers than a Whitechapel whore? That your father had the cocaine habit and died as a result? Suicide and vice run in your family."

At the mention of Thomas, Rhys's smile vanished, but his voice remained cool and nonchalant, with all the well-bred disdain worthy of his position. "You seem to have made quite a study of the De Winter family tree."

"And a weak, sickly tree it is. The moment I learned you were sniffing about my niece, I made inquiries. As a result, I am quite well-informed about you."

Though he seemed to have the facts straight about Rhys's parents, he wasn't well-informed enough to know the true reason Thomas had chosen to tie a rope around his neck and take a leap from the stair banister in his school dormitory two days before his return to Winter Park for the summer holidays. Thank God that was still a secret. "My, my, how forward thinking you've been to go about finding these things out," he drawled with mockery. "My hat's off to you."

Feathergill refilled his glass from the bottle on the table beside him, his hand shaking. "I shall see that the trustees are told everything about you and your family," he said, and took a swallow of port. "By the time I've finished, they will know all your sordid little secrets."

"Ah, but what of your sordid little secrets?" Rhys countered, his voice soft and suddenly dangerous.

Feathergill set his glass on the table with a thud. "What do you mean?"

Rhys pulled a folded letter from the breast pocket of his jacket, giving the squire a look of pity. "You didn't think you were the only one making inquiries, did you?"

"Pinkerton's is an amazing institution," Rhys said, watching the other man's florid face turn pale as he unfolded the document in his hand. "They can find out the most intimate details of a man's life."

Feathergill licked his lips. "Pinkerton's?"

"Mmm . . . yes," Rhys murmured, glancing through the papers. "I haven't a clue how you learned about my family history, but I can tell you that I've had a man following you for nearly a week. He's also been digging into your past."

He looked up, smiling. "Does your wife know how often you visit Mrs. Dryer's establishment? That brothel caters to a very specific clientele, I believe."

The other man was now sweating profusely. "I—I—"

Rhys winked, putting on his best jovial, man-of-the-world air. "Tying up young girls and spanking them?" he murmured with a grin. "How naughty of you, Feathergill."

He tilted his head, and his grin vanished. He leaned forward, moving in for the kill. "What would happen, d'you suppose, if your wife, your daughters, your friends and acquaintances were to learn of your . . . umm . . . interesting proclivities?" He tapped the letter thoughtfully against his palm. "I wonder how Edith would feel to know that while she's been pinching pennies and worrying about how to afford beef fillet for Sunday dinner, you've been coming up from Sussex every month to spend what little money you can manage to scrape together on lascivious games with prostitutes. Tell me, how do you explain these trips to town? Business matters, I suppose?"

"All right, all right," Feathergill muttered hoarsely. He pulled out a handkerchief and mopped at the sweat on his face. "What do you want from me?"

Rhys once again folded the document. "Not only will you consent to my marriage to Prudence, you will assure her of your wholehearted approval. How you explain your change of heart to your wife is up to you. Tomorrow, you and I shall pay a call upon the trustees of the Abernathy estate, where you will make your approval quite clear to them. You're pleased as punch about having a duke in the family. Then you and your wife will accompany Prudence and me on a tour of my estates, during which you will make no snide comments about their shabby condition. We will then return to London for the wedding. There will be no mention to Prudence or anyone else of the skeletons rattling around my family closet. Not now. Not ever. I hope we've come to a right understanding."

"Yes," Feathergill answered in a hoarse whisper.

"Good. In return for your discretion, you will be amply rewarded. I will provide you and the other members of your family very generous quarterly allowances. What you choose to spend your portion on, I don't really give a damn."

The other man nodded and started to rise as if to depart, but Rhys's next words stopped him.

"One more thing, Feathergill."

The squire sank back down in his chair, the picture of misery.

"I am outraged by your past conduct toward your niece, particularly your shameful neglect of her."

The other man started to protest, but Rhys cut him off. "I will not tolerate such behavior one moment longer. The quarterly allowances you, your wife's cousins, and the husbands of your daughters receive from the Abernathy estate shall be forever conditioned upon my approval, and I can assure you that approval will be influenced solely by your kindness toward her from this day forward. In other words," he added, smiling, "you, your wife, your cousins, and your daughters—Beryl, in particular—will do everything possible to make up for the wrongs you have done Prudence in the past. From now on you will live for the purpose of making her happy. If you cause her even one moment of vexation or anxiety, or if any of you insult her or bully her in any way, I will tear up the next quarterly bank draft you are set to receive without hesitation." He leaned back again in his chair. "I hope that's clear?"

The other man gave a wordless nod.

"Excellent. You may go. By the by," he added as Feathergill stood up, "I shall be dining with you tonight. The Savoy's very best private dining room will do quite well, I think. That, along with the congenial company of you and your wife, should make for a most pleasant evening." He paused, helping himself to Feathergill's port. "The company will be congenial, won't it?"

"Of course."

"Excellent. Then I suggest you go home to

break the happy news to your wife." Rhys tucked the letter from his steward about the drains at St. Cyres Castle back in his jacket as he watched the other man leave, and he laughed to himself. He'd love to be a fly on the wall for Feathergill's explanations to his wife.

There was nothing more enjoyable than a stroll on a fine spring afternoon. Especially when a girl was escorted by a man as handsome as Mr. Fane.

Nancy Woddell cast a sideways glance at the tall, brown-haired man beside her as they walked along the Strand, and as she always did when looking at him, she felt a little thrill of pleasure. He was a well-set-up fellow, with fine blue eyes and a strong chin. When he'd asked if he might escort her to second service this morning, she wasn't sure about it, for she hadn't wanted him to gain the wrong impression. She'd had chaps enough in her life thinking a walk alone together entitled them to get fresh. But Mr. Fane was so polite and elegant, very much the gentleman. And he was valet to the husband of a princess. Though he would have to give up that position if he married, Nancy couldn't help being impressed. And he hadn't cut up rough at all when she made it plain to him that she was a respectable girl, brought up right, the sort who expected marriage. In fact, he almost seemed offended by that statement, as if the idea that she could be anything but a respectable, marriage-minded girl had never occurred to him.

"Would you like a dish of tea?" he asked, gesturing to the tea shop at the corner.

"I would, yes," she answered. "Thank you, Mr. Fane."

She smiled as he escorted her inside and pulled out a chair at one of the tables for her. Such attentive manners he had. He knew how to look after a girl, she thought, watching him as he crossed the room to the counter and ordered tea for two. A man like Mr. Fane would make a good husband.

She settled her skirts and did a bit of furtive primping in a pocket glass as she waited for his return, sighing as she studied her reflection. She wished she had a complexion like her mistress's, she thought, aggrieved, as she tucked a few stray tendrils of carroty hair beneath her straw boater and bit her lips to add some color to their pale pink tint. Miss Abernathy's skin was creamy white, not covered with freckles.

"You've no need to do that."

The masculine voice of Mr. Fane interrupted these feminine disparagements, and she looked up to find that he was standing beside her chair, a tray of tea and cakes in his hands. "Do what?" she asked, pretending not to understand as she lowered her hands to hide the tiny mirror beneath the table.

"Worry about how you look."

She tossed her head with a show of bravado. "I'm not worried," she lied, shoving the pocket glass back into her skirt pocket.

"Good." He set the tray on the table and sat down opposite her. "You're the prettiest girl I know."

Heavens, this man was a dream come true. "Thank you."

"I am very happy you came out with me today," he said as she poured tea for both of them. "I've some news to give you, and I don't know if you'll take kindly to it or not."

A flicker of uneasiness marred the pleasure she felt. When a chap said something like that, the news could not be good. But she didn't show her worry. "It sounds like something important," she said, and took a sip of her tea.

"It is. I've changed my situation. I am no longer valet to Count Roselli."

"Oh." She felt a dizzying throb of hope at this news. Since a valet couldn't marry, perhaps he had changed his post to one that would allow him to wed.

Nancy crossed her fingers. "What is your situation now?"

"I'm now valet to a different gentleman."

Disappointment crashed down over her, replacing the elated hope of a moment before. "I see," she murmured, working to conceal her feelings. "Who is your new employer?"

"The Duke of St. Cyres."

Once again Nancy's emotions ricocheted, swinging toward relief. The duke was the man her mistress liked so much, and that would offer her far more opportunities to see Mr. Fane. An Italian count and an Austrian princess were all very well, but they were foreigners who would one day go home. "Being valet to a duke is a perfectly acceptable position, and very impressive, Mr. Fane. Why would you think I wouldn't like your new situation?"

"Well, now that your mistress, Miss Abernathy, and my new master are engaged to be married—"

"They are?" Nancy interrupted with a delighted cry of surprise. "How lovely!"

"They agreed on things this afternoon. You didn't know?"

She shook her head. "Sunday's always my day out, and I've not seen my mistress since I helped her dress for church this morning." Nancy laughed, truly glad. Miss Abernathy, she knew, was well gone in love with the duke, and since she was a generous and thoughtful employer, Nancy couldn't be happier.

"They're to be married in June, my master tells me," Mr. Fane went on.

"But I still don't understand why you think I'd be upset by this news?"

He gave her a rueful smile. "My master is

taking your mistress to view his estates. No doubt we'll be thrown much together over the coming weeks—traveling on the trains, being belowstairs together, and such. Our proximity will be even greater after they wed, and if you don't feel . . . " His voice trailed off and he looked away, jerking at his tie. "That is, if you don't enjoy my company . . . I mean to say . . . bound to be awkward, you know, if you don't reciprocate my . . . um . . . feelings."

Nancy's heart warmed at this awkward blunder of words from a man who was usually so self-possessed. She leaned closer to him and, under the table, dared to brush his knee with hers. "I like you, too, Mr. Fane," she said softly.

Rhys lifted his chin a notch so Fane could properly form the bow of his black silk tie. "So, Miss Woddell wasn't able to tell you how any of Miss Abernathy's family took the news of our engagement?"

"No. She didn't know herself that things had been decided between you and her mistress until I told her."

"A pity. I would have enjoyed hearing what Mrs. Feathergill's reaction was to the news."

"I'm sorry, sir." Fane gave the ends of the bow a tug to tighten the knot, brushed a speck of lint from Rhys's black evening suit, and stepped back. "In the coming weeks, I hope I shall hear other things from Miss Woddell you will find valuable."

"Is Miss Woddell a pretty girl?"

"I think she's very pretty, sir."

"I'm glad. I should hate to see you forced to do your duty to me by paying your attentions to a plain girl."

"I shouldn't raise much objection to that either, sir."

Rhys laughed. "You're the answer to a maidservant's prayers, Fane."

The valet looked rather alarmed. "Only if I actually had to marry one, sir."

Chapter 12

The marriage of the Duke of St. Cyres to Miss Prudence Abernathy shall take place June 17. This date is one fortnight before peers all over Britain must make their quarterly interest payments. What fortuitous timing.

—The Social Gazette, *1894*

Dinner that evening went far better than Prudence had expected. Aunt Edith had been told the news by her husband before Prudence returned from Little Russell Street, and she was uncharacteristically silent throughout the meal—for Prudence, a welcome change. Uncle Stephen, on the other hand, was quite jovial, emphasizing at repeated intervals how pleased he was to have the Duke of St. Cyres as part of the family. Millicent and Robert were absent altogether, Millicent pleading a sick headache and Robert choosing to remain by his mother's side at home. Rhys was as charming as ever to her aunt and uncle, smoothing over any awkward moments with such ease that despite Edith's resentful silence, the meal proceeded without incident, much to Prudence's relief.

Within two days the papers were filled with news of the engagement, but Prudence chose to ignore them, for she found the snide insinuations made by the journalists insulting. Not only did they put the worst possible connotation on Rhys's motives, they did the same to her, accusing her of being a common social climber trying to buy her way into the aristocracy. Faced with such drivel in every publication she saw, she stopped reading the newspapers.

During those two days, the marriage settlements were negotiated, and though her uncle's portion was generous, twenty thousand pounds per year did not seem to satisfy Edith, for dear, dear Robert received only five thousand, an amount she deemed a pittance. Her manner toward the duke remained icy, though out of necessity, she was forced to be scrupulously polite to his relations and acquaintances when they began calling at the Savoy to congratulate the bride-to-be. Much social damage could result from snubbing the relations of a duke, and though Edith disapproved of the match, it did not stop her from taking advantage of the opportunities afforded by the connection. Though Rhys's mother was not in London, other members of his family and many of his friends showered them with invitations to dinner parties, afternoon-at-homes, and receptions. Edith could not refuse them, for they came from people in a much higher social sphere than her own, but Prudence was amused to note that she managed to finagle invitations to many of the same events for Robert and Millicent, assisting them to rise in social status as well.

A wedding date of June 17 was set, and that added even more activities to Prudence's daily routine. When a girl married a duke, planning the wedding was a rigorous job. She found Woddell of great assistance, for the girl had been educated under the 1870 Education Act and could read, write, and do sums. Within days Woddell ceased to be simply her maid and became her social secretary as well.

Despite Woddell's assistance, there were so many activities—luncheons, balls, parties—that by the time a month had passed, Prudence was exhausted. Rhys assured her that the pace would slow down once they were wed, but those frenzied weeks gave her an inkling of the rigorous social demands of being a duchess.

Prudence noticed that Woddell handled the ever-expanding social calendar quite cheerfully, now that her own young man, Mr. Fane, had managed to secure a post as Rhys's valet—a delightful coincidence that gave Woddell plenty of reasons to smile.

For Prudence, however, life was not a bed of roses. Though she was happy, she found her new life strangely lonely. Despite all the people she met each day, she saw little of her own friends, for the girl-bachelors of Little Russell Street hadn't the leisure time to pay calls, visit the shops, and go to parties. She also saw little of her fiancé, who was occupied with the responsibilities of his title and other matters of business. There was no opportunity for quiet time and private conversation.

When the time came to depart on the tour of ducal estates Rhys had promised, Prudence was heartily glad to put the exhausting pace of London behind her.

They traveled on their own private train, a luxurious affair of nine carriages that included a dining car, a drawing room, a library, a smoking room, servants' quarters, a kitchen, and three sleeping carriages, each of which was a private suite comprised of a sitting room, bedroom, and bath. Prudence had one sleeping carriage just for herself, Rhys had another, and her aunt and uncle the third.

She and her maid looked around her compartment as the train pulled out of Victoria Station, awestruck by the luxury of it. There was a thick carpet, a bath of Italian marble and gilt fixtures, and furnishings of burled oak. Draperies of green velvet had been drawn across the windows of her sleeping berth. "Heavens, Woddell," she murmured as she tossed her hat onto the matching velvet counterpane of her bed, "it's the Savoy on rails."

A low chuckle sounded from the doorway, and she turned as Rhys entered her bedroom compartment from the sitting room. "It is rather like a hotel," he agreed, moving to stand before her. "Do you like it?"

"Like it?" She laughed, lifting her hand in a sweeping gesture of her surroundings. "Who wouldn't like traveling about the countryside in this manner?"

"I'm glad you like it, because it's yours."

"What?"

"Consider it a wedding present." He put his hands on her shoulders, bent his head and kissed her.

"Your Grace," she admonished, glancing at her maid. The girl seemed fully occupied with sorting through the trunks the porter had brought in, but Prudence still felt self-conscious. When she looked at him again, he was smiling, laugh lines marking the corners of his green eyes.

"Did I say something amusing?" she asked.

"We're engaged, Prudence. You are allowed to use my name. And," he added, his lips brushing hers, "because we are engaged, I am allowed to kiss you." He tilted his head the other way and kissed her again.

Warmth began spreading through her at the touch of his mouth, the same sensation she'd experienced when he'd kissed her that afternoon a month earlier in Little Russell Street, a sensation that made her feel as if warm honey was being poured over her. Delicious as that feeling was, Prudence was still acutely aware of the third person in the room. She stirred in his hold. "Rhys," she admonished, hotly embarrassed, and yet liking the intimacy of saying his name. "We're not alone."

He ignored that. "We're allowed to kiss in front of the servants."

"People don't, surely!"

He kissed her nose. "You, my sweet, are a prude."

"I'm not!" she felt compelled to protest, though she did it in a whisper. "I am just . . . discreet."

"Woddell," he said without taking his gaze from her face, "Mr. Fane wishes to show you the laundry facilities. Go find him."

"Yes, Your Grace." The girl was out the door in less than three seconds.

"Alone at last," he murmured. "You see how simple that was? Order servants to leave, and they go." He bent his head again, this time pressing his lips to the side of her neck just above the high collar of her shirtwaist. "As my duchess, you'll have to learn to order servants about, you know."

The feel of his lips on her skin was so intoxicating, Prudence felt dizzy, but she attempted to keep her wits about her. "Aunt Edith could walk in at any moment," she pointed out, flattening her hands against his chest with the vague notion of pushing him away, but she must not have been all that forceful about it for he paid no heed.

Instead, he cupped her face in his hands. "Your aunt's maid is keeping her fully occupied with unpacking her things," he explained, and began pressing kisses all over her face—her forehead, her cheeks, her chin, her jaw. "I'm assured that task will take at least an hour. Your uncle is in the smoking car, discussing the train with the steward and the barkeep, who between them will keep him busy for that same hour. It's amazing," he added as he trailed kisses along her jawline to her ear, "how much one can get done with a few well-placed quid."

"You bribed people to keep my aunt and uncle away?" she asked, her words coming out in a breathless rush at the feel of his lips against the sensitive skin of her ear.

"Absolutely." He pulled her earlobe into his mouth, scoring her skin ever so softly with his teeth, and all the strength seemed to ebb out of her. He caught her as her knees buckled, wrapping one arm around her waist. "You like it when I kiss your ear, don't you?" he murmured.

"I think—" She broke off, finding it hard to breathe in her tight stays and impossible to think while he nibbled on her earlobe. "I think you got what you wanted."

"What I wanted?" His voice was low and thick, his warm breath was making her shiver.

"That night at the opera, you said you'd like to see me tipsy." She moaned as he pressed kisses along her throat. "I think I'm tipsy now."

He laughed softly and slid his free hand into her hair, tilting her head back. "Then kiss me, tipsy girl."

Prudence stood on her toes and twined her arms around his neck. Her lips parted willingly beneath his, but when he deepened the kiss and his tongue touched hers, she stirred in involuntary surprise. She started to pull back, but his hand tightened in her hair to keep her where she was, and his mouth tasted hers in a lush, open-mouthed kiss that was so sensual, so blatantly carnal, she knew he must have learned it from those French cancan dancers. She feared she was equally carnal, however, for when he withdrew, she followed his move, pressing her tongue into his mouth.

That seemed to ignite something inside him, for he made a rough sound against her mouth and leaned into her, using his body to maneuver her backward. Before she could guess his intent, Prudence felt herself sinking into the softness of her sleeping berth.

"What are you doing?" she gasped, shocked by the masculine strength of his body as he followed her down, his weight pressing her into the mattress.

"You're already tipsy. I'm going to make you drunk." His mouth opened over hers and he began to fulfill that pledge, kissing her again and again—soft, slow, deep kisses that spread aching warmth through her from her head to her toes, making her feel as if she had indeed been drinking spirits.

There was a particular hardness in his body where he was pressed against her. Having lived in the country most of her life, she realized what it meant, and she knew she ought to stop him, but as she moved against him, it felt so good, she could not will herself to call a halt. She squeezed her eyes shut in shame and delight, and relished the feel of his body against hers. She must be drunk, she decided, for never, even in her most secret, romantic dreams, had she imagined a man could make her feel like this.

But as dazed as she was, as glorious as it felt, she hadn't completely lost her wits. When his hand slid between their bodies, she instinctively guessed his intent, and when he began to unbutton her jacket, she flattened her palms against his shoulders to stop him. It was a token resistance, however, for his kisses seemed to have robbed her of all willpower.

He ignored this halfhearted protest and continued to kiss her, sliding his hand inside the front of her jacket. He opened his hand intimately over her breast, embracing it through the layers of her shirtwaist, corset, and chemise. She moaned with pleasure as his hand began to shape and cradle her breast, but when he began to unfasten the buttons of her shirtwaist, she knew her virtue was in serious jeopardy.

She broke the kiss, sucking in a deep gasp for air as she once again pushed at his shoulders, more forcefully this time. "We have to stop."

"Why?" He tilted his head and kissed the base of her throat as he continued unfastening buttons. "This is what married people do."

"We're not married yet."

"The wedding is in six weeks. I think it counts."

She squeezed her eyes shut and shook her head, knowing that was nonsense. "I'm a respectable woman," she said, trying to remind both of them of that fact.

His hand slid inside her shirtwaist. "I respect you."

He sounded sincere, but no man, even a man as noble as Rhys, could be trusted on this particular point. Her own mother had discovered that painful truth about the male sex, as had many a girl-bachelor at the lodging house. She strived to remember all the times Mrs. Morris had sat with young women in the parlor of Little Russell Street, listening to tales of what men had promised, handing over handkerchiefs, inquiring about family, and sometimes murmuring a delicate suggestion that seven months or so of country air at a discreet place in Hampshire could do a broken-hearted girl a world of good. But with Rhys's fingertips caressing her bare skin just above the lacy edge of her undergarments, his palm cupping her breast, it was hard to remember cautionary tales.

Prudence began to waver. They were going to marry, it was only a matter of time. But perhaps her mother had thought that, too. The wedding her father promised had never happened, and she had been the result. Desperate, feeling a wave of panic, she seized his wrist. "We can't," she whispered, opening her eyes. "Not until after the wedding."

He stilled, his breathing hot against her throat. "Prudence, I want to touch you. I've wanted this, dreamed of it, from the very first moment I ever saw you."

His words thrilled her to the very core, but she tightened her grip on his wrist, clinging to virtue, trying to remember sanity.

"I won't let things go too far," he told her, nuzzling her throat. But when she still did not relent, he took a deep breath and lifted his head to look into her eyes, caressing her breast as he braced his weight on his other arm. "I give you my word. Just don't stop me yet." His hand tightened and he closed his eyes, swallowing hard. "For God's sake, not yet."

He was an honorable man. She knew that as surely as she knew anything. He wouldn't ever deceive her. Her grip on his wrist relaxed. "Not yet, then," she whispered, unable to deny him just a little bit more of what he wanted.

He shifted his hand, sliding it inside the top of her corset and chemise. His fingertips grazed her nipple and she cried out, her body jerking sharply. She wanted to pull away, but his hips pinned hers to the berth and she could only writhe helplessly beneath him as he rolled her nipple between two fingers. She began to moan low in her throat, and he kissed her, long and deep, taking the sounds of her agitation into his mouth as he groaned in reply.

As he kissed her, his hand tightened, shaping her breast and toying with her nipple within the tight confines of her clothing. She stirred beneath him, but the weight of his body on top of hers limited her movements, and a strange tension began to build inside her. What he was doing felt so exquisite, and she began to yearn for more. When he withdrew his hand and rolled to his side, she cried out again, this time in vexation.

He laughed, the wicked man, blowing warm

breath against her neck. "I thought you wanted me to stop," he murmured, and grasped a handful of her skirt in his fingers, pulling it upward. "Do you want me to stop now?"

She shook her head, unable to think clearly, knowing only how she felt. "Not yet," she gasped. "Not yet."

Rhys's hand slipped beneath her skirt and petticoat, then glided up her leg, across her hip and between her thighs, his touch scorching her beneath the thin lawn material of her drawers. The tension inside her continued to build as his fingers eased inside the slit of her drawers, and when he touched the dark curls there, she felt her whole body blushing in response.

"I could stop," he said, the tip of his finger caressing her in her most intimate place. "Is that what you want?"

She tried to speak, but a frantic, "N-N-N . . . " was all she could manage, for her body was on fire with shameful excitement, excitement that flared higher with each touch of his fingers. As he stroked her, she could hear strange sounds coming from her own throat, sounds like none she had ever made, primitive, high-pitched animal sounds. Her body moved in frantic little jerks that she could not stop.

"What, then?" he asked softly. "If you don't want me to stop, then what do you want, sweetheart? Hmm?"

Prudence didn't know how to answer him. Need clawed at her, need for something she could not name. She shook her head, desperate, helpless to articulate what she did not understand.

"Is this it?" His finger began circling one particular spot in a way that was feather light and yet made her sob with pleasure. "Is this what you want?"

"Yes," she panted, desperate, frantic, unable to say anything beyond that one word. "Yes, yes, yes."

And then the feelings swirling within her seemed to coalesce into a ball of fire. The pleasure became unbearable, and she cried out his name as everything within her flared up and exploded in a white-hot flash, followed by waves of the most exquisite pleasure she had ever felt, waves that seemed to go on and on as he caressed her and she gasped his name.

Afterward, as the wild euphoria ebbed away, she felt him withdraw his hand, and she opened her eyes to find him leaning over her.

"My goodness," she whispered, amazed by the extraordinary thing he had just done to her.

He smiled at that, and her heart twisted with the same aching sweetness she always felt when she saw him smile.

She smiled back. "You kept your word."

He kissed her nose and tugged her skirt back down. "Damned heroic of me, too."

His voice had that light, careless note, but his breathing was ragged, as if he'd been running, and she could still feel the hardness of him pressed against her hip. She thought again of the whispered stories at the lodging house about gentlemen's animal nature, and she knew it couldn't have been easy for him to keep his word.

"Very heroic," she agreed, and lifted her hands to touch his face. He held himself above her, motionless, as she traced the lean planes of his cheeks and the square lines of his jaw and the thick, blunt, brown lashes of his eyes.

This was the man who would soon be her husband. Of all the women in the world, she was the one he thought luscious. She was the one he wanted to marry, the one he had chosen to be the mother of his children, the one he wanted to share his life with. The way he had touched her was the most extraordinary thing Prudence had ever experienced. Her heart overflowed with happiness. "I love you," she whispered.

His smile vanished, and she felt a vague uneasiness ripple through her. But then he smiled again, lowering his gaze to her mouth. "Well, I should hope so, tipsy girl," he murmured, closing his eyes as he kissed her, "since you're marrying me."

With those words and that kiss, her momentary disquiet vanished as if it had never been, and her happiness returned tenfold. And when he deepened the kiss, Prudence's soul opened up, unfolding like a flower beneath the bright, golden rays of the sun.

Winter Park, located in Oxfordshire, was the property closest to London, making it their first destination. It had been built in 1820 and was one of the primary ducal estates, Rhys explained as they had luncheon in the dining car with her aunt and uncle, but he seemed reluctant to talk about the house in any detail.

"You'll see it for yourself soon enough, darling," he told Prudence, deflecting her questions. "We'll be there in time for tea."

His voice was light and he was smiling, but as she studied him across the table, she had the feeling that the smile was a mask. When he changed the subject and asked Uncle Stephen about his estate in Sussex, she was certain of it, and felt as she had the afternoon of their picnic—as if a door had just been closed between them.

By his own admission, the estates were in poor condition, and embarrassment could account for his demeanor, though she had the uneasy feeling there was more to it than that. She wanted to inquire further but had no intention of doing so in front of her aunt and uncle, and set her curiosity aside for the time being.

The train arrived at Dunstable Station that afternoon. Half an hour before tea time, their hired carriage pulled into the graveled drive before a massive, fantastical structure of gray stone that looked like a storybook medieval castle, but since it had been built less than seventy-five years earlier, it was not actually a castle at all.

Rhys's mother was in residence, they learned upon their arrival. Remembering what he had told her about the woman that day at the National Gallery, Prudence wondered in some amusement if Lady Edward De Winter were truly capable of devouring Aunt Edith in one bite, for it was something she'd rather like to see.

She doubted Rhys shared her amusement, however. By his admission, he and his mother did not get on. But if he was displeased by the news that she was staying at Winter Park, he did not show it.

"How delightful," he told Channing, the butler, as they paused in the immense staircase hall. "We shall see her at dinner, then?"

"I believe Lady Edward was thinking to be introduced to Miss Abernathy at tea, Your Grace. She is eager to meet the bride."

"Yes, I'll wager she is."

Prudence heard something different enter his voice with those words, something hard that echoed off the austere Gothic architecture of the hall, something so cold it startled her, and when she looked at him, he was wearing that mask of a smile. "Tea it is, then," he said. "Channing, show our guests to their rooms, if you please, and arrange for our things, will you?" He turned to Prudence and her aunt and uncle. "I shall leave you to refresh yourselves, and I shall see you at tea. Now, I must meet with my steward. If you will pardon me?"

He kissed her hand, but it was a perfunctory gesture, hastily done. He bowed to her and to her aunt and uncle, then departed, his boot heels echoing on the black and white marble floor with strides so rapid, he was almost running.

Prudence watched him go with a troubled frown, wondering what in such innocuous conversation had caused him to practically bolt from the house. She thought of that day in Little Russell Street, remembering his reluctance to even embark on this tour. He had only agreed to come because she had wanted it.

"This way, miss," the butler called to her, and Prudence turned to follow the others up the grand staircase. It was a fantastic structure of elaborately carved stone balustrades, newel posts, and railings. As they mounted the stairs, their footsteps echoing on the cool gray stone, she studied her surroundings and couldn't help feeling awed, for the house was a bit like a Norman cathedral. This wasn't even the primary ducal residence, but it was terribly grand, although she thought the gargoyles atop the newel posts were rather ghastly. It was a house that spoke plainly of the glory and power of an old, aristocratic family.

She caught glimpses of some of the other rooms as she followed the butler up the stairs and noted that though the furnishings were sparse, the carpets threadbare, and the draperies faded, the house was hardly the wreck Rhys had warned her to expect.

Her bedroom was an almost luxurious contrast to the rooms she had passed on the stairs, possessing thick Turkish carpets, pretty landscape paintings, and a mahogany four-poster canopied with ivory and teal brocade. Coordinating draperies bracketed the windows. Prudence walked to one and looked out over a weedy garden. Beyond it, a wide expanse of green turf speckled with dandelions was flanked by overgrown boxwood hedges. Past the lawn, there was a rectangular, moss-encrusted pond with a stone folly behind it. In the distance, park and woodland stretched for miles. Though it was somewhat neglected, it was a fine property, much more lofty than anything she was accustomed to. It was certainly a long way from Little Russell Street.

Of all this, and four other households, she was to be mistress. Like everything else in her life lately, it still seemed unreal that she was going to be a duchess. His duchess.

She stared out the window, and the view outside receded as an image of her future husband came to mind. Her cheeks grew hot as she remembered what had happened that morning in her train compartment, the things he'd done to her, the intimate touches that led to such an unexpected and glorious conclusion, a physical explosion like nothing she could have imagined. Even now her skin seemed to burn where he had touched her, and she closed her eyes, her breath quickening as she began to imagine again his hands on her body.

A scratch on the door interrupted this decadent daydreaming, and Prudence turned with a start, then ducked her head, her cheeks burning. She returned her attention to the view outside, but watched out of the corner of her eye as Woddell entered the room, followed by two other maids in gray dresses with white aprons and caps. They carried soap, towels, and pitchers of hot water. Under Woddell's direction, they placed the toiletries on the papier-mâché dressing table, dipped curtsies, and departed, closing the door behind them.

"What do you think of the duke's house, Woddell?" she asked, turning to lean back against the window behind her as the maid opened one of the trunks on the floor.

"It's a grand estate, isn't it, miss?" Woddell pulled a tea gown of rose-pink mousseline de soie from the interior of the trunk and held it up inquiringly. At Prudence's confirming nod, she laid the loose-fitting garment and its matching, floor-length jacket on the bed, then began pulling various undergarments from the trunk. "House seems a bit empty, though," she added, placing a pair of ivory satin slippers at the foot of the bed.

Prudence thought of Rhys's voice echoing up the gray stone staircase and shivered, as if a goose had just walked over her grave. "It's a cold house," she said, surprised by her own words. "Winter Park is a fitting name for this place. I don't . . . I don't think I like it."

Woddell paused and glanced around. "Your room's ever so nice, though. Mr. Fane told me His Grace ordered it all done up with pretty things for you."

"Really?" The maid gave an affirmative nod, and delicious warmth stole over Prudence at his thoughtfulness, banishing her sense of foreboding. But as she walked into the drawing room half an hour later for tea, she once again had cause to feel cold.

The icy atmosphere hit her like an arctic wind the moment she entered the room. Rhys was there, leaning against the fireplace mantel, his pose casual and indolent, yet she could feel his tension. As he performed introductions, she once again heard the hard inflection of his voice as he introduced his mother.

"My dear." Lady Edward De Winter came forward. Her hands were outstretched in a welcoming gesture and she was smiling, but as Prudence looked into the other woman's face, she was not deceived. When Rhys said his mother would slice Aunt Edith into pieces, devour her, and feed her bones to the dogs, Prudence had thought his words an exaggeration. She hadn't really believed him. Somehow, she believed him now.

Despite that, Lady Edward must have been a beautiful woman once. In physical appearance, she and her son were not unalike, but where Rhys's green eyes reminded her of the lovely autumn meadows at home, this woman's eyes were like icy green jewels. Rhys's smile warmed her like sunshine, but this woman's tipped-up curve of the lips seemed an effort, as if she feared her frozen face might shatter. Prudence, who believed strongly in her own first impressions, knew she had never met a colder woman than this one.

"How do you do?" she murmured, glancing at Rhys as he introduced Mr. and Mrs. Feathergill to his mother. She sensed that he had once again donned a mask, the mask of the respectful son.

Lady Edward poured tea, her demeanor attentive and interested as she made inquiries about their journey from town and their plans for the coming weeks. When she stood up and crossed the room to hand Rhys his cup, he accepted it with a smile. "Waiting on me yourself, Mama?" he inquired lightly. "Why, how . . . motherly of you."

"I've always done my best," she answered, returning his smile with one of her own.

"Of course you have."

Prudence watched them, sensing something else beneath this polite exchange, something almost violent, and as she observed them smiling at one another, she realized the truth in the space of a heartbeat.

They loathed each other to the very core.

Lady Edward patted her son's shoulder with all the appearance of maternal affection, then took her seat and turned the conversation to wedding plans. She offered to come to town and assist with the nuptials in any way she could. Prudence, however, still watching Rhys's face, decided that despite the demands the wedding was placing on her, she would not seek the assistance of her future mother-in-law. She murmured a polite, noncommittal reply.

Various cakes were handed around. Though everyone else happily partook of the offerings on the tea tray, Rhys refused, explaining he didn't care for any.

"No cake? No scones and jam?" Edith laughed. "How unusual. Most men have such a sweet tooth, they are often very greedy over their tea."

"Indeed?" Rhys said smoothly. "I've always preferred high tea myself. Boyhood memories, I expect."

His voice was so cheery, his smile so friendly, and yet, the hairs on the back of Prudence's neck stood up.

She strove for something to say. "I should dearly love to know what His Grace was like as a boy, Lady Edward. What foods did he prefer for high tea?"

There was a pause, then the other woman gave a little well-bred laugh. "I believe . . . yes, I think Toad in the Hole was always his favorite."

"Amazing that you know that, Mama," Rhys drawled, "since I don't believe you ever had high tea with us. In fact, I don't think you ever set foot in the nursery when my brother and I were boys. You were usually in Paris."

Beside her on the settee, Prudence felt Lady Edward stiffen, heard her sharp indrawn breath. The tension in the air became a palpable thing, and a sick little knot formed in Prudence's tummy, but she did not know why. Something was very wrong, but she did not know what.

"Uncle Evelyn, now," Rhys went on softly, "he loved having high tea with us. Why, that summer we were here, he visited us in the nursery every chance he had. He played games with us, too. Especially Animal Grab." There was a long pause. "Uncle Evelyn loved Animal Grab."

The clatter of porcelain had Prudence glancing at Lady Edward's hands. They were shaking as she held her teacup in its saucer, and the *clink-clink-clink* seemed to reverberate through the room like gunshots.

Rhys set his own cup and saucer on the mantel.

"Forgive me, but I must walk the park and see what needs to be done. Things have been so neglected since I was last here."

He once again bowed, turned on his heel and beat a hasty retreat. Prudence set down her tea, excused herself, and followed him. Somehow, she did not like the idea of him being alone.

Chapter 13

Miss Prudence Abernathy has embarked on a tour of her fiancé's estates. We can only wonder what changes she will make, though from what we have heard, anything would be an improvement.

—Talk of the Town, *1894*

It took only a few moments for Prudence to exit the drawing room, but Rhys had already vanished. She paused a moment in the corridor, listening, and thought she heard the echo of his footsteps on stone. She ran for that monstrosity of a staircase, and as she leaned over the railing, caught a glimpse of him descending—a golden seraph amidst the gargoyles. She grasped handfuls of her skirt to keep from tripping as she raced down the steps after him, calling his name.

He paid no heed. At the bottom of the stairs she came to a halt, for he seemed to have vanished. But in the distance she could hear the faint tap of his boot heels on those cold marble floors, and she followed the sound across the staircase hall and down a dim, narrow servants' corridor. At the end, she found a door to the outside standing wide open, and when she exited the house, she could see him on the other side of a weedy herb garden, wading through a field of lavender toward a small stone building. When he reached it, he opened the door and went inside.

"Rhys, wait!"

The door slamming behind him was his only reply.

His desire to be alone could not be more plain, and Prudence paused, uncertain what to do. But as she considered the situation, she remembered the terrible look on his face when he talked about childhood things like high tea in the nursery and games like Animal Grab, his pain like a tangible force, and she knew she had to do something.

Prudence drew a deep breath and traced his footsteps along the flagstone path through the herb garden, evading the column and sundial in the center. She picked her way through the field of weeds and lavender, and when she reached the small stone house where Rhys had gone, grasped the handle of the weathered oak door. She half expected to find he'd locked it behind him, but when she turned the handle, the door opened, the hinges creaking as she pushed it wide. After the brightness of the late afternoon sun, the room seemed dark, and she blinked several times as she stepped inside.

Even though she could barely see, she realized at once she was in a lavender house, for the scent of that herb permeated the room. The slats of the shutters across the two windows were only partly open, and the windows themselves were small and narrow, to keep out as much light as possible during the drying process. Long hooks to hold bunches of the flowers after harvest were bolted to the ceiling beams. In one corner she saw a still for making lavender oil, and along two of the walls, shelves held dozens of green glass bottles, waiting to be filled with the fragrant oil. Everything was dusty from disuse.

"I always liked it in here."

Prudence turned her head at the sound of his voice. He was sitting on a long, battered worktable against another wall, his back to the stone behind him, his boot heels on the table's edge, forearms on his bent knees. The light through the partly open shutters slashed across him in stripes.

"It's the only part of this damned house I ever did like," he added. "It always smelled good in here. Like summer ought to smell. Fresh, sweet . . . " He closed his eyes, inhaling deeply. "Like your hair."

She didn't know what to say. Words seemed inadequate.

"Oh, God, I hate that house." He leaned forward, cradling his head in his hands. "I hate it."

Prudence could feel his pain, and knew she had to find a way to comfort him, drive away whatever was haunting him. She slowly walked toward him, as one might approach a wounded animal.

"I tried to forget what a nightmare it all was." He leaned back against the wall, and as he lifted his head, she could see the weariness in his expression. "I tried so damned hard."

Prudence halted in front of him and laid her hands on his knees. "I'm sorry," she whispered. "I didn't know. You should have told me you didn't want to come here."

"I had to come. I had to see if the ghosts were gone. It's been twenty years, for the love of God. They ought to be gone. But they're not." His gaze looked past her and he swallowed hard, closing his eyes briefly. "I don't think they'll ever go away."

"What ghosts?"

He looked at her and smiled a little, reaching out to run one finger along her cheek. "I thought it would be all right if you were with me. I thought it would be different somehow. That you could wash it all away—" He broke off and lowered his hand to his side. He gave a deep sigh. "Stupid," he muttered, "to think it would be that easy. That it could ever be that simple."

"But what ghosts? Why does this place trouble you so much? What happened here?"

His smile vanished with her questions, and a frown took its place. "You should go back to the house."

"Rhys, I'm going to be your wife." She curled her arms around his bent knees, her palms on his thighs the closest thing to holding him at that moment. "We have to be able to trust each other. I've told you things about my family, about my life. Won't you tell me about yours? About this place?"

"This isn't about trust, for God's sake!" He sat up and grasped her by the arms. "I don't want to talk about it, Prudence. I can't. Don't ask me to."

The vehemence in his voice startled her. "All right," she said quietly. "We won't discuss it again."

His grip on her arms relaxed and then his hands slid away. "I'm sorry," he muttered, and again leaned back against the wall. "I never should have brought you here." With those words he fell silent, staring past her shoulder into space, seeing God only knew what.

She studied him, not knowing what was wrong or what to do, not knowing what would help or what would only serve to hurt him more. "We'll leave this place. Tomorrow, if that's what you want."

He didn't answer, he didn't look at her. Wanting him to see her, not his ghosts, she reached up and laid her palms tenderly against his cheeks, turning his face toward hers.

He flinched and leaned forward, grasping her wrists, pushing her hands away. "Go back to the house."

She shook her head in refusal. There were wounds in him, deep wounds somehow connected with this place, and though she knew she couldn't heal them herself, she could perhaps be a balm for them until time and love did the rest. "I'm not going unless you come with me."

He was rigid and still as she curled her arms around his bent knees again. She pressed a kiss to his knee, then rested her cheek there. "I love you," she said.

A tremor ran through his body, then he jerked with sudden violence. His feet came down from the edge of the table on either side of her and he slid forward, the insides of his thighs brushing her hips.

"I want you to leave," he told her. "Right now."

She glanced over her shoulder at the door across the room, where she could clearly see the latch and bolt. Returning her gaze to his, she shook her head.

"I said leave." But even as he spoke, his hands

gripped her arms, as if to prevent her from obeying his command.

"You don't want me to go," she said, reaching up to smooth back a lock of his hair. "If you didn't want me here, you would have locked the door."

"Damn it, Prudence, I'm not made of stone, you know. If you stay, I won't be able to keep to that promise I made you this morning."

She considered that for a moment, but oddly enough, the stringent moral principles with which she'd been raised seemed curiously irrelevant now. He needed her, and though she didn't know why his emotions were in such turmoil, no one had ever needed her before. "I understand that."

"Here? In this dusty old lavender house—is that what you want? Because that's what will happen if you stay. There'll be no holding back. No calling a halt."

"I won't call a halt." Her fingers tenderly caressed the nape of his neck. "I love you."

He wrapped his arms around her, pulling her closer, until her abdomen was pressed against the hard edge of the table. His thighs tightened at her hips, keeping her imprisoned between his legs. "God help you for it," he muttered, and captured her lips with his.

His kisses that morning had been lush and tender, but there was nothing tender about the way he kissed her now. Nothing in it to beguile or persuade. This kiss was hard and blazing hot, demanding and possessive, and if she hadn't already known there would be no going back, his kiss would have told her so.

Her eyes closed and her lips parted willingly beneath his. He gentled the kiss, relaxing his hold to slide his hands beneath her arms. His palms flattened against her back, his fingers pressing her shoulder blades, his thumbs brushing the sides of her breasts. Because she was in a tea gown, she wore no corset or corset cover, and with only a few thin layers of clothing between them, his touch seemed to burn her skin even more hotly than it had that morning.

As he kissed her, she raked one hand upward through the thick, silky strands of his hair. Her other hand touched his face—the sandpapery texture of his beard-roughened cheek, then the hard line of his jaw, then the velvety soft skin just below his ear. She breathed in the earthy, smoky scent of him along with the lavender in the room, the two fragrances a potent combination that went to her head like strong wine. His body was hard and aroused where he was pressed against her stomach.

Suddenly, he tore his mouth from hers with a groan. His hands pushed her back a step and he slid off the table, his feet hitting the floor. His arms still around her, he turned their bodies, slid his fingers into the knot of her hair and pulled her head back, then recaptured her lips in a deep, long, slow kiss that seemed to drive all the air from her lungs and spread aching warmth through her entire body.

He was so much larger than she. Prudence's arms tightened around his neck as if to bring him even closer, and she stirred in his embrace, glorying in the hard strength of his body pressed so intimately against her.

He groaned against her mouth. Still kissing her, he pulled back far enough to pull off his jacket. He tossed it onto the table behind her, then his hands opened at her hips, grasping fistfuls of her tea gown and petticoat. He caught up the layers of pink mousseline and white muslin, bunching fabric between their bodies as if to keep it all out of the way, then cupped her buttocks in his hands.

She broke their kiss, sucking in a deep gasp of surprise as his hands tightened on her buttocks and he lifted her onto the table. Her skirts fluttered down around her hips and over her knees in a puffy circle of silk and lace. His hands slid from beneath her, and he worked to unfasten the hooks that held up her drawers.

"Lean back and lift your hips," he ordered, and she complied, leaning back on her arms and raising her body. He tugged the drawers down her legs and over her feet, dropping the garment to the dusty stone floor. The silk lining of his jacket, still warm from his body, felt slick against her bare bottom as she sat up.

His fists closed over the lacy frills at the edges of her tea gown, and he slid the long robelike jacket from her shoulders and down her arms. She pulled her hands out of the sleeves as he began unfastening the hooks at the front of her bodice.

She looked up, studying his face in the afternoon shadows as he undressed her, and it struck her anew just how beautiful he was—sheer, masculine beauty like nothing she had ever seen in her life until she'd set eyes on him. His was truly a flawless face, grave now, with his attention fixed on his task, his long, straight lashes lowered over his extraordinary eyes.

As he unfastened the hooks of her gown, he slipped the tiny pearl buttons of her chemise free as well, his knuckles brushing her breasts. She gave a soft sigh, and he paused to look at her face as he slid his hands beneath the edges of her garments with purposeful intent. When his fingertips grazed her bare nipples, she moaned, closing her eyes against the shameful excitement that began flowing through her even as she flattened her palms on the table and arched her body toward him.

"Does that please you?" he murmured, and when she nodded, he rolled her nipples between his fingers as he had that morning, so tenderly and so sweetly that she moaned again, her hips stirring against the warm silk beneath her.

"What about this?" he asked, opening his hands over her breasts. "How does this feel?"

She made a faint sound, striving to answer, but as he shaped and cradled her breasts in his palms, the warmth within her deepened and spread, making her ache, and she couldn't seem to form a single word.

"And this?" He bent his head, opening his mouth over her nipple, and Prudence's whole body jerked at the sweet sensation of it. To her amazement, he began to suckle her, pulling her nipple with his lips, scoring it gently with his teeth, and the pleasure was so exquisite she could not stop the soft cries that came from her throat. "Does this feel good?"

She nodded, a quick, definite affirmation. "Yes," she gasped. "Yes."

He pulled and teased one nipple with his mouth and the other with his fingers, and as he did, she cradled his head, exhilarated by his touch. When he slid his free hand beneath her skirts, a powerful wave of anticipation surged through her, for after their experience that morning, she knew what he would do next.

But he confounded her, for instead of touching her as he had that morning, he ran his hand up and down her bare thigh in a light caress.

Her hips writhed, need clawed at her. "Rhys," she moaned, holding his head to her breast, her hands tightening in his hair. Each time his palm slid up her thigh, he came a little closer to what she craved, but it was a teasing that soon became unbearable. "Oh, don't! Don't!"

He lifted his head a fraction. "Don't?" he repeated softly. His tongue licked the pebbled skin around her nipple, and his fingers paused at the apex of her thighs, tickling. "I said there would be no stopping, remember?"

Stopping was the last thing she wanted. Desperate for the same sweet pleasure she'd experienced earlier, she reached for his hand.

"Touch me," she whispered, hotly embarrassed by her own lack of modesty, even as she pressed his hand to the place he'd touched before. "I don't . . . don't want you to stop." she managed, struggling to get the words out past her panting breaths. "Oh, don't stop."

Rhys pushed her back until she was lying on the table. He slid his hand between her thighs, but then he once again began to tease, caressing her in feather light circles all around that magical spot he'd touched so deliciously that morning. She arched her hips again, urging him closer to what she wanted, but he ignored her, still teasing. She groaned his name, a plea and a command, but he still didn't give her what she wanted. "Touch me," she ordered, desperate, unable to stand this sweet torture. "Touch me."

"I am touching you."

She shook her head, becoming frantic. "You know what I mean," she panted, her entire body flushed with heat. "Touch me the way you did before."

"No." He pulled his hand back, and she gave a cry of frustration that changed to a moan as he pressed a hot, wet kiss to her stomach. "I have something better in mind, tipsy girl."

She couldn't imagine what could be better than what he'd done to her on the train, but then his hands spread her thighs apart and he opened his mouth over the same special place he'd touched that morning.

She cried out, her body jerking at the exquisite sensation evoked by that carnal kiss, and he stopped, lifting his head a fraction. "Do you love me?"

"Yes," she panted, her hips writhing, arching upward. "Yes."

He raked his tongue ever so lightly over the spot where all her pleasure seemed centered. "Say it. I want to hear you say it."

"I love you, Rhys." Her fingers curled in his hair. "I love you."

He began to stroke her with his tongue, causing that indescribable pleasure to come over her once again, even hotter, even stronger, than before. Waves and waves of it, until she thought she would die.

Rhys heard the words of love amid the incoherent cries of passion that came from her, and the mingled sounds filled him with a satisfaction he'd never felt in his life before. God, she was sweet. So, so sweet.

He didn't know what had compelled him to demand her declaration of love so relentlessly, for he didn't much believe in love anymore, especially when, cynical bastard that he was, he suspected her feelings stemmed from the bliss of her first sexual experiences.

But even if her love wasn't really genuine, he'd needed to hear it, here at this place where there had been no love, only sick and twisted imitations of it. He'd wanted to hear it from her, for she was sweet and fresh and wholly unaware of the dark corruptions of his boyhood. Because she smelled fresh and sweet and safe like lavender, and because in the soft, genuine goodness of her, he had perhaps found a refuge far better than his childhood hiding place had ever been.

His body was screaming for release, but he held back, wanting to please her so she would tell him again that she loved him, and when she did, he savored it along with her climax as a drowning man savors a gasp of oxygen.

But finally he could hold back no longer, and he straightened, tearing at his trousers, undoing buttons with desperate haste. He was rock hard, wanting her so badly that he feared he might actually spill himself too soon, something he hadn't done since he was a skinny lad of fifteen bouncing his first mistress.

Rhys turned her body lengthwise on the table, then hoisted himself up, bringing his body fully over hers and bracing his weight on his arms. "Prudence," he said, reminding himself she was a virgin, thinking to warn her what to expect, wanting to go slow, but the feel of her, velvety hot and wet, against the tip of his penis was such an erotic sensation, he knew there was no time for gentleness or warnings. With one hard thrust, he entered her.

She cried out again, and this time he knew it was not with pleasure. Cursing himself, he kissed her, smothering the sound of her pain with his mouth, hating that he'd caused it, even as he relished the virginal tightness of her.

She turned her head, burying her face against his neck with a sob as her arms came up around his neck. He began kissing her everywhere he could—her face, her neck, her ear, her hair—as if that could somehow make up for the taking of her innocence. And when her legs wrapped around him and she began arching beneath him, pulling him deeper into her, lust inflamed him, burning away any momentary guilt.

He began moving, rocking his body against

hers, trying to go slow, but the feel of her tight around him was so delicious, he couldn't contain his moves. He lost himself in the softness of her, his thrusts deep and forceful even as he tried to tell her how luscious she was. He touched her breasts, kissed her face, murmuring words to arouse and reassure her, but he didn't even knowing what he was saying, because he was beyond any sort of control. And when he finally climaxed, the pleasure was so intense it was like pain, shattering him into thousands of infinitesimal pieces.

Even afterward, as the throes of orgasm faded away and he collapsed atop her in blessed release, he could not stop wanting to hear those words from her again.

"Love me?" he whispered, nuzzling her throat.

"Yes," she whispered, her fingertips caressing his face.

He lifted himself above her, kissed her, nipping her lower lip between both of his. "Say it again."

She began to laugh. "I love you."

He laughed, too, laughed, by God, in this place, where he'd never laughed in his entire life.

A wave of satisfaction rose up inside him, a wave so powerful it hurt deep in his chest. He kissed her again, hard, then slid his arms beneath her and held her tight, and he didn't care if her words stemmed from naive infatuation or not. He didn't care that he'd ceased to believe in love a long time ago and that even if it were real, he was utterly undeserving of it. All he cared about was that those words from her lips silenced all the ghosts that haunted him. At least for now.

Chapter 14

Rumor has it the Duke of St. Cyres and his bride will make their home at St. Cyres Castle after the wedding. Miss Abernathy's American millions will no doubt go a long way toward making a silk purse out of that sow's ear.

—Talk of the Town, *1894*

She was gone when he awakened. He didn't know how long he'd been asleep, but it had to have been at least several hours, for when he glanced at the window, he could see that it was twilight. He rolled onto his back, grimacing at the hardness of the table and the stiffness in his body from lying on it for so long.

He stared up at the rafters. They were bare, not laden with bunches of lavender as he remembered them. But then, it was only May, and he and

Thomas had come to Winter Park in June, after school had ended.

Evelyn had loathed the smell of lavender and hadn't ever come here, making this stone cottage a refuge of sorts. But boys couldn't spend their nights in the lavender house. They were supposed to sleep in the nursery, after high tea and playtime with Uncle Evelyn.

Memories of the summer he'd spent here heaved up from deep down where he'd buried them all so long ago, memories of boot heels coming up the nursery stairs, of high tea and Animal Grab.

Best not to think of those things. As he had so many times before, Rhys shoved the horror of that boyhood summer out of his mind and strove to regain his balance. He closed his eyes and took deep breaths, taking refuge from all that was sordid in his past by thinking of Prudence.

She was so lovely. An image of her came to mind, of her round, pretty face and big dark eyes. She'd wanted him to tell her what had happened here. How could he? She was so blissfully unaware of how ugly the world was, how could he tell her about the sordid nightmare of that summer? She was so innocent.

At least she had been, until he'd taken her innocence and given her pain. He knew all about both of those, and guilt nudged him. But then he remembered how she had wrapped her arms around his neck and welcomed him so sweetly, and he couldn't sustain remorse for what he'd done.

He took deep breaths, drinking in the scent of lavender as he imagined kissing her hair, and a feeling of peace settled over him, keeping the ghosts away until he once again fell asleep.

Rhys did not come to dinner. In fact, he did not return to the house at all that night, and did not sleep in the master's bedchamber. These facts, and the mystery of his whereabouts, had been much discussed belowstairs in the morning, Prudence's maid informed her, Mr. Fane having been ever so concerned about the matter. The housekeeper had been the one to put Mr. Fane's mind at ease, telling him at breakfast that the master was likely sleeping in the lavender house, for he and his brother had often done that as boys the summer they lived here. Upon investigation, Mr. Fane had discovered the housekeeper's guess to be an accurate one.

"Though what he slept on, miss, I've no idea," Woddell said, pushing a hairpin into the intricate knot of Prudence's hair. "Mr. Fane said there wasn't even a cot out there. Just a hard stone floor and an old table."

Prudence vividly remembered that table and the extraordinary things that had happened on it—how he kissed her and touched her in the most intimate places, how he demanded that she declare her love for him aloud, remembered his body on top of hers and the feel of him as he pushed that hard part of himself inside her.

That had not been quite as enjoyable as the other things he'd done, she was forced to admit, flinching a little on the vanity seat, for she was still sore where his body had invaded hers. But he had kissed her face and hair afterward, and the pain was forgotten, replaced by a passionate tenderness like nothing she'd ever felt in her life before.

Prudence closed her eyes, savoring again those special moments when she had stroked his hair and held him in her arms. Even now she felt herself blushing at the memory of his body on top of hers. Even now she could remember every word he'd said in the throes of his passion—how he loved her and how beautiful she was and how perfect her body. Those moments had filled her with a happiness even stronger than the exquisite physical sensations he'd given her, for she knew that in those moments, he had achieved what he'd been seeking—a way to forget. Just what it was he was seeking to forget, she did not know, but she promised they wouldn't discuss it and had to be content to simply hold him in her arms afterward and stroke his hair as the sun set and he fell asleep. She'd wanted to stay with him, but the absence of both of them for too long would have caused Aunt Edith to search for her.

They weren't married yet, and fear of discovery had finally impelled her to depart from the lavender house, leaving Rhys to sleep in the only part of this cold, cold place that he could seem to tolerate.

"And His Grace told Mr. Fane we'll be leaving today for Hazelwood, wherever that is," Woddell said, recalling Prudence to the present conversation. "He had Mr. Fane make the arrangements for the train. We're to be packed and ready by three o'clock, he told me."

Prudence nodded, not at all surprised by this news, and very much relieved. "I'll be glad to be gone from here, Woddell," she said. "Very glad."

Oh, God, I hate this house. I hate it.

His words echoed back to her, and she shivered, "But why?" she whispered. "What happened here?"

"Beg your pardon, miss?" Woddell paused in her task of dressing her mistress's hair and ducked her head to meet her gaze in the mirror.

Prudence gave a dismissive wave of her hand. "Nothing, Woddell. I was thinking out loud. That is all."

Satisfied, the maid tucked one last pin into the chignon and started for the dressing room.

Lost in thought, Prudence scarcely noticed. Whatever the cause of his antipathy for Winter Park, she knew his mother had something to do with it. Lady Edward was an ice queen if ever there was one. So different from her own mother, who had always been full of laughter and warmth and love. Prudence could not imagine Lady Edward ever laughing or being loving toward anyone. The late duke, too, was part of the puzzle. And what of Rhys's brother who had died?

"Would you like to wear the beige traveling suit today, miss?" Woddell asked, interrupting her speculations. "Or the buffalo red?"

"The red," she said, and stood up. "Definitely the red."

Wearing his favorite color was a woefully inadequate method of comfort, she thought, but at the moment, it was the only one she had.

During the two weeks that followed their departure from Winter Park, Rhys strove to regain his equilibrium. Though the other estates had no nightmarish memories, he found other, less expected ghosts waiting for him.

As they toured the various estates, Rhys's initial emotion was embarrassment. Things were every bit as dire as he'd been told, worse than he had described to Prudence, and painful to view with her relations, who knew damn good and well why he was marrying their niece and their resentment was palpable. Stephen, as promised, said nothing, but Edith could not resist commenting on the condition of the properties. He told himself he shouldn't care what they thought, but thick as his skin was, he was bothered by Feathergill's silent condemnation and his wife's snide little jabs more than he cared to admit.

Stripped of their furnishings and valuables over the years, ignored and eventually abandoned, none of the houses were fit to live in, except by the mice, beetles, and other vermin who had taken up residence. The De Winter family had once been one of the most powerful in Britain, with an aristocratic lineage dating back to Edward I, but in the rotting timbers of Hazelwood, the crumbling brick of Seton Place, and the wild, unkept landscape around Aubry Hill, only the echoes of that lineage remained.

Of all the estates, St. Cyres Castle proved to be in the worst condition. As their carriage pulled into the rutted, weed-choked drive and he saw the broken windows and rusted gates of the fortified manor house that had been his home as a small boy, he thought of his father, who had loved this house, and his embarrassment deepened into shame.

When he and Prudence paused in the Baron's Hall of the original keep, where cobwebs decorated the elaborately carved stone mantel of the massive fireplace and only the discolorations on the whitewashed walls marked where the arms and weapons of his ancestors had hung, he could almost feel his father turning over in his grave.

This is what it's all come to, Papa, he thought, lowering his gaze to the stone floor beneath his feet, a floor first laid in 1298. Five worthless piles of stones and weeds scattered across central England. It saddened him, and he didn't even know why, for he'd long ago turned his back on all of it and thought he'd ceased to care.

In the distance, Edith's high, arch voice and her husband's deeper replies echoed faintly to the keep from another wing of the house, but past their voices, he heard other echoes. He heard his father, telling animated tales of the family history to him and Thomas by that massive fireplace late into the night. He heard the sounds of wooden swords and cricket bats as his father played with them. He heard the laughter of two carefree, innocent boys who had played here with no idea what awaited them when their father died. Such a long, long time ago. He put his head in his hands.

"Rhys, what's wrong?"

He felt Prudence's hand on his arm and lifted his head. "Nothing," he answered, rubbing his hands over his face. "I was just remembering . . . things."

He didn't look at her but could feel her gaze resting on him, and he struggled for something to say. "There was a red carpet in here," he said, gesturing to the floor in front of the fireplace. "On rainy days, my brother and I would lie here on our stomachs by the fire and listen to my father tell stories."

She smiled, glancing around. "This was the house you lived in as a boy?"

"Until I was eleven. That's when . . ." He paused, staring at the massive fireplace. "That's when my father died, and my brother and I were sent away to school. I haven't been back here since."

She looked at him, head tilted to one side. "Did you like it here?"

He was surprised by the question, for he couldn't recall ever thinking of the ducal estates in terms of his personal preferences. They had always belonged to Evelyn, and now they were burdens, responsibilities, debts. "I don't quite know what you mean."

Prudence walked up to him and took his hands in hers. "We have to decide which of these houses is to be our home. Where we'll raise our children. Do you like it here?"

He stirred, uneasy. He'd had vague ideas of them living abroad, traveling to America and Europe, seasons in London on occasion. He hadn't thought about children at all, and certainly not about settling in one place to raise them. "I like it well enough, I suppose."

"When you lived here, were you happy?"

Happy? He pulled his hands from hers and walked to one of the windows. Propping a shoulder against the frame, he looked through the jagged, broken remnants of diamond-shaped glass panes installed when Elizabeth had been queen.

What would his life have been like if his father had lived? he wondered, staring out at an expanse of weedy turf, seeing a man and two boys fencing with wooden swords and shields, pretending to be knights of old. He hadn't known then, of course, that his father's restless, energetic temperament and insomnia stemmed mainly from the cocaine that eventually took his life.

He could still remember the rage that filled him when his mother shared that little tidbit with him a few years later, rage toward the man who had died and abandoned them to Evelyn for the sake of his cocaine habit.

On the other hand, Rhys reflected, he'd been terribly fond of absinthe in his Paris days, so who was he to judge? Staring out the window at the field where he and Thomas had spent so many happy days with their father, hearing the laughter that had echoed through this house so long ago, he found himself unable to summon the anger he'd once felt.

His father, he realized now, had loved them. Not even knowing for certain if they were truly his own sons, he had loved them and cared for them. Rhys closed his eyes as something hot and tight squeezed his chest. He'd forgotten, in all the shit that had come after, he'd forgotten that. He'd forgotten about love and affection and what it was like to be happy.

"You are very quiet," Prudence said, and came to stand by his side. "What are you thinking about?"

"Look there," he said, pointing to the lawn spread out between two overgrown knot gardens. "That's where my father taught us how to fence and how to play cricket. And beyond that, in the distance, do you see that crag sticking up on the hill? On the other side of it is the lake where he taught us how to fish."

"Perfect," she said, and grabbed his hand. "Come on."

"Where are we going?" he asked as she pulled him toward the door.

"We are going fishing."

An hour later Rhys was sitting on a grassy bank by the lake where he hadn't fished since he was a boy. But instead of his father and brother, the company was quite different this time—different, and thoroughly delectable.

He glanced sideways at the woman seated beside him on the grass. She looked as fresh and pretty as the spring day in her green and white skirt, crisp cotton shirtwaist, and boater hat of white straw. "So," he murmured, "you left poor Woddell to explain your disappearance to your aunt?"

"I have not disappeared." She turned her head to look at him, all wide-eyed innocence. "I am wandering about the house, making lists of furnishings to buy. Where are you?"

"I am working very hard. I'm studying the condition of the farms. At least that's the story Fane is telling. He is a most excellent valet, by the way—trustworthy, loyal, and a very good liar."

"What about you? Are you a good liar?"

His heart skipped a beat at that question, but he forced himself to look at her. "What do you mean?"

She tilted her head to one side, studying him. "They might question us when we get back to the inn, so we might have to lie a little." She gave him a dubious look. "You can manage that, can't you?"

He kept a straight face and leaned closer. "I shall endeavor to be convincing."

Her concerned expression vanished. "Good. These rules about chaperones are so silly, and Aunt Edith is so punctilious about it, but we do need to steal a little time for ourselves on occasion."

"I couldn't agree more." His gaze slid down over the pin tucks of her shirtfront, caught the shadowy profile of her breasts beneath the cotton. Just that was enough to arouse him, and he began to envision her pale pink aureoles and tiny, jutting nipples; pure imagination, of course. He knew Prudence well enough to know she had on layers and layers of underclothes. There would be yards of muslin he'd have to wade through to touch her bare skin, satin ribbons to untie, silver hooks and fabric-covered buttons to unfasten, lacy garters and silk stockings to pull off. . . . As he thought of removing those garments one by one, his body began to burn. He set aside his fishing rod, then moved closer, ducking his head beneath the brim of her straw boater to kiss her ear.

"Rhys," she admonished, shrugging her shoulder with a glance around, "that isn't what I had in mind."

"No?" He took her fishing rod out of her hands. "All this privacy and you're going to let it go to waste?"

She blushed, but was laughing as he leaned over her to set her fishing rod at her side. "You are a wicked man."

"Yes," he agreed, and pressed a quick kiss to her mouth. Then he lifted his hands to pull out her hat pin and remove her straw boater. "I warned you I was."

He dropped the enameled pin into the crown and set the hat aside. As he kissed her again, he grasped her shoulders and began to push her backward into the grass. To his surprise, she resisted, and he was forced to pause. "What's wrong?"

"We can't," she protested, her blush deepening, her body stiff. "It's broad daylight."

"That didn't stop us before." Those words did not seem to relax her, and he sensed that some slow, serious persuasion would be needed. He began pressing light kisses to her face. "Why let it stop us now?"

"But . . . before . . . at Winter Park . . . we had . . . we had shelter." Her cheeks were scarlet now, but he wasn't about to let maidenly modesty interfere with something as delightful as a tumble in the grass. He slid one hand into the knot of her hair and pulled gently, tilting her head back, then began to kiss her neck above the collar of her shirtwaist.

"Be-Besides," she went on, flattening her palms against his chest as if to push him away, "that isn't why I wanted us to have privacy. I wanted us to talk."

"Talk?" With a feeling of dread, he stilled, his lips against the side of her throat. "What about?"

"Nothing in particular. I thought we could get to know each other a little better."

He lifted his head, sure he couldn't have heard correctly. "You mean we sent Fane into the village for rods and tackle, thought up elaborate alibis to give your aunt and uncle to account for our whereabouts, and came here by separate routes for the purpose of being alone, and you want to make conversation?"

"Yes. We've known each other such a short time, and we need to become better acquainted."

Rhys had no intention of making conversation and every intention of making love, but it was clear that some talking as well as some persuasion was necessary before he could bring her around to his way of thinking.

He bent his head again to kiss her throat and lifted his free hand to give her prim little necktie a tug. "Why don't you introduce a topic?" he suggested, beginning to unbutton her collar as he ran his tongue along the side of her neck.

She stirred a little, and when she spoke, her voice had a breathy catch to it he found quite encouraging. "Rhys, what is a duchess supposed to do, exactly?"

His fingers slid into the opening of her blouse just above the lacy top of her corset cover. Her skin felt like warm silk. "What do you mean?"

She pushed him back so she could look at him. "When I'm your wife, I shall be a duchess, and I want to do it properly. Only I don't quite know how." A tiny frown knit her dark brows. "I should so hate to make a blunder of it."

She sounded so worried, he couldn't help laughing. "Darling, most duchesses are like most dukes. And marquesses and earls, etcetera, etcetera. We don't do anything. We lead terribly lazy lives in which we give and attend fabulous parties, gamble away our fortunes—if we have them—eat outrageously rich food, drink excessive amounts of champagne and port, travel the world, accumulate massive amounts of debt, and engage in outrageous exploits. All because the lot of us suffer from terminal ennui."

"I'm serious."

"So am I." He kissed her as he brushed the fingers of one hand back and forth across her collarbone and caressed the nape of her neck with the other. "Peers are the lilies of the field, my sweet," he said against her mouth. "We toil not, neither do we spin."

She leaned back a little, her weight on her arms, looking at him with a troubled expression. "Is that what we are going to do, Rhys? Be lilies of the field?"

That was what he'd had in mind, but he could see from her expression that that idea did not appeal to her. And there was all the ducal responsibility drivel he'd stuffed her head with that day in Little Russell Street. "Of course we shan't be idle," he assured her solemnly. "We shall . . . um . . . do good works."

"What good works?"

"Charities, of course." He pulled her shirtwaist wide open and returned his attention to the delectable task of kissing her neck. "We have heaps of money," he went on, tasting his way down to the satin and lace just above her breasts. "I promise we shall give plenty away to those less fortunate."

He opened his hand over her breast, shaping it against his palm. Her fingers curled around his forearm but she didn't try to stop him as he cupped and shaped it through the stiff fabric of her corset. "What charities did you have in mind?" she asked, her breathing uneven and quick.

"Any you like. Hospitals, Salvation Army, military widows . . . " He paused and lifted his head to press a quick kiss to her nose. "Affordable living quarters for girl-bachelor seamstresses."

"I'd like to do something for my friends at the lodging house in Little Russell Street."

Her voice had a breathless catch to it he found very promising. "Anything for your friends," he said, and lowered his head, nuzzling the shadowy cleft between her breasts.

She stirred with a little moan. "I thought . . . umm . . . I thought, perhaps, we could help them somehow." She gasped as he kissed the luscious swell of her breast just above the edge of her corset. "But they are so proud, they won't take money."

"We'll find another way," he promised, and turned his head to place a kiss just above her other breast. "So they won't think it's charity."

This time when he pushed her down into the grass, she sank beneath him without resistance. "Can we help orphaned children, too?"

"Absolutely." He opened his mouth over hers and slid his hand beneath her skirt. Through a thin layer of muslin he could feel the underlying heat of her body, and his desire burned even hotter in response. He deepened the kiss, savoring the lush taste of her mouth as he worked his hand beneath one leg of her drawers. When he slipped two fingers beneath the edge of her stocking above her garter and touched her there, the feel of her warm, silken skin nearly drove him mad.

He broke the kiss with a groan and once again began to kiss his way downward to her breasts, tasting her in small nibbles. At the same time, he caressed the sensitive skin at the back of her knee in lazy little circles.

She lifted her hands, raking her fingers through his hair, her body stirring restlessly beneath him, soft little moans issuing from her throat.

He savored the erotic sounds of her agitation, knowing she was as aroused as he. But he also remembered how he'd hurt her the first time, and he was determined that this time she would feel only pleasure. He withdrew his hand from beneath her skirts and finished unbuttoning her shirtwaist. He wanted to remove the garment altogether, but she protested so much that he left it on. When it came to her corset, however, he ignored her protests and some bit of nonsense she said about being too chubby without it.

"You're perfect," he told her firmly, and kissed her. "Luscious. Dancers at the Moulin Rouge would be as green as in that painting we saw—green with jealousy—if they saw you. And besides," he added, rolling her onto her side to loosen her stays, "a woman can't make love properly in one of these." With the stays loosened, he was able to unfasten the front hooks and remove the satin and lace contraption altogether, tossing it aside into the grass as he once again rolled her onto her back. He leaned over her, his weight on his forearm, and dipped his head to kiss her neck.

Her skin was hot, rosy with embarrassment, and she buried her face against the side of his neck as if trying to hide. "Oh, Rhys, don't," she whispered, shoving uselessly at his hand as he began to unbutton the front of her chemise. "Somebody might see us."

He laughed at that; he couldn't help it. But when she demanded to know what was so amusing, he shook his head, suppressed his laughter, and did not point out that when two people were rolling around in the grass, anyone watching would know precisely what they were doing, clothes or not. To distract her from all the spinsterish embarrassment, he began kissing her again, working his way slowly downward.

She was so lovely, half dressed like this, all pink and white and plump, her bare skin peeking here and there from beneath delicious bits of lace and muslin. He lifted himself above her, bracing his weight on one arm as he used the other to pull back the edges of her chemise, exposing her breasts to his gaze.

His throat went dry at the sight. "Perfect," he told her again, shaping her breasts with his hands, embracing them, relishing the feel of her erect nipples against his palms. He breathed in feminine warmth and scent as he toyed with her breasts, using his mouth and his fingers to tease and play. When he suckled her, working her nipple gently with his mouth and tongue, his own body felt the erotic answering pull.

She was shivering beneath him now, all embarrassment forgotten in the flush of arousal. He was not very cool himself; in fact, his whole body burned to have her. But he strove to keep his own desire in check.

He slipped his hand beneath her skirt and petticoat, gliding it upward along the plane of her thigh and across her hip to the place he wanted most to touch. When he shifted his hand and cupped her mound, her hips tilted up, pressing into that touch with gratifying eagerness. Slowly, gently, he pushed the tip of one finger past the slit of her drawers and into her tight sheath.

She was wet, deliciously ready, and he could no longer resist the need to be inside her.

"Come on top of me," he told her, rolling onto his back, and when she complied, he pulled her skirts up to keep them out of the way and spread her legs over his hips. He then reached between their bodies and hooked one thumb in the opening of her drawers, ripping the thin lawn fabric farther apart to give himself greater access. Gently, he spread her labia with his fingers and thrust upward with his hips, entering her fully.

She sucked in a deep gasp, and he went still. "Did I hurt you?" he asked, dreading that he had.

But she shook her head from side to side so emphatically that her hair came tumbling down to tickle his face. "No. Oh, no."

Relief flooded through him, followed at once by desperate, hungry need. She was so tight and slick, and she felt so delicious, he had to have more. He thrust up again, wanting to increase the pace, but her body moved on top of his with the awkwardness of her inexperience, and he knew he had to wait yet a little longer. He sucked in deep, steadying breaths to tamp down his own desire, holding back so he could show her how to take what she needed from him.

"Sit up and brace your weight on my shoulders," he told her, and when she did, he grasped her hips and lifted his own, pushing up in a slow, flexing move. Then he did it again, and then again, teaching her the rhythm, accustoming her to the feel of him inside her. Each tiny thrust was a lash of pure torture that forced a groan from his lips, but the torture was worth it.

He kept his eyes open and watched her as he stroked her clitoris with his thumb and stoked the flames of her lust. He watched her as she took the lead, guiding his hand with her own without even realizing it, her body moving on top of his in a demand that set the pace for them both. He watched her, and as he did, he knew he would never see anything in his life lovelier than her face.

She was blushing, her skin awash with a tint of soft pink in the afternoon sunlight. Her forehead glistened with a fine patina of sweat. Her eyes were closed, her dark lashes like tiny fans against her cheeks. Her lips were parted, and between soft, panting cries, she kept touching them with her tongue. Her expression was one of such erotic concentration, with everything in her striving to reach climax, it made him smile. And when she came, in wave after wave, her hand over his, her body clenching around his penis in convulsions that went on and on and on, he felt a pleasure greater than any he had ever known before.

And afterward, when she lay in the crook of his arm, nuzzled her face against his neck and whispered, "I love you," the warmth that washed over him thawed the icy chill in his soul as the gut-twisting heat of Parisian absinthe and the blistering summer sunshine of Italy had never been able to do.

"This is where we'll live," he said.

And as he kissed her lavender-scented hair and listened to the songbirds in the leafy English elms over their heads, Rhys de Winter thought that perhaps his own April had come at last. He dared to believe that he had finally come home.

Chapter 15

Marriage is a solemn vow. Engagements, on the other hand, are made to be broken.

—The Social Gazette, *1894*

Rhys proved to be a far better liar than Prudence would ever have imagined. He discussed the condition of the farms and the work to be done there with Uncle Stephen at dinner that evening in such detail, she was almost sure he'd actually been at the farms during the afternoon, the time she'd spent with him by the lake nothing more than a dream.

A very carnal dream. Every time she thought about it, she felt her body heating with embarrassment. And excitement. And a longing for more.

He wasn't at breakfast the following morning, and the serving girl at the Black Swan who served them bacon and eggs told them that he'd breakfasted already and would be conducting estate business all day.

"His Grace thought you might wish to shop in the High Street," she explained, taking the lid off a warming dish of hot buttered toast, "but he went to the estate on horseback and left you the carriage, miss, on the chance you preferred to return to St. Cyres Castle instead."

"Excellent. Thank you." Prudence reached for a slice of toast as the servant bobbed a curtsy and departed the dining room. "I'm so glad he left me the carriage, for I do want to go back to the house today."

"Go back to that horrid place?" Edith set down her teacup and looked at Prudence askance. "Whatever for?"

"That horrid place is to be my home, Aunt. The duke and I have decided to make St. Cyres Castle our primary residence, and there's much to do."

"Better to live at Winter Park," Stephen said, helping himself to more kidneys. "Closer to London, and that house is in much better condition."

Prudence thought of Rhys's face the afternoon they'd had tea with his mother, and she knew they would never live at Winter Park. "We want to live at St. Cyres Castle."

"Live at that drafty old place? But how silly." Edith gave a tinkling little laugh. "Why, it will be months before you can even move in. Not to mention the cost of repairs!"

Prudence smiled. "Then it's a fortunate thing I shall have such a large income, isn't it?"

Edith made a sound of exasperation. "It is a complete waste of money."

"Perhaps. But . . . " She paused over her eggs and bacon, her eyes wide as she looked at her aunt. "It is my money to waste, isn't it?"

"Of course it's your money," Stephen put in, his voice hearty and soothing. "Of course it is."

Prudence resumed eating. "Besides, I am sure Rhys will be very judicious in how the money is spent."

"I daresay he will," Edith snapped, "since he needs most of your income to pay his debts. And finance his gambling habit, and pay for his women—"

"That will be enough, Edith," Stephen cut in, giving his wife a long, hard stare. "We talked about this, remember? Prudence has made her choice, and we must accept it."

"Oh, I don't understand you anymore, Stephen, I really don't!" Edith cried, dropping her knife and fork into her plate with a clatter. "That Prudence has agreed to marry that man is incomprehensible enough, but that you should take his side and abandon poor Robert, who is to receive only—"

"I think I've had enough breakfast." Prudence tossed aside her serviette and rose to her feet, knowing if she stayed here any longer, there would be a row, and she was in too good a mood to let Edith ruin it. "I am going back to St. Cyres Castle. Alone," she added as her aunt started to rise.

A few seconds later she was out the door, but the arguing voices of her aunt and uncle followed her all the way down the corridor.

"He'll leave us to starve in the hedgerows once he's married her, Stephen! And there you sit, doing nothing about it. Oh, Prudence is blind, blind! And so are you, apparently."

"I hardly think we'll starve. The duke has agreed to give us twenty thousand pounds a year, a very generous sum."

"Generous? How can you say so? Why twenty thousand is nothing to what he'll receive. As Prudence's husband, he'll have it all, though he hasn't done a thing to deserve it, the conniving fortune hunter."

"There is nothing we can do about it, and when you oppose her, all you succeed in doing is alienating her further. Leave her be, Edith, for God's sake. Just accept the twenty thousand and be content with that."

Edith be content? Prudence thought with a snort of disbelief as she went down the stairs. That was about as likely as flying pigs.

She was still fuming as she stood in front of the inn, waiting for the carriage to be brought around. Just what entitled Edith to any of the Abernathy fortune? she asked herself. Not her tender loving care toward her niece, that was certain. And what of Robert? After his neglect of her all these years, why should he and Millicent receive anything?

A brougham pulled into the inn yard, and Prudence started forward, then realized the carriage was not her own and stopped. She folded her arms and leaned back against the wall behind her, still fuming as she watched a footman jump down from the dummy board of the brougham and roll out the steps.

A couple alighted from the vehicle, first a handsome man of around forty years of age, then a pretty, auburn-haired woman who seemed vaguely familiar. Diverted from her own thoughts for a moment, she studied the woman, but couldn't place her.

"Madeira, if you please, Mortimer," the woman said to the footman, and her voice added to Prudence's impression that they had met before, for she knew she had heard that voice somewhere. "I'm simply parched."

The footman raced past Prudence through the doorway of the inn, and the couple followed at a more leisurely pace, but as they approached, the woman made an exclamation of surprise.

"Why, I do believe it's Miss Abernathy, isn't it?" She stopped and stretched out her gloved hand. "You don't remember me, I expect," she went on, and it was her cheerful, friendly voice that finally sparked recognition. "I'm—"

"Lady Standish," Prudence finished for her, clasping the offered hand for a handshake and smiling in return. "How do you do?"

"So you do remember me? I thought sure you wouldn't, for you had that look on your face—you know the one I mean, where you are trying frantically to place someone who knows you but your mind is blank." She gestured to the man beside her. "This is my husband, Earl Standish. Darling, this is Miss Abernathy."

"How do you do?" The man tipped his hat, then looked at his wife. "You two will want to have a chat, no doubt."

"And you want a pint?" Lady Standish said, laughing. "Go on, then. I shall drink my Madeira out here and have a visit with Miss Abernathy."

Her husband departed and she returned her attention to Prudence. "It wouldn't be surprising if you failed to recall me. You were in rather a fluster the day we were introduced."

"It was a crush at Madame Marceau's."

"I should say! And all because of you, my dear. Marceau fawning all over you."

"Yes. I had suddenly become important, it seems."

The wryness in her voice was not lost on the other woman, who gave her a shrewd, understanding look. "That's human nature, I'm afraid. But you'll have to become accustomed to it, for it will only worsen once you become a duchess. You are to become a duchess, are you not? I heard you are to marry St. Cyres."

Prudence confirmed that news with a nod, and Lady Standish clapped her gloved hands together like a delighted child. "I knew it! I knew from the first that the two of you would make a match of it!"

"Did you?" Prudence felt a spark of curiosity, for she could only recall seeing Lady Standish the one time at Madame Moreau's, but before she could inquire further, another voice interrupted.

"Your Madeira, my lady."

Lady Standish turned to the footman, who paused beside them with a crystal goblet of liqueur on a silver tray. "At last!" She lifted the glass from the tray and took a sip, then breathed a gratified sigh. "Ah, this is just what I need. Thank you, Mortimer."

He bowed and departed as the countess returned her attention to Prudence. "One's so used to traveling by train, going anywhere by carriage seems a tedious business, doesn't it? One needs a bit of refreshment along the way, even when only going across a county or two."

"Are you merely passing through the village, then?"

"Yes. We're on our way to Tavistock for a house party and we should arrive in time for dinner. But enough about my plans. I want to talk about you, my dear. You and St. Cyres. I was thrilled to read about your engagement in *Talk of the Town*." Leaning closer, she added with a smile, "It's always so much more amusing to read gossip about other people than about oneself."

She gave Prudence no chance to comment, but rushed on, "I take full credit for the match, of course. Why, when the duke was looking at you through those opera glasses, I could tell he was already smitten, poor fellow. But he thought you were still a seamstress." She paused with a tiny frown, her glass halfway to her lips. "Though how he ever knew your profession to begin with, I haven't a clue. Anyway, I knew about you already, of course, for Lady Marley had told me the whole exciting story at the dressmaker's. I set the duke straight about the matter at once."

In this rapid gush, two words in particular struck Prudence with special emphasis. "Opera glasses?" she echoed as uneasiness danced along her spine.

The countess took another sip of her Madeira and nodded. "Yes, at Covent Garden. St. Cyres was looking through his opera glasses and spied you in the box across the way. When I asked him what he was staring at—"

"Wait," Prudence pleaded, holding up her hand and stopping the other woman in midsentence. There had to be some mistake. She had only been to the opera once, and she remembered the evening perfectly well. Some horrid German performance, and she'd seen Rhys at intermission. He hadn't known about her new situation then, and she had deliberately avoided telling him. He'd sent champagne up to her, and they'd raised their glasses together. Had Lady Standish been sitting with him that night? She couldn't recall, for she'd had eyes only for Rhys. The image of him leaning back in his chair watching her across the theater, that faint smile on his lips, was burned in her memory. Even now, the image made her heart twist in her breast.

She took a deep breath. "You told the duke about me," she said, trying to understand. "You told him about my father and my inheritance? At the *opera*?"

"Of course I told him!" Lady Standish looked thoroughly pleased with herself. "I could tell you'd caught his eye, but a duke can't marry a seamstress! Especially St. Cyres, for he's stone broke." She winked at Prudence in a confidential, woman-to-woman sort of way. "A dowry makes all the difference in the world to a girl, doesn't it, my dear? It can turn a seamstress into a duchess. I know a bit about that myself, for I had no dowry when I first met Standish . . . "

The countess's voice faded away as Prudence pressed four fingers to her forehead and strove to think, but she felt numb and a bit dazed. He'd found out about her money at the opera. Not in Little Russell Street. But that didn't make sense.

"My dear Miss Abernathy, are you unwell?"

The concern in the countess's voice penetrated her consciousness. She lifted her head and lowered her hand. "A sudden headache," she said with a deprecating little smile. "A trifle, really. Do go on. This is . . . fascinating. Quite, quite fascinating."

"He adored me, but I was penniless, Miss Abernathy, so we couldn't marry. But then my grandfather died . . . "

As the countess chattered happily on about her own romance with Earl Standish years before, Prudence smiled and nodded and didn't hear a word as she tried to stamp out the horrible, impossible idea that was snaking its way into her consciousness.

There had to be some sort of mistake. He couldn't have been told about the money at the opera. He hadn't known about it when they'd seen each other the next day at the National Gallery, or the next when they'd gone on their picnic, or at the ball. Pain squeezed her, a fist around her heart. He hadn't known. He hadn't known.

Unless he'd been lying to her all along.

With that thought, everything in the world shifted, changed shape and color and form. No starry eyes, no rosy glow, no romantic love. Just hard, glittering reality.

As if watching the pages of a picture book flip past her vision, she saw herself and him and everything that had happened, but saw it all in a whole new way.

He could have followed her to the National Gallery. Or learned somehow where she would be. Their encounter could have been arranged, yet meant to look like a happy accident.

Their picnic could have been a charade, with him only pretending to be enamored of her.

The ball and Lady Alberta and that afternoon in Little Russell Street . . . a farce meant to play on her emotions. Lying to her about his motives, yet giving it all a veneer of truth with his frankness about his financial woes. Simple avarice, yet meant to make him seem noble. Playing her like a pawn in a chess game.

Tarrying here only tortures me further, Miss Bosworth. Let me go.

Lies. All lies.

No. Everything in her cried out in denial. This was the man who had been chivalrous and heroic from the very beginning. She could not believe him capable of such deliberate manipulation, such deceit. She would not believe it.

There had to be some other explanation for what Lady Standish had just told her, for why he would pretend not to know about her money for so long. Desperate, she tried to think of other reasons for his actions, as doubt and fear warred with love and hope. But what other explanation could there be?

The church clock chimed the hour with gloomy relish. To Prudence it seemed like a death knell, the death of illusions.

"Heavens, is it noon already?" Lady Standish downed the remainder of her Madeira in a gulp. "I must find Standish. He's still in the tavern, I'm sure, having his pint and visiting with the locals. He loves that sort of thing, which is good, I suppose, for it gives us votes. But Lady Tavistock does hate it so if guests are late arriving. It delays dinner and causes no end of trouble for the staff. Forgive me, Miss Abernathy?"

Prudence forced herself out of her reverie. She tipped up the corners of her mouth in a perfunctory smile. "Of course. It was a pleasure seeing you again."

"And you. Give my regards to St. Cyres, will you? Come along, Mortimer." She started through the entrance of the inn, then paused, leaning back in the doorway. She gave Prudence a long, thoughtful glance, then nodded as if satisfied. "Yes, you and St. Cyres are perfect for each other."

"Yes, perfect," Prudence agreed brightly, striving to conceal the sickening fear within her. "We're a match made in heaven."

Rhys visited the farms that morning. He discussed crops and drainage with his land agent.

He met with the few tenant farmers that he had, examined livestock, and decided on repairs. That afternoon he determined the necessities of the household, touring the bakehouse, the brewhouse, the laundry, the stables, and the kitchens, making notes about all that needed to be done, how much staff would be required, and how to make St. Cyres Castle into a viable, working estate. More important, he thought about how to make it a home.

Home. With every decision that he made, that word thrummed through his mind in time with the beats of his heart. As he moved through the house and grounds, he thought of Prudence, who would be his wife. He stood in the nursery for over an hour, imagining the children they would have and how different their childhood would be from the hell that had been his.

And at the end of the day, when he was on his way back to the village, he paused on the crag at the top of the hill and turned his horse for one more look at St. Cyres Castle. Its limestone walls glowed like gold in the late afternoon sun, and he knew that within that pile of stones was everything he'd ever wanted, everything he'd stopped believing in, and everything that mattered.

The village of St. Cyres was quiet at sunset, and his horse was the only one on the High Street, for it was dinnertime. As he rode toward the inn along the empty cobblestone street, Rhys studied the vicarage and the village green and the smithy with the same sense of awareness with which he'd been surveying his own lands.

This village had first become prosperous in Tudor times, for the forests around St. Cyres Castle were a favorite hunting spot of Henry VIII. That prosperity had continued and grown, and St. Cyres thrived well into the reign of George IV. But during the past sixty years or so it had fallen into decay, due to economic conditions and the hopeless mismanagement of the past half-dozen dukes of St. Cyres. Now it was a quiet, run-down little backwater, but as he passed the dilapidated cottages and shabby shops, he saw what it could be.

All of these people are looking to me, waiting and hoping I can save them from these times of agricultural calamity.

His words to Prudence that day in Little Russell Street came back to him, and he smiled ruefully. Such a load of shit, he'd thought at the time. But now, as he looked around him, he appreciated the truth in it. He could make this village and all the other villages that were under his ducal leadership prosperous again. Not the old ways, not with feudal control, not with land rents, but a new way, a modern way. Factories, mills, industry.

There was also everything Prudence's father had built in America. That legacy had to be cared for as well, properly managed and passed on to the next generation.

A heady thing, so much responsibility, and a bit frightening. Good thing Prudence was so sensible and steadfast. She'd be an excellent duchess. She'd keep him on a straight course. She loved him.

At the Black Swan, he handed his horse over to a groom and went into the inn. A serving maid was waiting by the side door that led to the stables. "If you please, Your Grace," she said with a curtsy, "Miss Abernathy's waiting for you in the parlor."

He handed over his hat, his gloves, and his cloak. "She's not at dinner?"

"No, sir. Mr. and Mrs. Feathergill have already dined, but Miss Abernathy said she wasn't hungry and she'd wait for you."

"Did she?" He smiled at the knowledge that she'd waited for him. If they managed it right, talking in the parlor until her aunt and uncle and the other guests at the inn finished eating, they could perhaps dine in private.

Savoring that idea, he walked through the tavern, where a handful of locals were gathered around the tap, sipping their pints of bitter and ale. He crossed the corridor, leaving the tavern, and entering the inn's small parlor.

Prudence was there, staring into the empty fireplace, her back to him when he came into the room.

"Darling," he greeted, starting toward her. "Wonderful of you to wait your dinner for me."

She didn't turn around, and as he came up behind her, he saw that she was straightening the spill vases on the mantel. Her hands were shaking.

"Are you cold?" he asked in surprise, sliding his arms around her waist. "It feels like a warm, fine spring night to me, but if you're cold, I'll warm you."

He reached for her hands and pulled them down, entwining her fingers with his. "Sorry I'm so late coming back, but I had the most productive day. I think we'll plant flax next year and build a factory to make the linen from it. Can you imagine how this village will prosper with a linen mill?"

"I had a productive day, too."

"Did you?" He kissed her temple. "Shopping for the house, I suppose?"

"No. I wasn't shopping." She pulled her hands from his, grasped his forearms and pushed them down, gently extracting herself from his embrace.

He frowned, all his senses sharpening in warning as she walked away from him to another part of the room. "What's wrong?" he asked. "What's happened?"

"I encountered an acquaintance of yours today," she said over her shoulder. There was an odd inflection in her voice, one that he couldn't quite define. He felt a sudden sense of foreboding as she turned, lifted her chin and looked at him. "Lady Standish."

He sucked in his breath, not at her words, but at her face. There was none of the love he usually saw there. It had vanished, along with her adoration and her tenderness and that absolute conviction that he was her very own hero. Gone, all gone, all the soft, sweet things he'd never had until he met her, things that in two short months he had come to crave like an addict seeking opium. They were gone, and in their place he saw nothing in her countenance but icy composure. He tried to imagine what Cora might have said to make her look at him this way, but he couldn't, for his wits suddenly felt thick like tar.

"They were on their way to a country house party," she told him. "Lady Standish and I had a nice little visit while their driver changed horses. She takes full credit for our engagement, since she told you about my inheritance at the *opera*. The opera, where you pretended not to know anything about it."

The opera. *Oh, shit. Oh, shit.*

She took a step toward him, and as she looked into his eyes, emotion came into her face, an awareness and a certainty that cut him to the heart. "Oh my God, I knew it," she whispered, staring at him. "Until now, until this moment, I kept trying not to believe it. I kept trying to convince myself that Lady Standish made a mistake or lied or . . .

something. I've tried to find some other explanation, but there is none. When I told you about the money, you already knew. You've known all along, almost from the very beginning."

He opened his mouth to deny it, but the lie stuck in his throat.

"Meeting me at the National Gallery that day wasn't happenstance. You arranged it. But how?"

He drew a deep breath and admitted the truth. "Fane. He found out where you would be."

She stared at him. "Mr. Fane wasn't working for that Italian count at all, was he? He was working for you. Under your orders, he was deceiving Miss Woddell just as you were deceiving me." Her eyes narrowed. "My God, did you ever, at any point, stop to think of anyone but yourself? Miss Woddell is in love with Mr. Fane, but his feelings are as much a lie as yours. It's all a tissue of lies."

"Not all of it, Prudence. You see—"

"And our picnic," she interrupted. "That was a lie, too. You only pre... pretended to have a romantic attachment to me that day."

"I wasn't pretending. I swear to you." He started toward her, desperate to explain, but she wouldn't let him.

"And the ball," she swept on. "Paying your addresses to Lady Alberta was a farce, wasn't it? A way to play on my feelings for you and heighten my suspense. Then your declaration at Little Russell Street, and all that talk about ducal responsibility and needing to marry an heiress. You knew what I would do. You knew I would tell you about the money."

She pressed a shaking hand to her mouth, looking as if she would be sick. "You manipulated me at every turn, playing with me as if I were nothing but a pawn in some chess game!"

Rhys told himself he could make everything right if only he could find the right words to say. "I can explain—"

"How you must have laughed at the chubby, foolish, lovesick spinster making a fool of herself over you."

Rhys gave a violent start, and he felt as if he were coming apart. She was the sweetest, loveliest thing he'd ever come across in his life. That she could think he would ever laugh at her nauseated him. "I have never laughed at you. Never!"

With a sound of disbelief, she started to turn away, but he gripped her arms and swung her around to face him, knowing he had to find a way to explain it all from his point of view. "Yes, I did know about the money, I admit it. Cora told me at the opera, just as she said. Yes, I arranged things and manipulated the situation, but it was because I didn't see how I could be honest about my motives. You've got such romantic ideas, Prudence, and I—"

"Foolish ideas, you mean!" she cried with a sob. She wrenched free of his grasp. "I thought you were a hero. I thought you were a true gentleman, honorable and chivalrous. I thought you loved me!"

"I do love you." The moment he said it, he knew it was true. He loved her. And he knew from the hard glitter in her eyes that he'd realized it too late.

"You bastard." Her palm hit his cheek with enough force to swing his head sideways. "You lying bastard."

The loathing in her voice sent panic coursing through him, and he fought back, refusing to believe he was losing her now. Not now, not when everything to make both of them happy was right in their grasp. "Prudence, listen to me. I wanted you from the first moment I ever saw you. I always desired you. That was no pretense, I swear. I needed money, it's true, but I always wanted you." He took a deep breath, trying to think. He ought to tell her everything he felt, everything he'd thought about today, everything he envisioned for their future. But desperation was clawing at him as he watched the resentment and hurt in her eyes hardening into hatred. Finding the words for a long, poetic speech about his feelings proved beyond him. "I love you."

"Liar!" Her condemnation rang out like a knife twisting in his guts. She began walking backward, shaking her head as if in disbelief at his gall. "You are such a liar."

"I'm not lying!" he said, forcing the words out past the sick fear that gripped him. "I'm not!"

"And you expect me to believe you when I know you've been lying to me all along?" Her gaze raked over him with utter contempt. "It's the money you love, not me."

"That's not true."

"Well, you're not going to get any money from me," she said as if he hadn't spoken. "You'll have to go find yourself another heiress. After all," she added with a humorless laugh that cut him to ribbons, "you're a duke. You couldn't possibly earn your living the way most of us do. You have position, but without money, what are you? You're a lily of the field." With a sound of dismissal, she turned her back. "You're worthless. You're nothing."

He watched in despair as she walked away. Her rage, even her hate, he could handle, for they told him she still had a passion for him that could be turned to love. But her contempt was different. Without her respect, her words became true. He had nothing. He was nothing. Rhys watched her walk out the door, and he saw everything he'd dared to dream these last few days crumbling into dust.

Chapter 16

Abernathy heiress breaks her engagement! Jilted duke appears devastated.

—The Social Gazette, *1894*

Before confronting Rhys, Prudence had made preparations. She had already packed her things and settled her account with the innkeeper of the Black Swan. She had given Woddell the painful truth about Mr. Fane. She had endured the pleas of her uncle and the self-satisfied crowing of her aunt. She had arranged for a hired carriage to convey them to the village's tiny train station and for the train to be ready for departure the moment they boarded.

When she walked out of the parlor, there was nothing left to do. She departed from the inn and stepped up into the carriage beside her maid. She didn't know if Rhys even tried to follow her because she never looked back.

At the station, she boarded the train Rhys had bought her, but as it conveyed them back to London that night, she did not sleep in her compartment, for she couldn't bear to lie in the berth where Rhys had kissed her and touched her so sweetly. Instead, she sat alone in the parlor coach while the others slept, staring out the darkened window and trying to decide what to do next.

The Abernathy millions would be forfeit, for she couldn't see herself marrying anyone now. She could not imagine allowing any man to kiss her or touch her as Rhys had. And his betrayal had shown her that no man could ever be trusted with her heart when millions of pounds were at stake. She thought of the other people who had gathered around her these past two months—Edith, Robert, Millicent—people who wouldn't spare her a thought if not for her inheritance, and she felt a bitterness she'd never felt in her life before.

She had always assumed having money would be the most wonderful thing possible. How wrong she'd been. Maria and Mr. Whitfield both tried to warn her that money might not provide the happiness she expected. She hadn't understood then what they meant. She understood now, and it was a hard, painful realization. And though she'd enjoyed having pretty clothes and staying at the Savoy and having her own private train, none of that could replace the things that truly made a person happy.

Because of that, she didn't mind giving up the inheritance, although she regretted that she would be unable to help her friends as she'd hoped. But for herself, she had lived the life of a wealthy heiress for two months now, and decided she'd had enough. She just wanted to be herself again. Prudence Bosworth had been happy. She'd known her place in the world, she'd had friends—true friends—to rely on and a cozy little flat to call home. That and enough money to live on were all a person really needed in life anyway.

She'd have to find a new post, something perhaps that didn't involve working such long hours. Her allowance from her father's estate was hers to spend as she liked until the year was up. Perhaps she could use that money to finance a dressmaking establishment of her own. Her friend Emma, being a viscountess, might be able to help her establish a clientele. The train would have to be returned, and the legal terms of the engagement officially severed. She supposed Mr. Whitfield could take care of all that.

In making these decisions about her life and her future, she tried not to think of Rhys, but in the quiet darkness, with nothing to distract her but the rhythmic sound of the train, it was impossible to veer her thoughts in any other direction. Impossible not to remember the beauty of his smile and the magic of his touch, the hot, sweet feel of his kisses and the thrill in her heart when she'd believed he loved her.

She struggled to be numb, yet as often as she reminded herself he wasn't worth a single moment of pain, she could not be numb. Every part of her was bruised and battered and raw.

Kiss me, tipsy girl.

Prudence closed her eyes and a tear slid down her cheek. She brushed it away, but it was followed at once by another, and she got angry all over again, angry with herself for wasting tears on that lying, worthless cur of a man. Yet when the next tear spilled over, she didn't have the strength to stop it.

She curled up in a ball on the seat, hugged her knees to her chest and gave up, letting the tears fall. She cried for all her silly illusions, her romantic ideals, and the death of her dreams. Most of all she cried for the love that had existed in her heart but had never existed in his.

Day was breaking. Rhys stared out over the lake at the blue and pink shades of a pastel sunrise, but in his mind all he could see was love and adoration dying in Prudence's eyes. All around him was silence, but ringing in his ears was the sound of her contempt.

You're worthless. You're nothing.

She hadn't told him anything he didn't already know. He'd known for years his life was an utter waste of time. He thought of those days in Paris, drunk on absinthe. All those days in Italy—the gambling and the champagne and the sexual escapades. Numbing himself with any sensations that could help him forget that he'd failed his brother. Refusing to let anything matter to him because the things that mattered were impossible to hold onto. Building layers of cynical, man-of-the-world wit to form a shell around the emptiness that had been in him since he was twelve years old.

Liar. You are such a liar.

Prudence's accusation shouted through his mind, echoing back to years ago. Letitia saying the same when he'd tried to tell her about Evelyn, when he'd tried to save Thomas from a second summer at Winter Park. How ironic that the times in his life when the truth had mattered the most, he hadn't been believed. Rhys rested his elbows on his knees and cradled his head in his hands. He was so much better at lying, he thought wearily, than he was at telling the truth.

A chaffinch began to sing in one of the elms over his head. Rhys straightened, listening to that promise of home, and the sound was like another crack in his protective shell.

He stood up and began to walk. He climbed the hill, wanting only to get away from that sound, but as he reached the top of the tor and looked down at St. Cyres Castle, the place he and Prudence had decided would be their home, he felt another crack, another fissure of fear and despair that threatened to break him apart.

What would he do now? The past few days here with her had been the happiest of his life. But now she was gone, and he felt more lost and empty than ever before. He couldn't go back to the life he'd had before he met her, and he didn't know how to go forward into any future without her.

The sun lifted above the horizon and hit the stones of St. Cyres Castle, gilding them with light and warmth and the promise of home. He'd been yearning to find home ever since he'd lost it, but it had always been here, waiting for him and he would not lose it again. This was home, for him and for Prudence, the place they would live and raise their children, the place they would grow old together. He knew, as surely as he knew anything, that this was the life he wanted, and he was going to fight for it with everything he had. Prudence was the woman he wanted, and he was going to do whatever he had to do to get her back. But this time he could use no wiles, no tricks, and no lies. To regain Prudence's love, her trust, and her respect, he knew he would have to earn them.

Staying awake on a night train gave a woman with a broken heart plenty of opportunity to think, and by the time her train pulled into Victoria Station, Prudence had made her own plans for her own life.

The platform was crowded when they arrived, but there were plenty of porters waiting to assist them. Rich people with private trains evidently received more attention than ordinary folk traveling the rails.

"Yes, yes, all of them go to the Savoy," Edith assured the big, burly Cockney who'd won the honor of taking charge of their things. "All of these," she went on, pointing to the various trunks and cases stacked on the platform. "And these, too."

"No, Aunt." Prudence stepped forward and pulled one black valise from the pile of luggage. "Not this one. This comes with me."

"What do you mean?" Edith glanced at Stephen, then returned her gaze to Prudence. "You're coming to the Savoy with us."

"No, I'm not." She pointed to four of the trunks. "Porter, I want these delivered to 32 Little Russell Street. Prudence Bosworth. Can you do that?" When he nodded, she pulled her money purse from her handbag and, ignoring her aunt and uncle's protests, counted out the porter's fee, including a generous tip. "That should take care of transporting my luggage to Holborn, I think," she said as she put the coins in the man's hand. "And when my trunks arrive, there will be a fiver waiting for you."

"Very good, miss," he agreed with a happy smile and began separating her trunks from the others.

"What do you mean you're returning to Little Russell Street?" Edith demanded. "Prudence, what are you doing?"

"I'm going home."

"Home? But your home is with us now. Until you marry, at least."

"I'm not getting married, remember?"

"But you've eight months left before the terms of the will are voided. Surely before then you will find some suitable young man. Robert—"

"I'm not marrying Robert, Aunt Edith," she interrupted. "I will never marry Robert. Perhaps when April fifteenth comes you will accept that fact. And once the expiration date passes," she added with a cynicism that was new to her, "I'm sure Robert's affection for me will disappear, too, as quickly as it came."

"No one's demanding that you marry Robert, Prudence," her uncle said in a conciliatory voice, and she didn't miss the warning glance he gave his wife. "After all, the duke is the one you really love. It's clear you're still hurt by his . . . er . . . unorthodox methods of courtship, but he'll redeem himself, I daresay, if you give him the opportunity. He's—"

"I'm not marrying the duke either, Uncle, and you will have to accept that."

"But Prudence, you have to marry somebody!" Edith cried. "And you won't ever meet anyone of the right sort if you go back to living in that lodging house."

"Then I won't marry anyone, and the money will be forfeit. I don't much care."

"Let all that money go?" Stephen cried. "You can't! You're obviously upset, but once you've thought things over—"

"I have been thinking things over," she interrupted, and faced her aunt and uncle. She took a deep breath. "I have been thinking things over all night, and I've made some decisions. First, I am meeting with Mr. Whitfield this afternoon, and I shall make it clear to him that from this point forward, my allowance comes directly to me."

She allowed them no opportunity for argument. "The allowance of fifty pounds per month is mine to do with as I like from now until April fifteenth," she said incisively. "And I see no reason to spend it on lavish hotels. The two of you may stay at the Savoy until the weekend. If you decide to stay beyond Friday, you will pay for it yourselves. I am returning to Little Russell Street, as I said, and I should advise the two of you to return to Sussex. London is so expensive nowadays."

Prudence turned to Woddell, whose pretty, freckled face showed that she, too, had cried through the night. "I won't be needing a lady's maid anymore, Miss Woddell," she said as she once again opened her money purse. "But if you wish to accompany me," she went on as she counted out the amount of wages she owed the girl, "I'm certain my landlady at Little Russell Street could find a place for you until you get your bearings and decide what to do."

"Thank you, miss," the maid said as she took her wages and put them in her pocket, "but I've a sister in Clapham. I'll stay with her for a bit, until I find a new situation. If you could just see your way to writing me a recommendation, I'd be appreciating that very much."

"Of course. Come to my lodgings in Little Russell Street tomorrow. If I'm not in, I shall leave the letter with my landlady. Will that do?"

"Yes, miss. Thank you."

Prudence held out her hand. "It's been a pleasure, Miss Woddell."

The girl looked at her gloved hand a bit doubtfully, as if uncomfortable with the sudden transition from servant to acquaintance. She curtsied. "Good luck to you, miss."

Prudence let her hand fall. "And you as well. Good-bye."

Nancy Woddell walked away in search of the platform for trains to Clapham, and Prudence turned the other way, but she'd only taken one step toward the exit at the opposite end of the platform when Uncle Stephen put a hand on her arm.

"Prudence, be reasonable," he pleaded.

"I have been reasonable for far too long," she said, and pulled free of his grasp, "and I'm tired of it. From now on I'm going to do what I want, and I don't care a jot if it's reasonable."

"What on earth has gotten into you?" Edith asked in bewilderment. "After all we've done for you, this is how you repay us? Tossing us aside and throwing away all that money without even trying to find a husband?" She began to cry. "Oh, Prudence, I don't understand you anymore."

"That's your problem, Aunt Edith," Prudence said as she walked away. "You never have understood me. I doubt you ever will."

Number 32 Little Russell Street looked just the same as always, but though it had only been a month since she'd last been here, it felt like a lifetime. Prudence paused on the sidewalk, eyeing the familiar red brick building, dark green shutters, and potted geraniums with affection. It was good to be home, she decided as she opened the door and went inside.

"Hullo," she called, pausing in the foyer and setting down her black valise. "Is anyone about?"

Feminine voices answered back in the affirmative, and moments later Mrs. Morris came through the doorway, followed by someone Prudence had not expected to see.

"Emma!" she cried, crossing the foyer toward the slender redhead. She opened her arms and gave her friend a warm hug. "How wonderful to see you. When did you return from Italy?"

"We docked at Dover three days ago. It's wonderful to see you, too. I was so pleased when I heard of your good fortune. Congratulations, Pru. You deserve it."

"But the London papers said you were in Derbyshire," Mrs. Morris put in, "gadding about the countryside, visiting the duke's estates, being the grand lady. Not supposed to be back until just before the wedding, we read. Of course, you can't believe all you read in the papers, I know, but—why, my dear, what's wrong?"

Prudence shook her head, shoving down a momentary pang of heartache. "Nothing. It's just—" She took a deep breath. "I've broken my engagement."

"Oh." There was a pause, she and Emma exchanged glances, then she took Prudence by the arm and ushered her into the parlor. "Come and sit down, my girl. You need a glass of my damson gin."

"No, no," Emma interjected as Prudence sat down in her former place at one end of the horsehair settee, "tea's the only thing at a time like this. She needs a stimulant."

Mrs. Morris was a bit doubtful, but Emma was firm. She rang the bell for the maid. "Tea, Dorcas, if you please," she said when the maid appeared a few moments later, and as Dorcas departed to comply with this request, Emma sat down beside Prudence on the settee.

"Maria's not in, I suppose?" Prudence asked

Mrs. Morris as the landlady took her usual place in the chintz-covered chair on the opposite side of the tea table.

"At this hour of the morning? No, my dear. She's at the bakery, of course. She's eating in this evening, though, so I know she'll be home before dinnertime."

"Do you know if she has found another flat-mate yet?"

"No, but—" Mrs. Morris gave her a puzzled look. "Now, why would you be wanting to know that? Surely, you're not wanting to move back here into your old rooms? But my dear," she added when Prudence nodded, "you don't want to live here. You're an heiress now."

"I won't be an heiress for long. Since I'm not marrying, I won't fulfill the terms of the will, and the money will be forfeit."

The landlady gave her an indulgent smile. "That's a broken heart talking, I think. You wait, my girl, and see how things are in a month or two. You'll change your mind or you and your duke will patch things up."

"No, we won't, and I won't change my mind!" she said more sharply than she'd intended. At Mrs. Morris's startled look, she sighed and pressed four fingers to her forehead. "I'm sorry," she murmured. "It's only that there is no possibility of reconciliation."

"Even so," Emma murmured beside her, "are

you certain moving back into your old rooms is a good idea?"

Prudence lifted her head and turned to her friend, puzzled. "Why wouldn't it be?"

"I've been away, I know, but stories of your inheritance and your engagement to St. Cyres have been in all the papers, even the ones on the Continent. The London papers are filled with stories about you."

"I wouldn't know," she said wearily. "I stopped reading newspapers ages ago. But what does that have to do with me moving back into my old rooms?"

"The breaking of your engagement will also be reported. I fear you will be hounded by the London journalists if you stay here. Not those who work for Marlowe Publishing, of course," she added at once. "We can prevent that. But journalists from other papers will not be so considerate, I fear. If you stay here, there is nothing to prevent them from accosting you the moment you walk out the door. The lodging house offers much less protection for you than a hotel."

"I don't want to stay at a hotel. I've had enough of hotels and inns to last a lifetime. I just want to come back home."

"But Prudence," Mrs. Morris put in, "you're an heiress now. Staying here, you would have no proper chaperone. Wouldn't it be best if you continued to stay with your aunt and uncle? If not at the Savoy, perhaps you should return with them to Sussex for a bit?"

"No," she said decidedly. "Staying with my aunt and uncle is not possible. I don't need a chaperone, anyway, since I have no intention of going out into society. Please," she added as the landlady started to speak again, "I don't want to argue about it."

Emma put a comforting arm around her shoulders. "What if you came to stay with me?" she asked. "Our house in Hanover Square offers you a measure of protection you couldn't find here. I'm sure Harry would agree, although his competitors will certainly accuse him of hiding you away for the exclusive benefit of his own newspapers, but he won't care about that. And," she added, "I can act as your chaperone, if it should be necessary. You can return to Little Russell Street once the furor dies down and the journalists lose interest in you. A few months, perhaps."

"A few months?" Prudence was dismayed. "Will it take that long?"

"I don't know, but having worked for Marlowe Publishing, I have some experience with this sort of thing, and I suspect the London journalists will be watching you like cats around a mouse hole for quite some time."

Prudence groaned. "Oh, I wish everything could just return to the way it was before."

Emma gave her a look of compassion. "One can

never go back to the way things were, Pru. One can only go forward."

Prudence tried to resign herself to that inevitable fact. After all, she told herself, if going back meant reliving what had happened to her during the past two days, she'd just as soon pass it by. Even an uncertain future was better than a broken heart.

"Hard lines, my friend." Weston gestured to the bottle of port as the waiter at Brooks's decanted it for them. "You should have told me sooner. We'll need something stronger than port if we're going to get drunk."

"I don't want to get drunk." He looked at the waiter who was preparing to remove the empty container from the table. "Leave the bottle, too."

Although the waiter frowned in bewilderment, he complied and departed.

"You don't want to get drunk?" Weston eyed him dubiously. "The newspapers are saying your heiress jilted you. You've told me creditors will be swooping down on you within a few days to take everything you've got left. And now you've dragged me down to my club, but you don't want to get drunk? God, St. Cyres, you've a stronger character than I. I'd be three parts pissed already, if I were in your shoes."

"Thank you, Wes. Your optimistic view of my situation cheers me enormously."

"Sorry. It's just that nothing ever seems to rattle you."

Rhys didn't reply, but he wondered what Wes would have said had he seen him two days ago by the lake, falling apart.

"No doubt," the baron went on, "you've another heiress waiting in the wings."

He took a sip of port. "No, as a matter of fact, I don't."

"Got it!" Weston snapped his fingers. "You want to know if I'm acquainted with any heiresses, now that the Abernathy girl is out of reach."

"No."

Wes lifted his hands, giving it up. "Then why are we here?"

"I believe Viscount Marlowe is a friend of yours?"

"Marlowe?" Wes asked in lively surprise at the change of subject. "Yes, we're friends. Why do you ask?"

"I heard he's returned from Italy."

"Yes, I believe he is back from his honeymoon, although I've not seen him myself. Why do you bring up Marlowe?"

Instead of answering, Rhys gestured to the bottle beside the decanter on the table. "I believe Graham's is his favorite port?"

"I think so, but I'm all at sea. Why this interest in Marlowe and his favorite port? Devil take it, how do you even know what port he drinks? Fane, I suppose."

Rhys hadn't been able to assign that particular task to Fane, but he had managed to obtain the information on his own. "I want you to introduce me to Marlowe."

"I'd be happy to, but only if you satisfy my curiosity and tell me why."

"It's a matter of business."

"Business?" Wes began to laugh. "And you said you don't have another heiress in mind."

"I don't know what you mean."

"Marlowe has two unmarried sisters, and since he's rolling in money, their dowries are quite substantial, but with your reputation, he wouldn't let you within ten yards of either Phoebe or Vivian. He's very protective of his sisters."

"I'm not interested in either of the Marlowe girls," Rhys cut him off impatiently. "I am going to marry Prudence Abernathy."

Wes leaned forward in his chair. "The engagement's broken off," he reminded him.

"Just so. That's why I want to meet with Marlowe."

"You're being terribly mysterious, my friend, but if you wish to meet Marlowe, here's your chance. He's just come in." Wes stood up and left the table, crossing the room to greet a tall, dark-haired man who looked to be a few years older than Rhys.

As the pair came toward the table, Rhys stood up, and as they were introduced, he couldn't help noticing, with some amusement, Marlowe's wary expression.

"Join us, Marlowe?" He pulled out a third chair and gestured to the bottle on the table. "We've an excellent port, a Graham's 1862, if you care for a drink."

"Graham's 'sixty-two?" Marlowe glanced at the decanter and the bottle beside it. "A fine vintage," he murmured. "One of my favorites."

"Is it indeed?" Rhys pretended surprise. "Then join us, please, and have a drink."

As Marlowe continued to hesitate, Rhys decided subtlety was not going to work. "It took me all afternoon to locate any of Graham's 'sixty-two for you," he confessed with a smile. "You must at least have one drink with us, so my efforts do not go to waste. Besides," he added, lest the other man continue to fear for the virtue of his sisters, "I am celebrating my engagement to Miss Prudence Abernathy."

Marlowe sat down in the offered chair. "I heard that was broken off."

"I seem to be the only one unaware of that particular piece of news," Rhys replied as he and Wes resumed their seats. "I noticed the *Social Gazette* devoted their entire society page to the matter of our broken engagement in today's edition."

The mention of one of his newspapers made the viscount grin. "Are you denying the story?"

"Oh, yes. Emphatically. I am marrying Prudence Abernathy."

"The lady seems to feel otherwise."

Rhys attempted to look apologetic as he poured wine for their guest. "I have never handled rejection well. You may quote me, if you like."

"Is that why you went to all this effort to acquire my favorite wine and arrange an introduction at my club? A club, I might add, of which you are not a member. Because you wish to tell your side of the story?"

"Not at all. What your newspapers say about me, true or not, is of no concern to me."

"My newspapers only print what is true," Marlowe hastened to say. "But if that isn't your purpose, I must assume you are asking my permission to pay a call upon her at my home, though how you learned so quickly she was staying with us baffles me."

Rhys blinked. "I beg your pardon?"

"You didn't know?"

"I did not." He shook his head, utterly fogged. "Why would Miss Abernathy be staying in your house?"

"My wife is a close friend of hers and invited her to stay with us. Her trunks arrived this morning. I thought you'd found out somehow and were finagling for an invitation to call."

Rhys didn't know if Prudence staying with the viscount and his wife would help or hinder his plans, but at the moment he didn't care. He had other fish to fry. "No, I arranged this 'accidental' meeting with you, Marlowe, because I wished to talk with you about the business of book publishing."

Marlowe picked up his glass and leaned back in his chair. "If your intent was to pique my curiosity, Duke, you've succeeded."

"Good." Rhys smiled and lifted his glass. "Because it may prove quite lucrative for both of us."

Chapter 17

What is it about being in love that turns an ordinarily rational British gentleman into an idiot?

—Talk of the Town, *1894*

William Fane stood opposite number 32 Little Russell Street, his eye on the entrance to the prim, lace-curtained lodging house on the opposite side, trying not to pace back and forth and draw attention to himself. He'd been here for six hours now, his tension growing with each passing moment.

Every time he caught sight of a woman walking along the street, he caught his breath, hoping this time it would be Nancy. The servant at Miss Abernathy's former lodging house had not known the whereabouts of Miss Prudence's maid, but that disappointing announcement had been followed by the surprising news that Miss Woddell was actually expected at Little Russell Street. A letter was waiting for her from Miss Prudence, Fane was told, and she was expected to claim it sometime today. But as the minutes crawled by and she did not appear, he began to fear the worst.

Perhaps she was ill, he thought with alarm. He pulled out his watch. Half past three. Surely by now—

He glanced up and saw a woman in a willow-green dress coming along the opposite side of the street. He didn't need to see the flash of her fiery red hair beneath a prim straw bonnet to know it was Nancy. Her slender figure and the graceful way she walked told him that. Relieved, he put away his watch.

She entered the building and a few minutes later she reappeared, her letter in hand. He waited until she turned to start back the way she'd come, then crossed the street, quickening his steps to catch up to her.

"Miss Woddell?" he called.

She glanced over her shoulder, and when she caught sight of him, a scowl appeared on her freckled face and her pretty green eyes narrowed. But then she turned away as if she hadn't even seen him.

"Miss Woddell—Nancy, wait!" He walked faster, and so did she, but his longer legs gave him an advantage. He easily caught up and fell in step beside her. "I've been waiting all day, hoping for an opportunity to speak with you."

She didn't look at him. "We have nothing to say to each other, Mr. Fane."

"The policeman came by twice on his round while I waited. He gave me quite a suspicious glare the second time, and told me to move along. If he sees me still lingering in the neighborhood on his third round, I shall be probably be arrested."

"No doubt you would talk your way out of that with some story or other. Perhaps he'll be impressed by the fact that you are valet to an Italian count. Oh, no, wait." She shot him a resentful glance. "You're not really the valet to Count Roselli, husband of Princess Eugenie. That was a lie."

"You must let me explain."

"Must I, indeed?" She tilted her nose a little higher in the air. "Who are you to tell me what I must do?"

"You have every right to be angry, but please listen to me, Nancy. Give me the chance to tell you my side of things."

She didn't reply. Nor did she attempt to cross to the other side of the street to evade him, and William took that as encouragement.

"I was valet for Count Roselli prior to his marriage. When he wed Princess Eugenie, he wanted me to stay on, but I fancied a change, and that's when I became valet to the duke. I have been in his employ for five years."

She stopped at the corner, looked both ways, and crossed the street, pretending to be oblivious to his presence.

William persevered. "I've enjoyed my position with His Grace," he said as they both stepped onto the opposite curb, "and being his valet has given me the opportunity to travel a great deal. I've learned many things working for him—" He broke off, thinking perhaps he'd better steer clear of that topic, for not all the things he'd learned were quite aboveboard. "His Grace has been a good employer, very generous—at least, when he's in funds. He's easy to please and possesses a fine wit. And he is a duke, and a most affable, courteous gentleman in every way."

Those words generated a reaction, though not perhaps a favorable one. She made a sound of disdain. "That you would think so highly of a scoundrel, Mr. Fane, does not surprise me in the least."

She veered sharply to her left and marched into a small, modest dressmaking establishment. Without hesitation, William followed her.

"When I take on a position," he said, ignoring the stares he received from the ladies in the shop, "I do my duty to my gentleman."

Nancy glanced at him over her shoulder as she walked toward the counter. "Go away," she said in a whisper, looking appalled. "This is a ladies' shop. You can't be in here."

"I am a loyal valet," he said stubbornly, still following her. "When His Grace asked me to find out what Miss Abernathy's plans were, I did the best I could to fulfill his orders."

"Orders?" She stopped in the center of the room and turned so abruptly he almost cannoned into her. "You lied to me."

He looked into her face, and the pain he saw there hurt him, too. "I know, and I regret that, Nancy, believe me, I do. But it was necessary. Miss Abernathy might have discovered that the duke was—"

"Was what?" she asked when he stopped. "Spying on her?"

He swallowed hard. "Yes."

"So you lied along with him. Did you ever intend to tell me the truth?"

"No."

She made a sound of derision and started to turn away, but his next words stopped her. "I've left the duke's employ," he said. "I have resigned my post."

She paused. "Have you?" she asked, head turned to the side, refusing to look at him. "Why should I care?"

William ignored that question. "Given the circumstances, I feel I can no longer work for him."

"I don't see why not," she shot back. "Birds of a feather do flock together."

She turned away, and he couldn't bear it. He grabbed her arms to keep her where she was. "Nancy—"

"Let go of me," she said, and tried to pull free of his grasp, but William did not let her go, afraid that if he did, he'd never have another chance with her. And he wanted that chance more than he'd ever wanted anything in his life.

"Nancy, I resigned because I had to," he explained, still holding her arms and ignoring the appalled whispers of the ladies. "A valet can't marry. It isn't done."

She stopped trying to pull free. She stared up at him, her green eyes narrowing. "And who," she asked through clenched teeth, "do you think you'll be marrying?"

"You, if I can ever manage to convince you to have me. I love you." He kissed her, then he fell to one knee, keeping one of her hands fast in his. "I know it will take a miracle for you to agree to marry me, but I'll wait as long it takes. I intend to obtain a new post, because when a man falls in love, when he wants to marry and settle down to raise a family, he has to have a steady job with a reliable income. I intend to work hard, save my wages and find a way to buy a house for you. For us. And every day, for the rest of my life, I'm going to ask you again to marry me, hoping that one day you'll have a moment of madness and say yes. Will you allow me to do that?"

She bit her lip, staring down at him, but did not speak.

"Will you, Nancy?" he asked again, and then he waited, on his knees with his heart in his throat, sure that she'd never agree in a thousand years.

"Yes, Mr. Fane," she said at last. "I will allow you to do that."

He was on his feet in an instant. Pulling her hard against him, William Fane, gentleman's gentleman, shocked all the ladies in Mrs. Oliver's dressmaking establishment by giving Nancy Woddell, lady's maid, a most passionate kiss.

Just as Emma had predicted, journalists swooped down on Little Russell Street the moment *The Social Gazette* announced the dissolution of Prudence's engagement to St. Cyres. Hanover Square was a gated square in Mayfair and Marlowe's house there provided Prudence the protection Emma had promised.

Because of the situation, the tradition of Sunday tea at the lodging house was not possible, but Prudence needed the support of her friends more than ever before, and Emma's suggestion that all the ladies take tea with her in Mayfair instead was happily accepted.

As a result, four days after the dissolution of her engagement, Prudence found herself seated not on the horsehair settee in Mrs. Morris's parlor, but on an elegant white brocade sofa in the drawing room of Lord and Lady Marlowe, discussing her future plans with her friends, and finding some solace in their validation of her ideas.

Her decision to take charge of her own money was heartily approved by all. If anyone knew how to manage an income with thriftiness and skill, it was a girl-bachelor. Gentlemen, it was agreed, had no idea how to spend money properly. Race meetings, club memberships, and port could not compare to important things like good quality bed linens and a well-stocked larder.

Her decision to send her relations back to Sussex and her refusal to marry Robert also received their endorsement. It was agreed that perhaps people who ignored a member of their own family for eleven years, paying attention to her and caring for her only after she was set to inherit millions, could not really be trusted. And since all of her friends had met Aunt Edith, they couldn't help but deem Emma a far better chaperone.

Her plan to open her own dressmaking establishment met with unanimous approval, and Emma offered to assist by using her influence to gain Prudence clients in the top echelons of society.

These matters were easy for Prudence to discuss, but when it came to her broken engagement, she found the terrain much more difficult to navigate. She had vowed never to cry over Rhys again, and she knew that the pain was too fresh for her to keep that vow if she began to explain. Her friends, sensing her unwillingness to discuss the matter, took their lead from her and asked no questions.

Fortunately, Emma's return from Italy provided plenty to talk about, for to a group of girl-bachelors, honeymoons were a favorite topic of conversation. Only weddings and babies could generate greater interest.

"Did you really have a view of the Arno, Emma?" Miranda gave a dreamy sigh. "Oh, how I should love to visit Florence."

Emma crossed the room to a cabinet and removed from it a folio. "I have photographs. I purchased them from a photographic artist in Rome."

Exclamations of delight greeted this news, and soon views of the Arno, the Roman Colosseum, and various other sights lauded by Baedeker's travel guides and popular with English tourists were handed round.

Two months ago, viewing them might have been a welcome entertainment, but with every photograph, Prudence couldn't help thinking of Rhys. After her soul-wrenching night on the train, she'd had little time to think of him. She'd moved her things to Hanover Square, ignoring the imploring letters from her relations to reconsider. She'd ensured that her aunt and uncle had left the Savoy. She'd met with Mr. Whitfield, clarifying that the allowance of fifty pounds per month was hers to do with as she pleased until next April and never had to be paid back. The coming months would no doubt keep her quite busy as she established her dressmaking business.

Right now, however, as she studied photographs of Italy, Rhys dominated her thoughts. She couldn't help wondering if he had stood in that piazza, eaten at that café, bathed naked in that fountain.

Pain pinched her chest as she stared at an image of the Trevi Fountain in Rome and memories came rushing back of that day with him at the National Gallery.

How happy she'd been that day, never dreaming he'd arranged it all. Inquiring about her family and whether she still had to work as a seamstress, knowing all the while about her money, playing her for a fool. How smooth, how accomplished, a liar he was. It still amazed her.

I think you're luscious.

Another lie. The pain in her chest squeezed harder. Deep down she'd always known she wasn't really luscious, but how sweet it had been to hear lies like that.

She passed the photograph of the Trevi Fountain to Maria and took the next one from Mrs. Inkberry, but as she bent her head, she only pretended to study it. She closed her eyes instead, unable to bear any more views of Italy and thoughts of him.

Jackson, the viscount's butler, entered the room. "If you please, ma'am, the viscount has returned. He has a friend with him, and he wishes to know if they may join the ladies for tea?"

"That depends," Maria put in. "Is the viscount's friend a single gentleman?"

Everyone laughed at that except Jackson, who maintained the dignified, superior air of an excellent butler. "I couldn't say, Miss Martingale," he murmured and turned to leave.

Stifled giggles followed him out the door, but were silenced almost at once when Viscount Marlowe walked in. He was followed by the Duke of St. Cyres.

Prudence jumped out of her chair as if jolted by a shot of electricity. She felt no dizzying rush of euphoria at the sight of him, no heart-twisting pang of pleasure, no overwhelming longing. Instead, she felt only the deep, bruising ache of hurt and the blazing anger of betrayal. "What are you doing here?" she demanded, as the other ladies rose to their feet in a far more ladylike fashion than she had done. "Leave at once."

"Oh, Harry!" Emma wailed softly. "What have you done?"

"It's business, Emma," the viscount said, attempting to look innocent. "You know with me business always comes before any other considerations."

Prudence asked the question before Emma

could do so, but she asked it not of the viscount, but of Rhys. "What business could you possibly be conducting with Lord Marlowe?"

Rhys reached into his jacket and pulled out a folded newspaper. "The viscount conducted an interview with me for *The Social Gazette.* This is the first copy off the press. Would you care to see it?" Without waiting for an answer, he unfolded the newspaper and held it up so she and all the others could read the headline.

Wicked Duke Chooses Love Over Money!

Prudence stared at it for a moment, then looked at him. "What is this?"

"I told you, it's tomorrow morning's edition of *The Social Gazette.*" He nodded to the man beside him. "I gave Marlowe's paper an exclusive interview, making a public declaration that if you were to consent to marry me, I would not receive a single penny of your inheritance."

There were murmurs of surprise from the other ladies in the room, but Prudence merely folded her arms and scowled at him. "I don't care what lies you tell the newspapers. I am not marrying you! Why on earth should I?"

"I can't think of a single reason," he admitted. "I know I've lied to you and I've been an utter bastard, and you have every right to hate me, but in all of this, I've told you one true thing. I love you." He handed her the newspaper. "This was the only way I could think of to prove it."

"I don't believe you. This is a trick of some sort."

"It's not a trick. Read the interview and you'll see. Please, Prudence," he added when she made no move to comply. "Just read it."

Reluctantly, she glanced at the story on the front page of Marlowe Publishing's biggest newspaper, but before she could begin to actually read it, Rhys's hand appeared in her line of vision, pointing to one particular paragraph. "Here's the part where I declare that if Miss Abernathy agrees to marry me, the wedding will be on April sixteenth of next year."

She glanced up, uncertain she'd heard him correctly. "April sixteenth?"

"One day after the terms of Henry Abernathy's will go unfulfilled," he went on. "The money will, of course, be forfeit."

She frowned at him, still skeptical. "You're willing to do that?"

"It was the only way I could think of to show you I'm sincere. I could have agreed to give you total control of the inheritance in some sort of prenuptial agreement, but my creditors would still come after the money and demand payment of my debts, so you would always have cause to suspect my motives."

"Especially since the moment after we were wed you'd begin trying to sweet-talk your way into gaining control of it from me anyway," she accused. "You would just keep trying to trick me."

"I knew that's what you'd think, and that's why I did it this way, so there would be no doubt of my sincerity."

She still had plenty of doubt. She studied him, and though she saw no devastating smile, no blithe confidence, she knew he could lie with his heart in his eyes, and she still felt the pain of his deceit.

"Seems like an awful lot of trouble to go to for a charming fortune hunter like you," she said. "Why don't you just find yourself another heiress? Lady Alberta Denville would marry you, I've no doubt."

"I don't want Alberta. I don't want any other heiress, I don't want any woman but you. I told you before, I've wanted you from the very beginning, ever since I first saw you at that ball, but I was in desperate need of money, and I knew the only way out of that hole was to marry an heiress. When I saw you at the opera, and Cora told me about your inheritance, that was all I needed to hear. From that moment on, the idea of marrying any other woman—heiress or not—never entered my head."

She sniffed, unimpressed. "I don't suppose it ever occurred to you to be honest with me about your motives?"

"With your romantic nature, I didn't want to take the chance. I knew you thought of me as some sort of hero, and I thought wooing you through courtship was a better strategy."

"Lying is never a better strategy, and you lied." Prudence held up the paper. "After the things you've done, do you think this is all it takes to win me back?"

"No, but I'm hoping the next ten months will be long enough to convince you of my sincerity. I know I'll never be your hero again—" He broke off and glanced away for a moment, his fist pressed to his mouth. Then he cleared his throat and looked at her again. "I know I've ruined any chance of that, but I hope I can at least gain your respect."

He leaned over the paper and pointed to another paragraph. "This is where I tell everyone I'm going to earn my living from now on. I'll be writing books for Marlowe Publishing."

Prudence glanced at Viscount Marlowe, who nodded in confirmation, then she looked back at Rhys. "You're going to be a writer?"

"Travel guides to Europe. Witty books for aristocrats on how to traverse the globe for no money at all, and serious books on where to go and what to see. A bit like Baedeker, you know. I realize it's not much of an income," he added in the wake of her astonished silence, "but it's the only thing I'm remotely qualified to do, and I hope it will convince the woman I love that I'm more than a worthless lily of the field."

She swallowed and closed her eyes, remembering when she'd accused him of that, of being worthless. She'd said it to hurt him, to wound him as she had been wounded. He'd deserved it, too, she reminded herself.

"That's in here, too, by the way," he said, causing her to open her eyes.

"What's in here?" she asked. "That you're a lily of the field?"

"That, and that I love you, not your money. I didn't love you when we started, true enough, but I love you now, and I will love you until the moment I die. And that if you ever agree to marry me, you will make me the happiest man in the world."

Prudence looked down at the words printed on the page as he repeated them, and the newsprint began to blur before her eyes. Deep down inside she began to shake, for she could feel a spark of hope that he was speaking the truth, and it frightened her. She was still raw with pain and afraid such hope only made her an even bigger fool.

"How can I marry you?" she cried. "You deceived me so thoroughly, how can I ever be sure you won't lie to me again if it suits your purpose? How can I ever trust you again?"

A delicate cough interrupted any reply he might have made, and Prudence glanced around, remembering they were not alone. She returned her gaze to his and hardened her resolve. "I want you to leave."

As if she were speaking to them, her friends all stood up.

"No," she said in dismay as they began walking toward the door, "I didn't mean all of you." She waved a hand in Rhys's direction. "I meant him."

Her friends seemed to have gone suddenly deaf, for they continued out the door. Emma, the last one to exit the room, paused and glanced at Rhys. "I am acting as Prudence's chaperone, St. Cyres. I shall be right outside the door."

"No, wait!" Prudence cried, but the door swung shut behind her friend, leaving her alone with Rhys. She started to leave as well, but his arm caught her around the waist.

"Prudence, listen to me." He hauled her back against his chest. "I know you don't trust me, and you have every right, but other than giving up the money, I don't know how to regain your trust." He grasped her arms, turned her around. "Just tell me how."

She looked up at him, into eyes as silvery green as a Yorkshire meadow in autumn, remembering the man she'd first seen, the man she'd thought him to be. "I don't know," she whispered. "You are not the man I thought you were. I don't know who you are."

She turned and walked toward the door. This

time he didn't try to stop her. She reached for the handle and turned it.

"My brother killed himself."

The door handle clicked back into place, and Prudence turned around. "What?"

"He hanged himself from a stair rail at school because my mother was sending him back to Winter Park for a second summer holiday. Alone. She was sending him back alone. He couldn't bear it."

Prudence felt that strange eeriness along her spine, just as she had that afternoon in the drawing room at Winter Park. "He didn't want to go?"

"No." Rhys tilted his head back and stared at the ceiling. "There are some men, Prudence, who don't care for women. They have . . . other tastes. A taste for boys. Evelyn had such tastes."

"Oh my God." She felt sick. "No."

"It was just games at first, then . . . then other things. We were just boys, but we knew it wasn't right, and we used to hide in the lavender house. Evelyn hated the place and never went there. But hiding didn't always work." He lowered his head and looked at her. "You can't hide all the time."

"He hurt your brother." She swallowed hard, and forced herself to go on. "So, because of what happened to him, your brother killed himself."

"Yes."

"What about you?" she whispered. "What happened to you?"

He looked past her, staring at the closed door. "I stabbed Evelyn right through the hand with a fork the first time he touched me. Because of that, he locked me in a room for three days. Afterward, when Thomas told me what happened to him, we ran away, and I managed to get us to Hazelwood. My mother was actually in residence at the time. I tried to tell her what had happened, but—" He stopped and his face twisted, tearing at Prudence's heart. "She called me a liar."

Prudence pressed a hand over her mouth, fighting past the sick knot in her stomach.

"She sent Thomas back to Winter Park. She sent him back to that monster. I begged her not to do it. I begged her. She wouldn't listen." Rhys raked his hands through his hair and sank into a chair. "Not me. I was sent to friends in the north of Scotland because after what I'd done, Evelyn refused to have me back at Winter Park. I didn't even have the chance to try to protect Thomas. In the autumn, we had to go to different schools, because I was old enough for Eton. We wrote, but I never saw Thomas again. When spring came and he learned he was going back for another summer at Winter Park, he killed himself. I couldn't protect him from Evelyn. I tried, but I failed."

"You were a boy. It is your mother who failed." She walked over to where he sat and knelt down beside his chair. "Why didn't you tell me this before, when I asked you about it?"

"How could I?" He sat up with an abrupt move and rubbed his hands over his face. "For God's sake, Prudence, you're so innocent. I just couldn't bear to tell you something so sordid."

She laid her hand on his knee. "Yet you're telling me now."

He looked at her, and there was a spark of anger in his eyes. "I'm not doing it to play on your pity to win you over, if that's what you're thinking." He shoved her hand aside, stood up and walked away. "I haven't sunk that low, thank heaven."

"I wasn't thinking you told me for pity," she said, and rose to follow him. When he halted by the fireplace, she halted as well. "I simply wanted to know why you are choosing to tell me about this at all. You didn't have to."

"I've never told anyone why Thomas killed himself. The rumors have been flying around for years, but no one knows the truth. No one knows Evelyn was such a sick bastard. No one but my mother, and to this day she still denies it, even to herself. I am trusting you, Prudence, with the ugliest, most sordid secret in my life, and I'm hoping that shows you that you can trust me, too. You said you felt as if you didn't know me. That you had no reason to trust me. And you were right. People who are going to be married ought to trust each other. Not that I'm taking anything for granted," he added at once. "I'm not assuming you're going to say yes. But I'm hoping you will."

She gazed up at him, and she believed him. She believed every word. She knew that some women might think that made her twice a fool, but she didn't care. She loved him. She always had, from the first moment she'd laid eyes on him. She still did, despite his wicked ways.

"I'm not any sort of bargain, God knows," he went on in the wake of her silence. "You could have your pick of chaps, and I have nothing, absolutely nothing to offer you. When this newspaper comes out tomorrow, the creditors will immediately call all my loans and take everything I own, which isn't much, I grant you. They'll strip Winter Park, the only estate with a single thing of value left. They'll take all the lands—except St. Cyres Castle, of course. They can't take that because it's entailed. The only point in my favor is that they can't take my title. I am a duke, with my very own castle."

She tilted her head, acting as if she hadn't yet made up her mind. "Owning a castle does have a certain cachet, I suppose," she murmured.

"Not that it will do us any good. You saw yourself it's not fit for dogs to live in, and I doubt it ever will be. What with all my debts, and earning my living as a writer, if you marry me, you'll always be poor."

She drew a deep breath. "Goodness, when you decide to start being frank, you do it thoroughly, don't you?"

"I suppose I do." Then he gave her that smile, that devastating smile that always gave her heart a painful, pleasurable twist, only this time there was none of the pain. That was gone. Perhaps because she'd survived her broken heart with her love for him intact. "No point in lying about St. Cyres Castle anyway," he added, his smile widening into a rueful grin. "You've seen the place. But if I work very hard and write heaps of books, I might earn enough that we could fix the roof, buy some furniture, and repair the fountain."

She began to smile. She couldn't help it. He was so outrageous. "The fountain?"

"For bathing naked," he confirmed.

Despite everything, he could still make her laugh. "A fountain is important, I suppose."

"Things aren't quite as grim as I've made them out to be," he went on. "We would have a couple of servants. Fane and Woddell are getting married, and they want a home of their own. So, I've offered to give them their own cottage on the estate and a bit of land, and in return they're willing to stay on for next to nothing in wages. Absurd of them, but there you are. They're in love, the fools, and if they stay in domestic service working for anyone but us, they can't get married. Woddell has assured me she can cook, by the way."

He cupped her face in his hands. "I love you, Prudence Bosworth. If you marry me, I'll protect you and take care of you, no matter what I have to do. I swear it on my life. And you'll be a duchess, for what that's worth. No one but a princess will ever outrank you, so no one will ever dare look down their noses at you because your parents never married. And no matter what I have to do, you'll never have to be on your knees taking abuse from horrid people like Alberta Denville. So . . . " He took a deep breath. "Come April sixteenth, if I prove myself to you, will you marry me? Or am I an utterly lost cause?"

She looked up at him, looked into his beautiful green eyes, and knew why he was so notorious. What woman could resist him? "Yes, Rhys. I'll marry you."

He blinked. "You will?" When she nodded, he began to laugh. "I'll be damned," he muttered.

"You seem surprised," she said, entwining her arms around his neck. "After that public declaration that's going to be in all the papers tomorrow, did you really think I'd refuse you?"

He bent his head. "I thought I didn't have a chance in hell," he admitted, and kissed her.

And with his mouth on hers, Prudence reflected that April 16 seemed a terribly long way off. Ten months would crawl by. Postponing the wedding, she told herself, wasn't absolutely necessary.

She broke the kiss, pulling back to look into his eyes. "Waiting until April sixteenth to give up the money won't prove a thing, you know" she told him. "I met with Mr. Whitfield yesterday, and he said that even if you and I mended our quarrel and went ahead with our original plans to marry on June seventeenth, it wouldn't matter. Your duplicity makes you a wholly unsuitable caretaker of the Abernathy fortune. He has withdrawn his approval, and since the consent of the trustees must be unanimous, the money will immediately go the relations of my father's widow."

"I'm not surprised. If I were a trustee, I wouldn't approve a fortune-hunting scoundrel like me." He lowered his arms and eased them around her waist. "If the money's forfeit anyway, would you consider marrying me now? I mean, why wait if we don't have to?"

She smiled sweetly. "You'll be getting a letter from Mr. Whitfield in a few days, formally declaring you an unfit candidate. Don't think you can get 'round that somehow, marry me early, and get the money that way."

"I welcome their letter if it means I can persuade you to marry me now." His hands caressed the small of her back, slid along her hips. "Waiting would be agony. After all, to prove I'm a changed man, I'd have to be thoroughly honorable the entire time."

"True." She frowned, pretending consternation. "I hadn't thought of that."

He tilted his head and began pressing kisses to the column of her throat. "All I shall be allowed are a few chaste kisses from you until the wedding. Assuming we can even manage to escape the journalists, for they will be following us everywhere, waiting to see if love truly conquers all." He licked and nuzzled her throat. "The sooner we get married, the sooner I can begin to prove my love for you in ways that are worthy of my wicked reputation."

"Hmm," she murmured in agreement. "What woman could resist that argument?"

He drew back. "So, do we go ahead with the wedding, or do we wait? It's up to you."

"Oh, all right, I'll marry you now," she said, seeming to be won over at last. Reaching up, she raked a hand through his hair and started to draw his head down so he could kiss her again, but he paused, his lips an inch from hers, smiling.

"What did I do to deserve someone as luscious as you?"

"You tricked me," she said, and pressed a kiss to his mouth. "How else?"

Epilogue

The Duke of St. Cyres and Miss Prudence Bosworth-Abernathy were married this morning at St. Paul's Cathedral. Three hundred eighty-six people attended, probably to witness for themselves an event that just one month ago seemed highly unlikely to occur at all.

—Talk of the Town, *1894*

The wedding breakfast, a much smaller affair than the wedding itself, took place at Milbray's town house. It went against all rules of etiquette to have such a meal at the groom's home, but the Savoy was out of the question. The bride's relations couldn't afford the expense.

After the meal, Prudence left the dining room first, accompanied by her head bridesmaid, Miss

Martingale, to change her dress. Rhys exited the room shortly afterward to change out of his wedding suit, but as he passed the open doorway of the study on his way to the stairs, he stopped. Through the doorway, he stared at the desk on the other side of the room.

Its surface was piled with unanswered correspondence, for both he and Fane had been busy the past four weeks. Rhys knew amid the invitations and letters there were also overdue bills and demands for payment, but though he knew he'd probably be in debt for the rest of his life, he hadn't a jot of regret.

He entered the room and walked to the desk. On top of the pile of correspondance, he could see the letter from Whitfield, Joslyn, and Morehouse, Attorneys-at-Law, which had come only a few days after his interview with the *Social Gazette,* and the announcement that despite rumors to the contrary, the Duke of St. Cyres and Miss Prudence Abernathy were intending to be married June 17 as planned.

He picked up the letter. Unfolding it, he walked around the desk and sat down, smiling as he read again the typewritten lines that said the trustees of the Abernathy estate could not in good conscience approve his marriage to Miss Prudence Abernathy, and that if the couple went forward with their plans to marry, they would receive nothing from the late millionaire's estate.

Still smiling, Rhys folded the letter and placed it back on top of the pile. Perhaps he and Prudence should make a fire in Milbray's fireplace tonight and burn it, along with all the bills. He thought about all the money he'd inherited from his father, money he'd thrown away, chasing happiness he'd never found. Now, when he didn't have a shilling, he'd never been happier. Perhaps honesty was the best policy. He began to laugh.

"What are you laughing about?"

He glanced up to find Prudence standing in the doorway. She had changed into a pink traveling suit, but his mind flashed back to three hours earlier when he'd watched her coming up the aisle of St. Paul's on her uncle's arm in her white silk bridal gown. At that moment, he'd felt a piercing, painful joy in his heart like nothing he'd experienced before, and looking at her now, he felt it again. She was the loveliest, sweetest, most luscious thing he'd ever seen in his life, and he still couldn't believe he had won her with nothing but love.

She gave him a puzzled look. "Aren't you going to tell me why you were laughing?"

He picked up a handful of correspondence and grinned. "I was thinking of a bonfire. We could make it a party. Invite my mother, and your relations, and all our indebted friends. They could bring their bills, too, and we could throw them all on. There would be so much to burn, we'd probably end up burning Milbray's house down. That could be a lark."

She studied him for a moment without speaking, then closed the door. To his surprise, she locked it before crossing the room and moving around the desk to his side. When he rose to his feet, she entwined her arms around his neck. "Any regrets?" she asked him.

"Not a one," he assured her, and slid his arms around her waist. "I've never given a damn about paying the bills. I just hope you don't come to regret marrying me. It isn't going to be easy, you know."

She smiled at him. "It's going to be far easier than you realize."

He found that enigmatic remark and the smile on her lips baffling. During the past four weeks, they had discussed their financial situation many times, deciding which debts to pay, making a stringent household budget, determining how to survive during the coming months on the advance Marlowe had paid him for his first book. "We'll barely have enough to live on," he reminded her. "What's easy about that?"

"No, no, we'll have plenty, my love. You see . . . " She paused and took a deep breath. "We still have the money."

Rhys stared at her, uncomprehending. "Darling, what are you talking about?"

"All that business about the trustees disapproving you? That was . . . umm . . . rather a deception on my part."

"A deception?" He stiffened, pulling back from her. "You lied to me?"

She nodded, still smiling. "Yes."

"But what about the trustees?" He picked up the letter from the pile on the desk. "I have their refusal to approve right here."

"Well, yes, but that's a lie, too. Mr. Whitfield agreed to play along with my idea, and wrote you that letter at my request."

"What?" That a lawyer would lie didn't surprise him in the least, but Prudence? He couldn't credit it. She had a hopeless sense of middle-class morality. "You lied?"

She bit her lip and nodded in confirmation. "I'm afraid so, yes."

"For four weeks now you have been leading me to believe that we are going to be poor as church mice, and all the while—" He stopped, unable to quite believe how thoroughly he'd been duped. "All the while, you were deceiving me?"

She gave him an apologetic look. "I had to do it, Rhys. I had to know for certain if you were genuinely in love with me."

"But all you had to do was agree to marry me in April after the money was forfeited."

She shook her head. "That would never have worked."

"Why the hell not?"

"Darling, I'd never have been able to hold out against your charms until April! You'd have finagled your way into a wedding by Christmas, and the shadow of doubt would have remained in my mind, no matter how I tried to ignore it. I had to be *sure*."

Rhys shook his head, trying to understand the consequences of what she'd done. "You're not joking about this? We really do have the money after all?"

Her smile widened. "One million pounds per annum, give or take a few thousand, of course."

"My God." He rubbed his hands across his face. "My God."

She laughed, her arms tightening around his neck. "Speechless for once?" she teased, and kissed him. "No glib answer? No charming offhand remark?"

"Not a one. You've flummoxed me. Absolutely flummoxed me." Rhys looked into his wife's big, beautiful dark eyes, where he'd seen no trace of deception whatsoever during the past four weeks, and he shook his head. "You lied to me," he murmured and frowned. "I'm not sure I like it. Doesn't seem like quite fair play, Prudence, really. We were supposed be learning to trust each other, remember?"

She sighed, studying him with concern. "Oh, dear."

"What's wrong?"

"Please don't go all upright and honorable on me now. I love my devious duke and his wicked ways."

"Oh, I'm still wicked, darling," he assured her. "And I'm going to spend the rest of our lives showing you just how wicked I can be."

"Starting tonight?"

"No." He slid his hand down her hips. "Starting right now. You did lock that door, didn't you?"

"I did."

"Then kiss me, tipsy girl."

And when she did, Rhys enjoyed the lush taste of her mouth so much, he knew he'd learned the wrong moral lesson from this entire affair. Honesty might be the best policy, but wicked ways were a great deal more fun.

978-0-06-052513-2
$13.95 ($16.50 Can.)

978-0-06-133527-3
$13.95 ($16.50 Can.)

978-0-06-087608-1
$13.95 ($16.50 Can.)

978-0-06-114874-3
$13.95 ($16.50 Can.)

978-0-06-082972-8
$13.95 ($17.50 Can.)

978-0-06-123221-3
$13.95 ($17.50 Can.)

Visit www.AuthorTracker.com for exclusive information on your favorite HarperCollins authors.

Available wherever books are sold, or call 1-800-331-3761 to order.

ATP 0108